The Look of Love

The Look of Love

A Novel

Jill Egizii

Brown Books Publishing Group
Dallas, Texas

The Look of Love

© 2010 Jill Egizii

Manufactured in the United States of America.

For information, please contact:

Brown Books Publishing Group
16200 North Dallas Parkway, Suite 170
Dallas, Texas 75248
www.brownbooks.com
972-381-0009

A New Era in Publishing™

ISBN-13: 978-1-934812-54-9
ISBN-10: 1-934812-54-4

LCCN: 2009937054
1 2 3 4 5 6 7 8 9 10

Dedication

To my beautiful children

and all alienated parents and grandparents,

who have had to endure the pain of a broken heart.

And to my husband who makes my life such a joy to live.

CHAPTER ONE

I HATE YOUR GUTS

Anna knew she'd better swing back out to the farmhouse and clean up. She and the kids ran late this morning leaving dirty pans and dishes scattered around. If…mind you, if…Erik managed to get downstairs she didn't want the kids to have to listen to him throw a fit later. She scans the room for evidence of his presence as she tiptoes in the back door.

"Anna!!!" He booms from somewhere above. "Annie!!!" He knows she hates that nickname. She waits a few ticks to see if he'll shut up or if she'll have to go deal with him. Their so-called separation hadn't kept him from leaning heavily on her because of his stupid, unnecessary, hypochondriacal, operation. Of course he managed to find doctors who said 'how high' when he yelled 'jump.' So surgery it had been. But he isn't going to suck her into being his slave today.

Finally after weeks of sending out résumés and making follow-up phone calls Anna has two job interviews lined up. Today of all days she isn't going to get dragged into his drama. She's tired of living in her Mom and Dad's empty house in town, driving back and forth to take care of the kids. A job held the promise of money that would buy her freedom.

Erik, as good as his threats, allowed her absolutely nothing; not a thin dime out of his several millions. Anna only discovered his betrayal when the grocer refused to take her check.

The embarrassed store manager drew her aside to show her the previous two checks the bank returned. Erik stopped payment. He changed all the credit cards. Now Anna has nothing but what she carried out the door six weeks ago. She arrives at the house every morning before the kids wake up and leaves in the evening after dinner is cleaned up and homework is finished. Most nights she stays until Betsy and Drew are asleep. Thankfully Erik either stays at the office late or haunts their regular round of dining emporiums. Most likely drinking his way through every menu, leaving a trail of abused waiters and offended chefs in his wake. As a result Anna and Erik rarely cross paths.

"ANNNIIIEE!!" He bellows, following up with a rapid fire succession of increasing volume. "ANNIE, ANNIE, ANNIE, ANNIE, ANNIE." She is sorely tempted to walk out and slam the door. Let him know she's blatantly ignoring him. Erik's bellows are more grating than the lowing calves when first separated from their mothers. The thought gives her a small chuckle. It is in that instant of mirth in which she relents. 'Oh what harm could it do to get him a fresh glass of orange juice and track down his remote?' He most likely flung it across the room in a fit of pique last night while watching the political pundits.

She bounds up the steps shaking her head. Boy oh boy once she's gone…really gone that is…would he ever learn. Well once he's gone that is. He refused to move out to make their separation 'official' until he bought another house. When Anna couldn't stand his presence anymore, couldn't live with him one more day while he studied the market, she started staying at her parents to get away from him. They were in Florida most of the year anyway. Plus it was only temporary until he moved out. 'And once he does' thinks

Anna, 'he'll realize that it's me that holds him together.' Literally. Frankly she looks forward to the day he realizes how truly helpless he is without her at his beck and call. She collects Betsy, Maggie, and Drew's stray things from the steps as she goes up, dropping a pile of lost belongings in each child's doorway.

"Annie!" he's a little more contrite in tone now. Good.

"Anna?" Even close up he's quiet. Amazing. She peeks around the bedroom door to find his bed empty. Odd guttural sounds draw her attention to the bathroom. Something liquid trickles from under the door, glistening in the light. Did he try to take a bath? That idiot! Everyone knows you don't put fresh surgical staples in water. As she gets closer, what she thought was water takes on a distinctly more sinister appearance. 'Oh! That's blood.'

"Erik?" She says rushing through the door. "Uh gah-uck," she chokes back the bile that rises in her throat at the sight of him. Despite her years on the farm, the blood everywhere frightens her. He's somehow managed to tear open the entire incision across his belly. It's deep. His surgeons cut efficiently at least, that's for sure. Much to her chagrin, Anna discovers that far worse than the blood is the pulsing viscera he juggles with little success. It looks as though his entire inside has flopped out.

She grabs the nearest towel and approaches him in a wary crab walk. He's panting and writhing, furious at the betrayal of his own flesh, pissed off at the devilish innards trying to abandon ship. She never imagined so many shades of pink and red, nor the various qualities mucus could display. She puts some pressure on the bulging membranes in an effort to shift them back behind the flesh but the blood makes everything slippery and she's shaking and choking on bile. Not to mention scared within an inch of her sanity. He's saying...something, "Arh- agu, abageehee u biss." You bitch. That much she gets.

After doing what she can to stanch the bleeding and wrap him up she remembers her purse, her cell phone. She calls his doctor; Cudahy, then an ambulance and the hospital all while continuing to try to truss him up. He keeps pushing on her trying to stand up. The slime everywhere keeps them both trapped. Anna yanks down the rest of the towels spreading them over the floor; a new kind of red carpet for his royal highness.

Of course he can't wait. He's grabbing onto her, shaking and pulling. He's white as parchment, his gut gaping like an open mouth and still the little dictator. She does what she can to wipe him down before wrapping him in a dark robe. He insists on hobbling down the stairs. His obvious intent to get to the car.

Her hands still quake as she fires up the ignition. He sprawls out in the passenger seat which is flung back and cranked to recline. He's still blathering at her. With one hand on the steering wheel the other groping for the cell phone she manages to roll out onto the main road into town. Cudahy is talking in Anna's ear as she struggles to maintain control of the car and herself. The shaking spreads from her hands to her chest. She realizes her ribs are shaking. Why is she so cold? Erik is roving in and out of consciousness. Blood trickles from the padding around his middle down his thigh. This single driblet somehow horrifies her, mesmerizes her.

"Anna…your incompetent driving is going to kill me before this gash does. Pay attention won't you! You always were a terrible driver I don't know how I ever even let you drive those kids to school…it's amazing you haven't gotten them killed…I'm gonna take away your car after this, if you don't kill me that is…"

He rambles on and on as she shakes violently willing her eyes to stay glued to the black road ahead of her.

Their arrival at the emergency room is a blur of noise, rushing bodies, endless questions, and papers to sign. Doctor Cudahy has a room staked out in Emergency, prepped and ready for Erik's privacy and comfort. Doc Cudahy insists Anna leave the room while he assesses the damage. As she turns to leave she sees Erik whispering in Doc Cudahy's ear. Outside Anna slumps in a plastic chair facing the nurse's station. She stares at the wall covered in preventative propaganda. "Never shake a baby," warns one particularly graphic poster tacked up among many. The idea of shaking draws her attention to her still trembling hands which to her surprise are covered in blood and various unidentifiable fluids of life.

Her hands shake more violently as her gaze travels up her arms. She examines her sweater and the front of her jeans to discover she is smeared in the rust ochre of Erik's drying blood. She touches her face and feels the clumps in her hair. She tries to rise to find a bathroom, a shower, a hose anything that will get the blood off her hands, out of her hair. She must look a fright. Her wobbly legs won't lift her and she sinks back down the few inches she managed to hover while attempting to rise.

Anna glances around to see if she's frightening any children. She recognizes the nurse approaching her with a stack of towels and clean scrubs. Her deep sigh of relief opens the floodgates to tears. She's in full wracking sob mode in an instant. No amount of willpower can stifle the heaving cries that escape her. In fact she fears she may throw up...again. The nurse's steady reassuring hand on her shoulder brings up a deep shame that urges Anna to resent the woman's kindness, but she can't. She wants to resent the nurse's solicitude but is too weak. This only compounds her confusion, exacerbates her imbalance, makes her cry harder.

Cudahy comes out of Erik's room at that moment. His bulk looming over her at least halts her heaving sobs. He spouts a string of incomprehensible noise at her sounding like honking adults from the Charlie Brown cartoons. Anna is certain her forced smile looks more like a grimace but she keeps at it. As he talks at her in his officious fashion she continues smiling and nodding until he abruptly strides away. Two orderlies wheel Erik from the room, tagging along behind Cudahy's waddle.

"See everything's going to be fine," the nurse suggests. "They're taking him into surgery now." Anna returns her gaze to the reassuring posters on the wall. "Pregnant women should not smoke." "Heart disease in women…the silent killer."

"Ok why don't I show you where you can clean up…doesn't that sound good?" the kind nurse asks gently shaking Anna's shoulder and offering her the clean scrubs.

TIME HAS LITTLE MEANING TO ANNA hovering in the hallway between the family waiting room and the coffee stand. She feels self-conscious in the scrubs. She's afraid some frightened mother or sister will accost her demanding answers about Michael's gallbladder or Steve's prostate.

If for nothing more than the sake of appearances she knew she'd better stay put at the hospital, although she did wish she weren't alone. She was tempted to drive to the school, pull Betsy from class, and bring her to the hospital to wait with her. After all it is her father in there. Maybe the kids should be there? But Anna recognizes her true desire is simply to have Betsy at her side so she won't have to endure this alone.

Anna straightens her shoulders, reminding herself that she's an adult. She can handle this. If being married taught her anything it's self-sufficiency and how to think on her feet.

From week one she had to use her wits and creativity. She thinks back to the night on their honeymoon when Erik took her to an exclusive restaurant on the other side of the island. She wore a strappy evening dress and strappy sandals. Delighted to be shown off and showing off in the finest, most expensive place on the Island. That night Anna even wore the diamond earrings her grandmother had given her as a wedding gift.

To this day she can't remember how it started...had she shushed him when he was raising his voice to the server? Did she decide to choose her own dessert? It could have been one of the million things Anna eventually learned to 'manage' over the years so as not to set him off. But this was the beginning, back before she learned to deflect his ire.

It ended with Erik stomping out of the restaurant, hopping in the rental car, and driving away leaving her there practically naked, definitely lost, and utterly alone. She didn't even bother to bring a handbag so as not to break the charm of her ensemble. There she was nineteen, abandoned in skimpy evening wear on the far side of a tropical island, without a dime, a credit card, or key to her hotel if she should somehow make it back. He might as well have tattooed 'victim' on her forehead and shoved her out into passing traffic on the way home.

But she managed. Anna made a deal with one of the busboys. He drove her back to the hotel on his scooter and she had the concierge pay him and charge it to their room. She made it...she figured it out. Looking back it seems so much clearer, so much more sinister and cruel on Erik's part. But back then...back then she cried and cried and blamed herself, just as he wanted her to. For most of their years together Anna had been so busy, so preoccupied using all her energy and effort to maintain her own balance, and then the kids, that she failed to realize it was not simply stormy seas rocking the boat; all along it was their captain Eric.

A pang of guilt undermines her renewed feeling of self-sufficiency when she remembers asking Erik's secretary to tell her mother-in-law, Mother Reinhardt about Erik's emergency. So okay she's mostly an adult. But Mother Reinhardt scares most people, aside from Erik's long time gal Friday; Marge. Marge frightens most people too. Anna thinks of the pair of old biddies as peas in a pod...well not really more like two dried up prunes in a tapioca.

Or more like two dark parentheses closing in on Anna and Erik's life from either side; work and family. 'Whew! Where'd that come from?' Anna wonders.

She shakes her head wondering if another cup of coffee will bring her back to earth. As she stands debating she catches a glimpse of Cudahy's distinct waddle passing along a far hallway. She hustles after him, finding him oddly quick for a squat, stocky man. She calls out to catch his attention but he's yapping into his cell phone and can't, or won't, hear. Eventually he ducks into a room. Anna closes in right behind pulling the door open before it even clicks shut.

Initially she's embarrassed. She thinks for an instant she's followed Cudahy into some stranger's room. The woman she assumes to be the solicitous wife leans over her husband covering his face in kisses, hiccupping, murmuring, "Oh I'm so relieved you're going to be all right. Thank heavens. Oh I'm so lucky" as she mwah mwah mwahes her way around his face. But the face… it's Erik. Not as pale and peaked as he'd been last time she'd seen him, but definitely Erik.

"Ahahah hem hem," Cudahy's not so subtle warning to Erik and…whoever she was…that 'trouble' had just arrived froze them in mid kiss. Cudahy simply rocks back on his heels clasping his hands behind his back awaiting the requisite drama with obvious anticipation. Whoever-she-was stands, straightens her polyester suit jacket, and sends Erik a meaningful glare as she musters her remaining dignity to flee.

Anna makes a show of stepping aside to clear the woman's exit.

"Don't worry Hon, I'll call you in a little bit," says Erik in his courtroom voice as he pats Whoever-she-was' hand.

Anna stopped giving them names a long time ago, about seven years ago…the time of their first divorce.

CHAPTER TWO

CO-CO VAN

Crisis of mortal proportions averted and maximum humiliation achieved. All in all, not a bad day for Erik. Even while flat on his back he still managed to attain his daily quota of irking Anna and keeping her distracted from her own life. As she left the hospital she at last remembered to call and apologize for missing her interviews but the icy tones of the receptionists made it clear that bridges had burned. And these were the only two interviews her father's aging political reputation managed to catch for her.

Because she married at nineteen, Anna's actual résumé is nonexistent. She had her degree yes, that's true. After all, she went away to college at sixteen. When she married Erik she had four credits outstanding to earn her diploma. It took her five years to find the time to take that last course to earn her B.A. in political science. But she did it after both her stepchildren started school and before Drew and Betsy were more than vague ideas in her imagination. All this made finding a job in the politically charged state capitol even more difficult. Anna's father retired from state politics just long enough ago to make pulling any strings for her difficult. Oh, the glory of the small town culture of the state capitol.

Although it's just past one in the afternoon she's had enough of today to last a few weeks. Anna does what she always does to cheer herself up. She plans the evening meal. Well…since Erik won't be there she won't have to make red meat, for a change. What did she need after such a harrowing morning? Comfort food, absolutely…ah ha! She knows exactly what she'll make, her version of 'chicken soup' and Betsy's all time favorite. This, of course, is the only reason she dared to bring it to the table a second time.

Anna has time to kill before getting the kids; Betsy and Drew from the middle school, her stepdaughter Maggie from the high school. Her stepson Greg already moved on to college. So Anna, in no hurry, takes the long way to the market. After all, she really only needs two things: red wine and fresh leeks. For the umpteenth time in memory she drives past the location, her location; the perfect spot for the comfort food café she began conceptualizing years ago when her children were just born. Early in married life Anna worked her way day by day through each of the gourmet recipes in Julia Child's biblical, *Mastering the Art of French Cooking*. As a result Anna indeed developed a mastery in the kitchen. With experience she even dared to alter, amend, and adapt her newly honed skills and Ms. Child's recipes to the family table.

Erik bought the building for her restaurant three years ago. Allegedly keeping the promise he made when she finally agreed to remarry him after four years of pseudodivorce. In her mind she refers to it as the 'pseudodivorce' because it was kept an absolute secret. This time, though, would be vastly, incredibly, remarkably different. See, already she's moved…to her mom and dad's yes, but farther than she'd gotten last time around. Much farther.

Despite being 'divorced' seven years ago, they continued living together, went to church together, attended charity events and public galas together. Not even their children knew, although they may have wondered why Mom and Dad slept in different wings of the house. Not even her parents and especially not his mother were ever to find out. Those were his conditions for agreeing to divorce her. That she maintain the status quo, keep mum, and live 'as if.'

At the time she hoped the divorce would have earned her some sense of autonomy, some control over the direction of her and her children's lives. She agreed to his conditions because they enabled her to have her cake and eat it too, or so she thought. She negotiated several months' worth of courses with top chefs in cities around the world into the deal for herself. She'd be able to live comfortably and raise her children well, and she wouldn't be obligated to serve as Erik's virtual slave as she'd been conditioned over the years.

Yes she is fully aware how mercenary the restaurant for remarriage sounds but, really, what does it matter now? For three years he strung her along with promises. First he needed to get the zoning rules changed. Rallying the city council behind this decision alone took over a year. Then the building was supposedly condemned by initial city inspectors, which she should have realized was suspect as Erik golfed with the state supervisor of building inspectors—their ultimate boss. As a powerful personal injury attorney, he knew everyone who was anyone in local and state government and was in bed with most of the movers and shakers in town in one way or another. She only began to understand these symbiotic, under the radar, relationships once she started paying closer attention to his associates and their comings and goings.

His vast, often hidden network of connections is also probably why Anna struggled to get even an interview for decent full time job. She'd probably been blackballed in advance by Erik simply saying in passing at some fundraiser, "You know now Anna's got it into her head to get back into politics after all these years. I mean yes…she did ultimately finish her degree, but you all know how strongly I feel about the sanctity of the family and the Godliness of a loving home for the sake of the children…" And she believed in it all too…once upon a time, long, long ago.

Then there was the series of contractors Erik swept through, firing each one before they could actually make any headway on reconstructing the café building. Today she parks in the weedy asphalt lot, another zoning issue there; parking. Today she wants a good long look. The whole thing just looks forlorn and sad from every angle. The layer of plaster over the concrete block is peeling off the exterior. The awning frame is rusted and caved in through the middle. It never did see the lovely canvas design she spent hours choosing colors for.

Anna picks her way through the muddy trenches that were once intended to be home to full-size trees and perennial gardens. She clambers through the hole a truck created in the picket fence around the al fresco deck. From there she can see the interior through the wide windows. Of course she tries the door handle to no avail. The place may be abandoned, but Erik still keeps it like a fortress. Even his discards warrant lock and key.

Surveying the dozens of varieties of tables, chairs, booths, and counters scattered about breaks her heart for the umpteenth time. As always she envisions the warm atmosphere inviting friendly faces in out of the rain. Anna's hopes and dreams still materialize in the fog where she breathes on the window.

"Oh Anna it smells so delicious! What's on special today? Did you make soup? Oh of course you did, you have a sixth sense don't you. You always know what we'll want!" dotes her neighbor Karen as she helps her elderly mother to her seat, their usual table. Anna in an apron her grandmother wore hugs them both and helps Karen's mother settle in comfortably. She has ingeniously arranged the seating rooms so that loud clamoring tables with small children (who…don't get her wrong, she adores) are far from the tables for adults. She even designed an area that naturally attracts the teens and preteens after school. Instead of gourmet coffees, Anna designed 'gourmet' cocoas and tea and juice blends the kids can ohh and ahh and brag about. Anna's milk and fruit juice–based blends are actually healthy and invigorating.

Seeing her hopes for the future in the dust, ladders, and fallen bits of ceiling is far more devastating than seeing Erik's intestines fall out. She remembers each chair and each plate service she'd narrowed down as her finalists. Creating the perfect atmosphere, attaining just the right balance between welcome comfort and tasteful elegance became a passion. Once she realized she would never have the marriage and the husband that would provide her children with the kind of family she dreamed of, she diverted all those thwarted hopes to the restaurant. The truth of all those losses, all her mistakes and misjudgments about Erik, confront her daily. Seeing this last costly dream neglected casts a shadow over Anna that she cannot shake. She wipes the steam from her breath off the window with her palm, wiping the slate clean.

But of course…there is dinner to make. The kids'll be upset about what happened to their dad and will need something hearty and comforting after dropping by the hospital to see him. Anna reminds herself to ring his room as they head over there after school. She'd hate for the kids to stumble into what she had. That would be too confusing.

Watching his saccharine performance during Betsy, Drew, and Maggie's visit to the hospital only makes her more determined to get free.

"Oh and you should have seen what a trooper your mom was guys…" he boasts to them. "If she hadn't come home just then, who knows what might have happened to old Dad?" Their 'marriage' seemed to have devolved into a theatrical competition. Whichever one of them would crack and betray the truth in front of the kids, Mother Reinhardt, or anyone else would be the loser. Who could appear the most solicitous, convivial, and happy despite the abyss of lies and emptiness that lay beneath? Of course Anna was losing this battle, because she in fact has a heart left. Or rather she hopes she has a heart left.

The whole show reminds her of the night she met Erik. She was nineteen and went into the hottest restaurant bar in town with her older brother who'd just finished law school. She felt privileged and special. She was in fact taken aback by the glamorous appearance of all the other patrons, most of whom were around her father's age. Their expensive suits and custom tailored shirts. She knew how to spot quality of course, thanks to her father's impeccable taste.

But they noticed her…oh yes…they all noticed her in her green dress that brought out the color of her eyes and highlighted her natural auburn hair that she wore piled high on her head. The hair, along with the stilettos, were adopted to make her look taller, so she wouldn't be mistaken for a high-school girl.

Anna remembers her first sight of Erik holding court at the far end of the bar. The apparent gathering place of the 'young bucks,' considering not one of them looked over thirty. Half a dozen men gathered around to be regaled by the tall dark-haired hero of the bunch. Anna couldn't tell what he was saying but she could see the interest with which the company was listening, hanging on his every word. Anna thought they must be strategizing or discussing politics to be that intent. At the end of his monologue the onlookers let loose with sincere chuckles and a few guffaws.

The most handsome and flashiest, the one who'd been telling the story, Erik finally turned around to take in the effect his compelling tale had on the rest of the patrons. Anna almost giggled when he gave an almost imperceptible nod of acknowledgement to her brother.

"Do you know him?" she pressed.

"Sure…I know him, everyone knows him. That's Erik Reinhardt. You know those ads for The Enforcer?" he asked. Anna nodded enthralled. "That's him," her brother said with a wave of his hand to indicate her entrance into the big leagues. Erik made some space for himself. Then, taking a long look at his chunky metal (and Anna assumed expensive) watch, he realized he had somewhere else to be. Much to Anna's surprise he paced to the booths behind the bar and extracted a woman who must have been his date—tall, thin, blonde, and obviously drunk. As he escorted her to the door he grazed by Anna saying something she couldn't hear to her brother. Then he was gone.

That didn't stop Anna from watching out the front windows as he loaded the blonde into a dark green Jaguar sedan parked right out front and zipped away. Anna was dazzled by the sight of the man who looked as though he had it all, a modern day Cary Grant. Anna recognized how he had the clothes, the car, the money, the career, the looks, the attitude…everything that indicates power and success. All the things Anna was accustomed to having in her experience, in her life. Teamed up with a star like that Anna could easily imagine being welcomed by the whole town.

The very next day her brother got an unexpected phone call from the alpha male himself, inviting him to interview at the firm. "I heard you recently graduated with honors from law school and…oh and by the way who was that delightful redhead you were with last night?" That was the beginning of the end for Anna. She shakes her head to set the old memories free.

Betsy, Drew, and Maggie feel more relaxed, more at ease, more themselves as they pull into the driveway. Knowing Erik won't be there to reign over the dinner table, or make an unexpected appearance as they sprawl about doing homework (or later as they watch a bit of TV) seems to put them at ease. So it seems to Anna anyway.

This is what she imagines a real divorce will earn her this time. Get them free from his palpable influence. To Anna Erik has become a thing, an energy, a bad odor, a distinct tang polluting the air whenever and wherever he was present. Her weakness was she felt sorry for him, wanted to show him, felt obligated to prove to him that life could be joyful, that love meant giving. So she gave and forgave, and buffered him from the things she knew set him off. She took on this Herculean task for years, until those years became decades that eventually became a way of life.

Betsy and Drew, after a bit less prodding and bribing than usual, dutifully spread their books and papers over the kitchen table as Anna pulls out her ingredients. Maggie, the oldest in her senior year, retreats to work in her room where, as she often reminds everyone, she can work in peace and quiet. Maggie claims the chattering of the kids and Anna clattering pots and pans make it impossible for her to study in the kitchen. Anna chalks the attitude up to Maggie's age.

She knows Maggie longs to break free, to experience life beyond their tiny country club village. Maggie swore over and over, up and down that she would never settle for such a backward, dingy place for her life's adventure. Anna quietly applauds her. Does all she can to make it possible for Maggie to break out by slipping university brochures for California and Oregon into her room. Of course, in one of her moods Maggie accuses Anna of wanting her gone because she's an evil stepmother, which they all knew is a wild exaggeration…Anna raised Maggie and her older brother Greg from ages nine months and two years, respectively, after their mother died of breast cancer.

Anna sautés cubed bacon, from their own hogs, in garlic oil she infused herself. The scent of the heavy saltiness steeped in garlic draws her back into herself; back into her body, her kitchen, her life. To Anna it's the scent of home, her home. She skins and debones chicken thighs and breasts adding them in chunky slices to the sauté. As she strips and slices thin disks of fat leeks, Betsy recognizes the wafting scent of her favorite dinner.

"Ohh Mom, is that what I think it is?"

"That depends…what do you think it is?" Anna asks in return. Betsy makes a gleeful squeal abandoning her math book to join Anna at the stove.

"What can I do? I want to help," Betsy wants to know.

"Oh, hey Mom can you put in extra mushrooms?" Drew interjects, engrossed in his work.

"Extra mushrooms? Since when are you a huge mushroom fan?" Anna asks.

"Oh please Mom." Drew says with an eye roll. "I'm fourteen now. I'm the one that always liked mushrooms…remember? It's Betsy who didn't, that is until she turned twelve and started copying me." Drew informs his errant Mother. Of course Anna knows this, but she just loves to hear him tell it.

"Here Bets, do you want to stir in the leeks?" Anna asks. Betsy deftly tips the small cutting board over the heavy pot and slides the pale green circles into the mix. "Look Mom pink and green, just like my bedroom curtains," Betsy says putting her face in the steam and inhaling deeply. As Anna opens the tall green bottle she gestures to Betsy. Betsy nods taking the bottle carefully from her Mother.

"OK, but you stir while I pour Mom, I don't want to add too much. I don't like mine soupy." Anna obliges, gently stirring while Betsy slowly fills the pot with the red wine. After adding the extra mushrooms they bring it to a simmer and clap on the lid. Now they have about forty-five minutes to finish schoolwork before Anna needs to make the noodles.

Together the four of them enjoy Anna's stripped-down version of traditional coq au vin. Betsy's toddler name for it, 'Coco Van,' somehow stuck. In fact it was the inspiration for Anna's still secret name for the restaurant; Coco's Café.

They while away their evening in the normal way, Anna nagging them in turn to get off the phone while she checks over their assignments. Anna negotiates which shows are Ok and which are not. Eventually they all settle in together to watch a few recorded episodes of their current family favorite—the show about the teenage girl who is given 'odd jobs' by God in the form of various normal looking people.

CHAPTER THREE

IN THE DARK

"Well are you ready?" Anna asks as Betsy runs up to the car window after school.

Betsy looks confused, "Ready? For what? I just came to tell you that I forgot to tell you that our intramural volleyball game is today...so...sorry Mom but I have to stay. I am our only decent defensive player after all."

"Betsy," Anna chides. "We are supposed to go get your first-grade art portfolio from Grandma's today...right now. She's expecting us."

"Aww Mom!" replies Betsy. "Can you just go? I mean I'm sorry but I forgot about the game this afternoon. And I need need need those files. The project is due in two days. I'll only have today and tomorrow to work on it as it is. Please..." Betsy asks. A few girls come clamoring out the door calling Betsy, urging her to hurry. The game is starting any minute.

"Fine. Fine. I'll go get what I can find. But don't blame me if something's missing." Anna says.

"Thanks Mom." Betsy throws over her shoulder as she bolts away. She stops when she reaches the glass doors and turns to shout. "Oh and Mom, you will be back to pick me up at 5:00 right?"

Anna nods. As soon as the girls trail out of sight Anna lays her head on the steering wheel and takes seven deep breaths. She remembers hearing something about seven being the key number.

Anna dreads the errand. In fact she's been putting it off for days, ever since Betsy told her she needed her elementary school art files. Together the two of them searched every nook and cranny of the basement, attic, and storage in the barn hoping they were wrong. But to no avail. The kids' elementary school files with their report cards, homework highlights, stage programs with their names in them, and what Betsy needed now, artwork, are stored in Erik's childhood home. Apparently these are in the few boxes left behind after being stored with Mother Reinhardt during the renovations to the farmhouse.

Betsy's assignment is to update an early work of art for class demonstrating the skills she's acquired and how much she's changed. 'What kind of teacher requires eight-year-old artwork?' Anna wonders as she heads for the gray house on Holt Avenue. She is sorely tempted to go home and scrawl on construction paper in crayon with her wrong hand and try to pass that off as Betsy's. But of course Betsy has in mind a particular item she remembers. If it was for anything else but homework Anna would do just that, but she's trying to teach her kids to take assignments seriously. What kind of role model would Anna be if she didn't even try?

The house sits on a vast corner lot in one of the oldest neighborhoods in town. A stone tribute to eras gone by. Before she ever met Erik she'd thought of this gray monument on Holt as her personal image of *The House of Seven Gables*. She just happened to be reading the gothic tome for her college coursework at the local university when she was learning her way around town and spotted the thing.

She spent her sixteenth and seventeenth years at the big state college which both she and her parents realized was too much too soon. Then, at eighteen, Anna moved to Cambridge to work part time at her Dad's state rep office while finishing up her classes at the local university. He'd been the state representative for their rural district for as long as Anna could remember. For most of her life he lived away half a year at the capitol, coming home only every few weekends during voting sessions. At the time she was thrilled to finally get a close look at how the system worked. Working with her father was what inspired her to change her major from theatre to political science. She was in fact making up humanities credits that first semester, reading Hawthorne. Never in a million years could she have anticipated that her very own local gothic mansion would be her future husband's childhood home.

As she rolls up the long driveway Anna sees Mother Reinhardt hovering in the doorway. She takes more deep breaths on the walk to greet her, hoping it will keep her voice light and keep her from chewing a hole through the inside of her mouth.

"Oh Anna! Hello. You're late dear. I'm afraid I have to leave this minute. I'm already late for Helen Gilchrist's husband's wake. Mrs. Delahey and Mrs. Rossi have been ringing my phone off the hook wondering where I am." She practically shouts all this as Anna walks through the door. Mother Reinhardt has her overcoat on and is halfway out the door. "Oh dear, Anna. You just need to move your car for me. See you've blocked me in. I'll leave the back door unlocked for you on my way out to the carport. If you could just...oh and be absolutely sure you lock up when you leave. You can't be too careful these days you know." Mother Reinhardt says pointing at Anna's car with her keys.

Anna obliges with all requisite haste. She is rather relieved at not having to keep company with Mother Reinhardt, but not at all pleased to be in the house alone. Anna pulls her car all the way around after Mother Reinhardt's ancient Mercedes sedan clears the driveway.

The word mausoleum pops into her head, which is odd as Anna had never actually been...no wait that's right in Italy in the catacombs. She tries to keep her mind on Italy, the trip Erik sent her on years ago after...after...after she had that fling; the unmentionable affair. Granted she was only twenty at the time, married and raising the two children of a woman she never met. But that was no excuse. The whole incident still filled her with shame and if she was truly honest with herself, a little bit of excitement. Peter. She still runs into Peter now and then, but not so often since his lobby firm went national. He matured into a good man. Although Anna made it a policy to never regret anything, giving up Peter is the closest thing to regret she ever felt. But she made her choice.

She made her choice when Erik begged and bargained for her loyalty. He said he loved her, even though he often called her by his first wife's name...in bed. He said he loved her and would do anything to convince her. He suddenly decided it was time for Anna to take her European tour to Italy, France, and Holland. "Take some time," he said. "Think it through while you're away. Take Janet with you, take Lena, whoever you like, take Evelyn." He insinuated this would help her grow up to his mental level. He was, after all, ten years her senior.

Of course the friends he encouraged Anna to invite were essentially banned when Erik or his kids were around. She took all three of them with her. But Anna never made it out of Italy. Maggie, only two years old at the time, came down with the measles and Erik had a conference in South Carolina. So Anna went home early leaving Janet, Lena, and Evelyn to finish the five star, first class, prepaid tour without her.

'Oh what is it with this house?' wonders Anna as she makes her way to the basement door. She doesn't want to disturb any of Mother Reinhardt's knickknacks or raise dust from her ancient carpet runners. Anna takes a deep breath as she ducks down the narrow steps into the basement. Wait hang on. Anna jogs back up the stairs into the kitchen. She finds a taper candle, lights it, and takes it back downstairs with her. This will help. Sure, yes the lights are on and it's broad daylight but…but…

Now where are those boxes? Anna tiptoes around trying to imagine where the stack of boxes they left behind might be. She finds some boxes, but not the right ones. If she remembers correctly she put the kids' portfolios in Rubbermaid containers to protect the art from the damp in this old house. She heads further into the gloom away from the stairs and utility sink out from the shelter of the antique furnace, exposed to the light seeping in the filthy window wells.

Oh that's right there's a so-called storage closet behind a wooden door in a crumbling brick wall at the far end of the basement. Anna makes her way across the dusty floor. As she walks she gropes the air for more light bulb strings that might be hanging. But all she gets is handfuls of cobwebs. Now she feels pretty smug with her candle. See, it came in handy.

It takes some doing to get the door open, simply from disuse. Yep, there they are—stacks of blue and gray Rubbermaid boxes in the corner. Anna is just about to fully enter the vast closet when she remembers a precaution. She finds an old brick not too far away and props the door open. Better safe than sorry she thinks. As she checks through the boxes to find the one or two she needs she thinks she hears a noise; a slam or a thunk. Well the closet door is ok. She waits to hear footsteps. Maybe Mother Reinhardt forgot something. After a few moments of silence Anna rifles through the boxes faster. Since she's here she isn't about to leave without her booty. But wait. What's that? It sounds like a 'ka-ching' metal striking a pipe maybe? Still, no footsteps or other sounds.

Anna starts dragging the stack of blue boxes toward the door.

No need to do this here. She can take them all and find what she needs later. She gets them over the threshold of the closet and goes back for the other stack. Luckily they aren't too heavy. She gives the stack of containers a lift over the threshold and goes back for the last stack. Then she hears it, a clear distinct slam. A door shutting. A click. A metal clanging. She checks the closet door. It's still open.

Oh no, the door at the top of the stairs. Anna creates a flotilla of Rubbermaid boxes, blows out the candle and puts it on top. She slides the whole thing across the expanse of the basement toward the light. Doing this kicks up a lot of dust, but it's quick. Anna is close to the finish line when she sees a shadow from the corner of her eye. Something blocks the wan light from the dirty window on her right.

Instinctually she crouches behind the stacks of boxes and peeks around. The shadow is the shape of a tall, tall man. He appears to be doing some kind of dance, his midsection swaying just a bit. Although she's frightened, it comes to her that this isn't a person. It's definitely not a dimensional living breathing human. It must be a garment bag or something she didn't notice on her way in. She shoves her pile of plastic boxes, keeping it between her and the shadow. At last she reaches the anteroom bound off by the utility sink, the furnace, and the ring of light over the steps.

She bounds up the steps to get—wait. The door's shut. The door is stuck shut. She wrenches the handle this way and that, yanking and pulling the door with her five-foot tall frame and… nothing. Deep breaths. She tries turning the handle both ways, this time more calmly. Nothing. Goose bumps ripple across her skin. She feels them crawl across her back and over her stomach. She sits on the steps and peeks over at the hulking shadow. Now the dust motes she raised swirl everywhere.

She remembers something…feels a sense of déjà vu she can't quite…yes she remembers now, finally. This inspires her to throw herself at the door one more time, again to no avail. This happened to her before when she was pregnant with Betsy. This happened before, but last time it wasn't an accident. All those years ago. Erik trapped her down here. He was drunk and they were watering the plants and taking in the mail while his mother was out of town.

He wanted to convince Anna that he grew up under the oppressive presence of his father, and he succeeded because there it was again. It was no garment bag. It was Erik's father, the shade of the man hanging by the neck from his belt, secured over the water pipe. She peeps over the banister in his direction, and faint and shady though it is, he is there. He's little more than an outline, the shadow of a large man's body hanging from the neck, dead.

How could she forget this? How? How? She'd been seven months pregnant when Erik terrified her by locking her in the basement for what seemed like hours while he paced and ranted and raved about his father. Erik had been only seven when he'd discovered his father there in the basement. At first she screamed and begged to be set free, but she quickly realized she was wasting her breath. Erik would never hear her over his own shouting. And even if he did hear her he wouldn't let her out until he was good and ready. She gave up and sat on the middle step, right where she sits now.

How many times did he tell her that story? How many times did the pitiful image of that brokenhearted little boy trapped inside the man convince her to forgive, to forget, to show godly compassion toward the victim.

He came home from his paper route to a strangely silent house. Normally his mother would be clamoring around frying eggs or if he was lucky bacon. His father would be reading the paper muttering about the news. They might argue about some unimportant detail. Then again they might scream and yell and lob pots and crockery at one another. But silence was a rarity.

That particular morning Erik junior came home to silence. He tiptoed around the silence to find his mother. She wasn't in the kitchen or the bathroom by the back door. He took the hallway towards her bedroom. Perhaps she was sick, lying in bed. She wasn't there, but he was shocked. The room was torn apart. Every drawer was pulled out, every shred of clothing flung about. Lamps were overturned, and the mattress almost shoved off the frame. He was young, but not naïve. Once he was certain she wasn't there hiding somewhere he headed back to the kitchen. There he would telephone his aunt as his mother had instructed him to do in an emergency.

But something caught his eye, drawing him instead into the sitting room (what his mother called it anyway). More overturned lamps and end tables. Ahh, there she is. He caught sight of her shoes and ankles from behind the reading chair. "Mother?" he cried out. "Mother, are you alright? Shall I call Aunty Jean Mother?"

As he rounded the couch and could finally see over it he realized mother was not fine. Mother was awash in a pool of blood bubbling from her head. He knew immediately she was dead because she wasn't moving, or talking, or screaming. She must be dead. There was so much blood. Blood everywhere.

Erik junior realized he was standing in a puddle of his mother's blood and leapt free only to realize he was leaving tracks. This made him realize there was another set of tracks already there. Bigger tracks heading…he followed them…toward the basement door, which was flung open.

The tracks disappeared, worn away, nothing left. But momentum carried little Erik forward through the door, down the stairs. At first he saw nothing amiss. Figured he misunderstood the tracks, and he turned around to retrace them. Out of the corner of his eye he saw it, the dark shadow where streaky light should have been. His father dead, hanging by his neck from his black leather belt absolutely still, silent.

Erik junior didn't call Aunty Jean. He called an ambulance. Then he called the police. Then he went to get Mrs. Hartford next door, and she called Aunty Jean who took Erik home with her where he stayed for nine months while his mother recovered from the two gunshot wounds to her head and spent some time gathering herself in a sanitarium. Erik senior was quietly cremated and his ashes buried unceremoniously in a rural pauper's graveyard, where they could bury sinners and those certainly damned to hell.

Anna couldn't count how many times he had slurred his way through that story in a drunken stupor. How central that story was to the man he'd become was clear to Anna perhaps for the first time as she sat staring at the shadow in the dim light. Only now, she can see there is nothing more than a shadow, a memory, a dense fear hanging like a ghost in the dusty air.

Anna shakes her head at her own naïveté. How had she managed to forget that her own husband had locked her in a basement he believed was inhabited by the ghost of his homicidal father? How had she managed to use this childhood incident to excuse every terrible thing Erik had become?

What she sees now for the first time instead of pity, sorrow, compassion, or anything else is that Erik is potentially dangerous. All these years she felt only for the pain of the boy, never fully realizing the boy had become a man—a man who had inherited a wide streak of family madness with the potential to inspire mortal hatred.

No longer afraid, Anna carries her strength to the door and not surprisingly this time it opens…as if by magic. She does, however, prop it open before she retrieves her boxes of memories from that dingy basement once and for all.

CHAPTER FOUR

DECLARED INVALID

Weeks go by and the weather changes from cold and snowy to chilly and damp. During this time not much changes for Anna. She has been urging Erik to get a place of his own and sending out feelers for a job. She still drives back and forth to care for the kids, make meals, and run them to and from school, practice, and various lessons. The list never seems to end but, honestly, Anna doesn't mind.

She's had a few so-called meetings with Erik; a few lunches and dinners to discuss their divorce, which only remind her of their early dates, each one to more and more expensive, more exclusive restaurants or events. Just like now. Erik recovered nicely despite the incident and was gradually spending a few more hours a week at the office. Today they had the restaurant practically to themselves. The state Senate and House of Representatives were out of session and therefore the downtown steakhouse was unusually empty. Anna treads carefully, noting that Erik (despite doctor's orders) is on his fourth scotch rocks.

"OK, so what I'm going to do Anna is go back to our former divorce agreement and simply have the remarriage of three years ago invalidated. That way, the original divorce will simply stand." Erik says.

"I'm not sure what that means 'invalidated.'" Anna replies. Over the years she learned it's best not to ask questions directly or insinuate that he was unclear or wrong. Sure, operating this way is slower and more cumbersome, but it's also less likely to inspire an outburst…especially after four scotch rocks.

"It means, simply, dear that our remarriage will be declared farcical, nonexistent…for all intents and purposes, invalid." He replies.

Anna has a million questions but dares not pose them now. She gestures to the waiter, who is chatting with the hostess, that they'd like their check. "So…OK then Erik. I'll come to the office next week to get a copy of the paperwork. Now Maggie has a campus visit scheduled this weekend so I'll be taking her to the airport around dinnertime on Friday. And Drew wants to talk to you about going to some golf camp over spring break in a few weeks." With this she stands up to take her leave.

"Oh don't worry dear, the paperwork will be ready long before next week. In fact, I'm waiting to hear from Judge Ouray in Keskert County. It should be all wrapped up any minute. He's agreed to seal the whole mess under lock and key so none of my colleagues or judges I work with will have to know the gory details. Remember, I have friends everywhere dear." With that Erik slaps his platinum card onto the leather folder the waiter is slipping on the corner of the table.

"Quickly please if you don't mind. I have an appointment to keep." He nods to the waiter who hies away to do as bid.

THREE DAYS LATER, at one in the morning, Anna answers her cell phone to wild raving. From what she can gather even Erik's pocket Judge Ouray, all the way out in Keskert county where Erik owns half the grazing cattle and the grain elevator, even that Judge Ouray finds it impossible to invalidate the remarriage and enact the old divorce without potentially being in hot water.

"Who'd you hiir?" Erik slurs over the phone. "Whodja get ta bail you out? Who tha hall dja manage to convince to go upaganst me? Huh? Who?"

Anna knows better than to argue or rationalize, or even to try to placate him at this point. These are the watering nights. Nights back when they were living together, back when they shared a room. These were the nights Erik would be so drunk that he'd piss the bed. She'd be wakened by a creeping warmth dampening her night slip, a creeping warmth spreading to encompass her entirely.

It took her a while that first time to figure it out. It just didn't seem possible that a grown man, soused or not, wouldn't wake up. She only wished she were able to get that drunk herself; then, time after time, month after month she wouldn't be wakened by a hot puddle of recycled Johnnie Walker Black. Worse yet were the nights his noise and nonsense would wake her up despite the earplugs and she would get snared by a hug, or he'd throw a leg over hers and she'd be trapped. She could choose to either risk waking him up by moving (never a good idea) or laying there wide awake waiting to feel the spreading warmth. Then at least she'd be sure he was dead asleep and she could finally move. To do so beforehand was too costly—she'd learned that the hard way. The glamorous charm he exuded in public became something quite different behind closed doors, something manipulative and insistent, something capable of punishing determination.

She actually grew to prefer the nights he simply wet the bed. On other nights when he wasn't quite so drunk, his urge would wake him and he'd stumble blindly around thinking he was in the bathroom. The first time it was Drew's dirty clothes hamper. Next it was the linen closet. This went on until Anna simply learned to shut the bedroom door so he wouldn't sense the opening and wander around the house. Then she managed to restrict his nocturnal accidents to his and her clothes hampers and closets. On rare miraculous nights he did her the favor of accidentally pissing in the bathtub. Still it was disgusting, but much easier to clean.

She's glad she's as far away as her mother's house, but she's not so relieved that the kids are in that house alone…with him stumbling around blind drunk. Maggie is used to it by now and she is old enough to know what's going on. Maggie's also a light sleeper and would be sure nothing bad happened to Betsy or Drew. Anna is almost sure Erik'd never do anything to harm the kids intentionally, but accidentally? Who knew?

Maybe she should get a lawyer and aim for sole custody? But how the hell can she manage that without money? Besides she spent almost twenty years hushing up, covering up, and keeping his problems secret. How can she expect anyone to believe her now?

WHAT SEEMS LIKE ONLY A FEW HOURS after the drunken call from Erik, Maggie phones bright and early to tell Anna she'll be driving the kids to school. Today is a rare occasion. Her dad is letting her take a car into town. Despite his tendency toward ostentatious wealth, he never bought his children their own cars. Sure, there were extra cars in the garage they were sometimes allowed to use. But he doesn't want to be perceived as 'spoiling' them.

"Is everything OK Maggie?" Anna asks in code, hoping the relationship to last night's bender was merely a coincidence. It isn't unusual for Erik to be in such an extra kindly mood after a night like last night.

"Sure, everything's fine. Dad left early for golf I think. He left me a note with the keys to the Escalade." Maggie exclaims. Anna can hear the squeal in her voice. Maggie always begged her dad to let her drive the Escalade, but he never would. "And it says… you should come by the office to pick the kids up at four." Maggie adds.

"Really?" Anna asks. "Are you picking them up from school then?"

"Ummm" Maggie hedges. "No, not that I know of. I guess he is or something."

"Alright, thanks for saving me the trip Maggie Mae. I appreciate it. Did everyone-"

"YES," Maggie interrupts her, "We all ate, everyone is wearing clean clothes, and we all have our homework...OK?"

"OK...thanks" Anna replies.

PROMPTLY AT FOUR ANNA SWINGS into the parking lot of his office building. She's already planning dinner. Since the weather is nicer she's thinking she'll surprise everyone by firing up the grill. Thyme and lemon marinated steak. All the receptionists nod at her as she strolls back toward his office suite. Hmmm and green bean salad maybe, Anna's thinking, when Marge shouts her name, "Anna, oh, excuse me...Anna." Marge is practically shouting at her. Anna wonders what has come over the woman. Is Marge suddenly going deaf?

"Yes what is it Marge. Erik knows I'm coming. I'm here to pick up...see there they are." Anna can see Betsy and one or two of her friends standing around in Erik's glass office. The blinds are only partially turned. Anna waves but gets no response. So she starts forward again. Marge appears from nowhere to block her.

"Marge?" Anna says. "Is something...is everything..."

"Now!" Erik shouts as he steps forward to block the doorway to his office. "Help!" he shouts. "Help! Betsy. Marge. Somebody. help."

Anna simply stands there gaping, wondering what the hell is going on now. More of Erik's drama? Anna tentatively tries to make her way around him toward her daughter.

"She's beating me up. She's trying to kill me. Help. Betsy, call the police immediately. You mother is drunk and trying to kill me."

For a second Anna starts laughing thinking the whole thing

is some practical joke gone awry. She can see Betsy through the office window. Anna waves the universal sign for 'come on.' Betsy, however, seems to ignore her as she dials the phone.

"See! See!" he cries as she tries to pass by, "She's beating me about the head and face. She's using her fists! Help somebody, call the police. She's drunk. I can smell the stench of alcohol on her. She's drunk." Now he also starts jerking his six-foot four-inch frame and flailing around in the doorway.

Anna makes a split-second decision to ignore Erik's one man melee. She gives up trying to get around or now over him and simply calls, "Betsy. I'm here to pick you up...you guys ready to go?" She tries to make herself heard over Erik's shouting.

"Betsy," she shouts. Because Erik stopped wailing at the same instant, it comes out sounding louder than she anticipated. "Come on honey let's get..." The only other sound she hears is Betsy sobbing. Through the glass Anna sees the girls huddle together to comfort her daughter. Erik's bulk is the only thing keeping Anna from giving in to her motherly instinct to rush to her crying daughter.

Anna takes a long glance at Marge, who looks pale. The older woman's hands are shaking as she punches numbers into the phone pad. "Hello building security..." Marge says into the headset.

After surveying the scene unfolding around her, girls cowering, Erik half crouched in the doorway, and Marge speaking shakily to 'security,' Anna makes a second quick decision. She simply strides out of the greeting room, all the way out to her car. She couldn't think of anything useful she could do that would diffuse the situation. Let Erik face the embarrassment of explaining his odd behavior to those girls' parents. More than likely they'll be scarred for life. This wasn't Betsy's first time witnessing Erik's outrageous behavior. What Anna couldn't figure out was...why didn't she come? What kept Betsy from slipping past her father and walking out with her? Was she embarrassed in front of her friends? Was Betsy trying to manage Erik's 'mood'…as she'd learned growing up at her mother's side?

Anna drives straight to her parent's house and starts making a list of lawyers she knows personally that she can call for a reference for a divorce lawyer. Obviously Erik is losing his mind. She has to get the divorce settled and get the kids away from him.

She has a total of sixteen names jotted down when the doorbell rings. Anna puts down her pen and skips to answer it before the annoying bell went off again. She opens the door and finds herself laid flat on her stomach with some man pushing on the back of her head, slamming her face into the foyer tile. Anna struggles and kicks and tries to draw the attention of anyone who might be walking by outside with their dog. What she sees in the doorway frightens her more than the potential rapist on her back. She sees shiny black shoes and navy blue uniform trousers. Beyond that she sees a police car has pulled straight up onto the front lawn.

"Hold still," the rabid rapist perching on her back shouts in her ear. "Hold still, or we'll take you into the station." Anna stops struggling. It's no rapist ramming her head into the floor, it's one of Cambridge's finest.

She hears the other cop standing in the doorway hiss under his breath saying, "Enough…Ricky…enough."

That prompts one more solid head shove into the ground before 'Ricky' gets off Anna's back. Then she feels the cold metal slip around her wrists. She tries to jerk away one last time before she hears the click. It takes both of them to drag her out the door and throw all five foot, one hundred pounds of her up against the car. The more level-headed cop is looking around at the crowd gathering in the street. Neighbors, dog walkers, passers-by, all start assembling to rubberneck. Anna tries to scan the faces for someone she recognizes, but the way they have her pinned she can't see clearly.

"So rich bitch tried to kill her husband this afternoon and thinks she can just walk away? Huh? That right?" says Ricky, who turns out to be not much bigger than her.

Anna says nothing. It's her instinct to shout, to call to the people on the street for help, to struggle, to fight, to do something. But she stands stock still, staring straight at the other officer's fourth brass button and saying absolutely nothing.

When Officer Ricky stops shouting and poking his finger in her face, she calmly looks Officer 'Not Ricky' in the eye with a cool level stare. Officer 'Not Ricky' looks about as old as her stepson Greg. She can see that he still misses spots shaving.

As the silence grows more and more uncomfortable and she can feel Officer Ricky starting to twitch next to her, she finally says, "If you're charging me, take me to the station. But before we go I want you to write down your badge numbers for me, fellows."

As she suspected 'Not Ricky' goes pale, drags her five feet away from the car, unlocks her cuffs, and walks around to get in the driver's seat.

Ricky steps up into her face and says, "My badge number is six- six- six, bitch. I bet you'll never forget it." And then he scrambles to the cruiser with his head down.

CHAPTER FIVE

SANCTUARY

Once she slams the front door behind her Anna leans against the thick sturdy wood thinking, 'Thank you, oh thank you, thank you.' She's fully aware things could have been far worse. Anna recognizes that in other countries even today women are dragged from their homes and murdered in the street for less. But this isn't Baghdad. This is the capitol city…law and order rules here. Anna thinks 'I'm going to report those little snot-nosed wanna-be cops… how dare they…don't they know who—ah yes. Of course.' She's no longer the wife of one of the wealthiest attorneys in the city, in the state even. No longer Mrs. Reinhardt, wife of prominent attorney and philanthropist…well fair's fair. Now that Anna's gone Erik will no longer be a philanthropist. It was Anna who managed all the charity work and donations. As his wife, his better half she'd become a professional volunteer, one of the ladies who lunch.

As the full impact of the day's events sink in Anna slides to the floor, relieved when the sturdy ground lands under her. What was the story with the cops? A gentle signal sent by Erik to remind her what it's like to be out from under his wing of protection?

Officer Ricky and his pal obviously weren't serious. Otherwise she'd be in custody, down at the station facing charges. What charges would they be...battery...assault at worst? Would his accusations require proof? Would Erik need to come forward to display his alleged bruises or broken bones? Any judge in the world seeing her five-foot, hundred nothing next to his six-six in cowboy heels would look at him cross eyed for wasting the court's time... right? Anna could no longer guess what Erik might be capable of, what else he was up to.

Impotent tears of rage come as she sits with her back pressed up against the front door. Sobs wrack her as the fragility of her position, the limits of her resources, creep into full realization. Her impulse is to call someone, but who? Her parents are in Florida. Besides, all she'd do is worry them. Her brother...well, her brother now worked for Erik at the firm. He'd be hamstrung by the new house, the arrival of the twins, and his wife's predilection for shoes; expensive shoes. Brother or no, it's unlikely he'd threaten his cushy position to help her at the moment.

Her sister all the way in Chicago...she'd only say 'I told you so.' Anna's sister Katherine despised Erik on sight. In the few weeks Anna brought him around before their wedding, her sister Katherine practically growled at him whenever he entered a room. When Anna pressed her, Katherine said "I just feel it, he gives me the creeps. There's something seriously not right with that man sister. My advice, run as far as you can in the opposite direction."

Of course, it was easy for Katherine to say. Even back then Katherine was already well on her way to following in Mom's footsteps. Twenty years ago, when Anna married Erik, Katherine's husband ran for state representative. Part of Erik's appeal way back then was that he seemed to have the same potential. He appeared to be cut from the same cloth as men like her father and brother-in-law, only more raw and flashy. In fact, Katherine's husband was no longer a mere state representative as the girls' father had been. He'd eventually won a seat as a state's senator in Washington D.C.

Considering her current hysterical state, Anna reasons that calling her sister is unwise.

Anna needs someone to encourage her to scream and yell, someone to feed her vodka (heavy on the orange juice) and stay until she falls asleep. Anna needs a friend. She dials Janet, but no answer. She doesn't bother with a message. Anna needs help but only too late she realizes the bulk of her relationships, her friendships somehow revolve around Erik, either through his business, his political intrigues, or his farm and livestock interests.

Nearly everyone Anna spends any time with, beyond planning charity events or sharing a fundraiser table, is the hired help. Housekeepers at one time came and went through a revolving door. Anna eventually gave up on the idea of 'help.' After she'd get a new one all set up in the family routine and with good rapport, Erik would lose his temper or otherwise scare them away. Anna wasn't particularly interested in the details.

Back when Anna's hopes were still high, when her kids were toddlers, there was Dorthea, who stayed longer than any others. Dorthea was the one who found Anna a few times a week hiding her tears from the kids by crying in the back basement stairwell. Dorthea, unlike the rest of the planet, was not fooled by the grandiose size of the house or the garages full of shiny cars.

"What'd that man do this time? Huh?" Dorthea'd ask. "You know, one of these times he's going to make that leap from shouting and waving his arms in the air to putting his hands on you...or one of those babies of yours. Before that, you better stand up and muzzle him once and for all. Show him who's boss around here. He's nothing but a man. You're a woman, and that means by nature you're stronger and smarter." Evidently Dorthea's knew more about Erik than Anna had realized.

But Dorthea had been wrong. He never did make that transition. He kept right on yelling and screaming and frothing at the mouth any time his ire was triggered. Anna asked herself all the regular questions following the horror stories she'd seen on Oprah. Anna asked herself time and again if this was abuse? If she was a victim? But because he never hit her and...because she chose him, for better or worse, she couldn't see herself as a victim.

She most certainly was not a 'battered wife,' absolutely not. Anna lived well, travelled, came and went as she pleased...for the most part. She came from a well-to-do, well-educated family. Anna was self assured, not the type likely to fall prey to such...to such... to such...

Early on, the only marital problem Anna thought they had was that Erik 'didn't love her enough.' She'd wheedled and cajoled, went through the entire gamut of Julia Child recipes, lost weight, gained muscle, studied his likes and dislikes, ultimately devoting herself to being the best stepmother (then, eventually, mother) in the world...in repressed hope of winning his respect.

Within weeks of marriage it became all too obvious that he had no respect for her. Once, when she cried because he called her by his first wife's name in flagrante, he snapped at her, "Oh Christ shut up about it already...don't act like you didn't know I was marrying you to get a live-in nanny for my kids. Besides I would never compare you to her, you'll never live up to her." Anna remembers thinking at that time...'I'll show you.' She showed him alright. She showed him she was taking on his challenge. She was going to prove him wrong. She intended to make him recognize how worthy and giving and caring she truly was.

Anna sits on the floor of her parents' entryway absolutely dumfounded at what has become her life. She thinks now of Erik's first wife, the dead one...as the lucky one. Occasionally she wonders about her death. At the time, in the early eighties, the entire world seemed to be offering alternative cancer cures. Erik chose for his beloved wife of barely four years, the mother of his two infant children, a Laetrile clinic somewhere in South America. After five months the breast cancer allegedly overwhelmed her. But Anna always wondered about this mysterious woman whose place in life she took over. The woman's shoes were still warm when nineteen-year old Anna stepped into them.

Such thoughts are not helping her get off the floor. In fact, she's rather encouraged to sprawl out further, get lower, sink deeper into feeling sorry for herself. How can her world be crashing in around her like this?

Anna spent so much of her time over the last few years feeling sorry for herself she'd become a veritable professional. But it was, and is, always in secret. Feeling sorry for herself had become her hidden talent. She never confessed honestly to what was happening, even to Dorthea. They never discussed any of it outright, just inferred in general terms.

When the kids were old enough to go to school Anna recognized she would never get the kind of love she needed, the kind of love she envisioned all her life, the kind of love she wanted from him. So she opted to simply steel herself against Erik. By that time she recognized he would never love her. And, frankly, that was fine. But he did love his children the best he knew how, and Anna could fault him less on that front. On that front, at least, there still seemed to be some hope.

What small portion of his life he spent playing father is what kept her from tearing their family apart. No matter how much she wanted out of their marriage even when she did 'divorce' him last time she chose not to rock the boat, not to interference with the sanctity of the Christian household or something like that...Erik had been going through a congregational phase. He must have read somewhere that big zealous churches were somehow good business. Anything that improved his bottom line was considered. The congregation turned out to be an insular community teeming with deformed and diseased relationships, which to Erik was hog heaven.

He is or had been a mostly decent father—particularly to Drew, who at the time of the secret divorce Anna felt needed Erik more than her oldest step-son, Greg. Her predecessor's oldest, Greg, hadn't returned since leaving for college three years ago. Greg was raised in the early years when Anna was still striving, still working furiously to win Erik's love, approval, and respect. She wondered if that striving, that urgency hadn't somehow made her a better parent, a more engaged mother to the older kids. But her own son Drew, years younger than Greg, somehow turned more to his father than the others. However, Betsy was Anna's through and through, all out all in. Betsy and Anna together were bugs in a rug.

It was about when Drew and Betsy started school that Anna came to the conclusion she'd been gypped, tricked, ripped off, sold a bottle of snake oil, or somehow been beguiled by him, by her ideas about marriage, by love, or by all three.

Anna felt bereft of love, affection, partnership, teamwork, understanding…things she should have been granted by virtue of his vows. But Anna failed to recognize that simply by virtue of his vows at the altar she had been entitled to be loved, honored, and cherished. She hadn't needed to earn it, win it, or gain it. Erik promised to offer her these gifts freely, without reservation or judgment; then he failed abysmally. This was one of the few valuable insights she gained from the innumerable counselors, therapists, and ministers they tried over the years.

She lies on the cold tile wondering what Erik could possibly be concocting. A hot stab of fear spreads through her body as the question 'What is he up to?' forms in her mind. The marble chill eases the impulsive flames of fear a bit. Her knees are Jell-O. For an instant she's glad to be sprawled on the entryway floor, saving herself the trouble of falling.

Anna feels threads of speculation roping her down. Her mind throws out questions, each one an anchor. He could be...what if he's...What do I do if he...He might...He could just...Just inviting the numberless possibilities to mind burdens her so much it's impossible for her to sit up, stand up, and simply put one foot in front of the other. Truth is, Erik could be up to anything.

That's the way the whole thing started, after all. From the very beginning Erik had been up to something, alright. Initially, that 'something' revealed itself in the shape of a guerilla wedding. He asked her at a fine restaurant, offering a modest promise ring; promising fireworks and full carats within weeks of their first date. At a cocktail party a few weeks later, when asked for the hundredth time in that short span, "So Erik...when's the big day? Eh? Did you set the date yet?" Erik snapped, "...A week from Sunday." And that was that. Anna was convinced he was driven by the urgency of his passion for her, his urgency to begin their adventure together.

Anna had thirteen days to plan her wedding, find a church, rent a hall, print and mail invitations—eh, scratch that—announcements. Find a dress, a florist, music, food, and napkins, choose entrees, plan a honeymoon, and decide where they'd live. At the time Erik and the kids were living with his mother. Since his wife's death in the Bahamian cancer clinic, he'd retired to his mother's to regroup.

Why was that bizarre wedding not some kind of omen to Anna? No, not entirely true...she was aware of some nagging drawback at the time. She remembers asking him more than once, "Why Erik...why do this in such a hurry?" The only response she recalls was, "Before I change my mind."

But she thought he was joking. He said it like he was joking.

Oblivious to his cruel frankness at the time, Anna felt only vague warning impulses from the back of her mind. Some warning signal...but she was too busy planning the wedding and organizing their life to pursue the reticent alarm buzzing low in the tenders of her gut. She had no time to investigate wild hunches or illogical wondering—at the time, she targeted her skills toward contacting a minister, fielding phone calls, and registering for gifts. It was a mad dash over the threshold, a leap of faith, an adventure, a commitment, a cliff. Anna dove in—fish to water, like the stocked pond past the west pasture.

In a heap on the foyer tile, in a postdusk haze, Anna breathes deep. No magical epiphanies blossom in her mind as she lies penitent and shocked. Right now her impulse is to crawl to bed and get a much needed night's sleep. Things may or may not look better in the morning...but morning would indeed still come.

In the void before sleep, Anna decides to behave 'as if' tomorrow at the house, when she goes to make breakfast. This was an often useful strategy she'd perfected over the years. Behave 'as if' he'd never said it; as if he'd not crossed the line, again; as if he'd not taken a brutal swipe, made a bruise, or sucked the wind from her sails with nothing beyond his glare and his words. Never raising a hand or snapping into a lunge. Well no, not never, but rarely, hardly ever, surprisingly isolated instances, considering. Considering how effectively he managed to sap her life force, tapping her like a sugar maple. He continued antagonizing her to keep her emotions boiling so he could leach more of her energy from her.

There were less than a few isolated instances of physical contact from him. A rare swipe or push, but they hadn't frightened her, rattled her, or confused her in any way. She was almost relieved to have her suppressed suspicions portrayed in flesh, in three dimensions. The confusion descended after the instant confirmation, after the truth was revealed.

This raw truth did not compute with the idea that she'd chosen him. His callousness and narcissism were such a constant surprise and shock, so contrary to the glib and charming man she'd met, that Anna never quite fully believed what she was experiencing.

This paradox pinned her there in limbo. How could two such conflicting truths exist? The truth was, once upon a time…she trusted him. Despite her long ago intuition not to trust him with her hopes, Anna made a choice to share her life with him, to confide in him. Admitting that her choice was wrong would take years to fully wrap her mind around.

Admitting that she betrayed her own best interest, her own best potential, by choosing him would have destroyed her back then. Staying with him, growing immune to his faults and weaknesses, compensating for his breaches, filling his gaps, and in general running around plugging up holes in his dike was easier than admitting she'd deluded herself. How had she fooled herself effectively enough to let a man who turned out as he had, to father her children? It took her years to compile enough evidence for logic to overwhelm her emotions and wrench her from delusion.

As she floats in her parents' empty house in the dark sea before sleep, Anna recalls the precise instant the tide turned. She pinpoints the second the camel's back broke and she came face to face with the folly of staying married, of staying with him. She registered the cost and the consequence of not leaving Erik, getting the kids away from Erik sooner the instant she recognized in Drew his father's subtle attack, his father's derisive words toward her. When she recognized in Andrew's manner a miniature reproduction of Erik's conceited tolerance of her, any illusions she'd been secreting away shattered.

Her life irrevocably altered. Her perspective drastically changed the afternoon Anna recognized Erik's barely tangible sneer on Drew's face. Two years ago, when Drew turned old enough to play league golf at the country club, the two of them became immensely closer. Anna guessed that Erik encouraged Drew to develop a taste for what Erik considered the finer things in life…expensive cigars, expensive whiskey, expensive meals, and the finest brandies and wines.

When she confronted Erik about Drew being too young to 'taste' the wine and whiskey, when she suggested that he was too young to distinguish a 'true' Cuban cigar he balked. "Are you crazy?" he asked her. "Do you know how far ahead in life I would have been if I'd had someone to teach me these things...you're never too young to learn what quality is." Somewhere in the back of Erik's mind, he longed to be one of the 'Park Avenue Set' from the black and white movies of his childhood.

Erik liked to pretend to know about the best vintages and classic art, but he'd gleaned what little he knew from skimming glossy magazines. He thought of himself at times as a Midwestern branch of the Rat Pack—slick, smooth, and top of the line. Other moments he portrayed himself as some twisted Rhett Butler. She'd heard him brag about confederate roots, boast about being descended from slave owners. And these attitudes were suddenly also a part of Drew when he turned into a real teenager last year.

Of course, because Erik's favored object of mockery and derision was Anna, she wasn't sure why she was stunned when Drew turned to strike her in Erik's fashion. Back then, as Anna'd laid yet another exquisite evening meal on the table, Erik turned away in distaste, asking Drew..."Don't you want some decent food for a change?" Drew sneered at her, "What, is she trying to make the rest of us as fat as her...please...I'd rather have Steak N Shake Dad. Can we please?" And Erik would get up and reward his son with a chuck on the chin and throw his arms over the boy's shoulder as they strolled to the Porsche.

That particular evening as the two 'guys' turned their backs on her, Anna realized that she'd irrevocably lost some portion of Drew forever. Recognizing this in Drew finally gave her a hint to the true danger of staying as long as she had. She wondered if it was maybe too late to extricate her children from Erik's overriding negative imprint, and knew they would wear scars despite her strategy of throwing herself on every land mine and into the crevice of every conflict with Erik.

Until that moment she'd mistakenly believed that she stood as a bulwark between Erik's less exemplary self and the kids for all those years. Coming face to face with the fact that she hadn't succeeded inspired her push for a real divorce, a true divorce this time. This time he was moving out. Sure, she'd been at her parents for a few months now, but this time it would be fair and not a secret and Anna would have her house…maybe even her restaurant pending the settlement.

Visions of her own kitchen, her own home, her own life lull her as she lies exhausted from the strange day. First being accused of assault and drunkenness, and then being harassed by Cambrige's finest. To get free is Anna's focus as she slips into unconsciousness.

CHAPTER SIX

BAG LADY

Despite getting plenty of sleep, Anna rolls out of bed at the last possible minute. "Shoot," she says to herself, "Now I'm going to have to really hustle." She hurries to get out to the farm, make breakfast for the kids, and get them to school on time.

Anna coasts a few right-hand turns hurrying out to the house. Her head is still fuzzy and a bit numb in places from yesterday. She reminds herself over and over to behave as if nothing at all happened yesterday. Anna would not ask Betsy to explain, or confront her with any questions. She decides ignoring the whole debacle is her wisest choice. And that's that.

When she arrives, the house is still dark. No sign of life or movement anywhere as Anna shifts to park. She glances at her dashboard clock. "Oh, this is going to be just great," she thinks, fuming as she approaches the back steps. She shakes her head again at the collection of overstuffed black garbage bags sprawled on the back stoop. Anna wonders if Erik went on a manic purge of some kind, or had a party or something.

The black garbage bags crowd her as she fumbles with her key. She turns the knob and leans in, but nothing happens. She checks to be certain it's the right key. It is. She takes a deep breath and carefully reinserts the key, only to realize it's not going all the way in…or something. She pulls the key out and examines it for bends or dents. Nothing.

She tries again, this time turning the key left to see if it will slide in, then right. She thinks to try the door without the key. Maybe it's not locked or something? Nope.

As Anna raises her hand to knock, thinking she'd have to wake up the kids, a large envelope taped on the door finally catches her attention. She shakes her head to clear it, wondering how she overlooked the thing in the first place. "To Anna" in Erik's hand. Uh oh.

Peeling open the big envelope, Anna finds a handwritten letter from Erik on top of a pile of stapled bundles, one or two with suspicious lawyer-blue bindings.

Dear Anna,

I am as always, darling, willing to put all aside and start again.
I forgive you and want you back in my life and in our home.
I've only ever wanted to be a Godly man, a leader of a
wholesome household, and a strong father. I know
I have fallen short on many—

Anna flips it to the bottom of the pile—nothing new there. His standard boilerplate apology letter, ultimately shifting the blame for breaking up the family onto her.

The next one says it's an 'Order of Protection' barring Anna from being within 500 feet of…

The next one lists a courtroom, judge, and hearing date… accompanied by a thick list of complaints and charges being brought against her…

The next one declares that Anna will not be receiving any maintenance or financial support from Erik as the divorce is pursued…

Another one states that as a result of the attempted murder charges being filed against her, Anna is barred from entering their shared home...

She flips back to the letter, scanning it for some verification of the pieces beginning to fall together.

...until you cease trying to tear our family apart...
I am not safe when you are like this...the children were so frightened...think it's best that you stay away...I hated to do it, but had to for our security and protection...

Anna lunges at the piles of black plastic garbage bags tearing at random to confirm her suspicions. One bag gives way spilling her sweaters and sweatshirts out onto the porch. Anna lunges for another one. She discovers some of her shoes and a few purses. A third spills out jeans and what looks to be winter coats.

Collapsing in the pile of bags Anna crams the papers back into the envelope so she won't have to look at them. Her Comden Apple Knockers sweatshirt tangles around her foot as she...Anna remembers helping her daughter count the apples in the tree on her sweatshirt during long drives. Oh how Betsy loved that sweatshirt. Even this memory can't reduce the impact of her belongings piled on her own back porch.

Anna is tempted to unleash her rage by shouting the sky down or beating the door down or, something. While she's certain that whatever strange confusion ruling the moment would soon be erased by the truth, this guerilla attack has succeeded. Insanity of this caliber could not be sustained. The truth would set the record straight. A reality check would soon dissolve Erik's wild accusations and even wilder actions.

But that knowledge does little to alleviate her more immediate rage and shame. Did he empty Anna's closets and dressers himself? Or did he make Maggie and Betsy do it?

An impulse of fury at Erik's pure audacity, his presumptuous-

ness, shakes Anna's frame. The fact that this confusion would soon
be ironed out and order soon restored does not buffer the sting of
betrayal. The effect of Erik's attack is not diminished by her aware-
ness of its falseness.

Shaking from deep in her bones, Anna rises from the black
plastic garbage bags with mounting anxiety. She's tempted to
scream as she tosses the mutilated envelope and its contents in the
driver's seat. Opening the trunk to load her sad pile of belongings,
she's tempted to tear at her own hair and beat on her breasts as
they did in the bible, but instead she takes off running from the
car and all it now holds of her life. The decision was so quick,
so instantaneous, so instinctual she's past the storage buildings
and rounding the stable before she's fully conscious of what she's
doing. She circles around the stable and strolls in the far entrance,
moving more calmly so as not to spook the horses.

The scent of childhood afternoons greets her. She inhales the
mingled odors of the stable and remembers sunlit afternoons from
her own childhood overlapping with memories of Maggie and
Betsy's horse years. Anna stands and breathes, collecting herself.
Curiosity propels her to greet her tenants. Well no, not anymore.
Not her tenants—Erik's. She wishes she could get all sentimental
about being torn from them and missing them, but that wasn't
true. After Betsy's interest in riding waned, Anna generally ignored
the horses except when noting the cost of their feed and keep on
the monthly budget.

She strokes and nuzzles those that come to greet her. Inspired
Anna decides to have a last gallop. She also decides to take Erik's
mount just because no one is ever allowed to. They were never
particularly hard to handle or fiery horses. Erik just could not
share. Even after he put his chosen horse aside, he often sold them
off rather than let someone else take them over.

Anna savors the wind in her face and sets the horse loose to lead the way. Heading for the wooded stretch separating properties Anna adapts to the horse's natural rhythm. Once beyond the fence lines and barriers the horse tears loose into a full flat-out gallop. Thrilling at the speed and sheer joy of movement, Anna laughs out loud. The clean air, the ruffling breeze, the green filling her brain from horizon to horizon eases her mind and helps her feel glad to be alive. Her horse falls into a rhythm with the prairie equivalent of waves; the shushing and clattering of millions of leaves on the wind.

Out here she can believe that everything will be OK, that everything will work out. She repeats this to herself over and over again willing her heart to grab onto that belief—to take it in, savor it, and remember what it feels like.

Her horse picks through the woods, getting a bit careless as a matter of fact. Anna recognizes that the horse has tired herself out. She hops down and leads her out toward the dirt road through the meadow on the other side of the woods. It'll be an easier walk home.

As Anna rounds a curve a fence-post crew appears ahead. She tries remembering exactly who owns that property. She thinks she recognizes the antique pick up truck, the green lettering. She orients herself, thinking they came out of the woods there...the burnt out trunk up here on the right is where a kind of hidden track veers off to the right to enter her own property from the west. The mint-colored truck rolls slowly to meet her halfway. She waves. He waves. She wishes she could remember...

"Is everything alright?" The driver asks as soon as the truck rolls within earshot. Anna gives an exaggerated nod and smile, waving widely to let him know she isn't hurt or anything, just heading for the turnoff she knows is so close. Habit forces her to assess her appearance. She inwardly rolls her eyes...a mess, ugh. She hates that feeling.

As they close in on each other, the driver comes more clearly into view. Anna has a vague hit of recognition but that's it. The logo on the side of the truck, "D'ELLARTE PRODUCE" she remembers...what, from childhood?

He speaks as they meet. "Carlo Dellart," he says sticking out his hand with a glint in his eye. He knows she doesn't...that's nice thinks Anna. She responds in kind, "Anna Reinhardt."

"I know," he nods. "Nice to see you Mrs. Reinhardt. Anna. We've met actually."

Anna cocks her head, knitting her brows, but she knows him, she knows she knows him. "Ah ha." Is all that escapes her. She's still clutching his hand.

"Oddly enough we were neighbors up in Grando County as well. Actually I just bought this place here." He says, politely taking his hand back to gesture around.

Anna nods.

"Nothing's wrong with your horse there?" Carlo asks.

This snaps Anna back to consciousness. "No, no she's fine. Just a little tired I think. It was so beautiful out I—I wanted to give her a little break."

Carlo nods in understanding. There's still a cat-ate-the-canary glimmer in his eye that keeps Anna off balance.

"So...heading for the track around to your back fields?"

Anna smiles thinking yes of course...that's what I was doing. It seems since he appeared she's forgotten where she is standing, where she's headed, and even what she's been doing. Somehow she just expects him to keep talking as if he were going to burst into a fairy tale...or something.

"Yes." She nods. "Yes...I am. It's just up here the turn off, on the right past a blackened elm. I remember even though it's been a while."

Carlo smiles even wider, "Why don't I walk with you...make sure it's up there?"

"You don't have to do that." Anna says with a dismissive wave. But he's slid the truck off to the shoulder, shut off the engine, and is emerging from the driver's door. She changes her opinion to, "Great! Thanks. Yes." She's grinning like an idiot and can't quite put her finger on why.

He's not a large man. Not like Erik. But Carlo is more solid, more down to earth somehow, Anna senses. His presence by her side is new and interesting.

"Do you ride often?" Carlo asks.

"Afraid not. This was just a…a spur of the moment. An impulse kind of thing." Suddenly an image of the car trunk gaping open, ding, ding, dinging to remind someone there's a key in the lock. The black plastic bags piled on the stoop. The spill of clothes… for an instant Anna loses her breath, missteps, stumbles a bit. She's nearly forgotten what's waiting for her. Now suddenly she's in a rush, feeling frantic almost to hurry back and try to fix everything, mend it all up as quickly as possible. She's alarmed and even more distracted, if that were possible.

Carlo sustains a gentle patter of comments and observations that do not require her response, for which she is grateful. He really is intuitive and kind, incredibly kind. She's relieved to spot the track turnoff not much farther past the post-holing crew. Now she can return the kindness and turn her full attention to the gentleman on her left.

She takes a long look at him, thinking about the name, Dellart. D'Ellarte. Still nothing. She gives up on figuring out how he knows her and focuses on what he's saying.

"Are you going to be in town full time these days?" He's asking.

"Oh. Yes, yes I'm in town for some time now," she replies.

"Why don't I do this…let me put your name on the list for the opening. I'd love to hear your observations on the restaurant. It's only the test run, but it should fare well. The only drawback is the preview's tonight. Sorry about the short notice."

"The restaurant…tonight," says Anna. Suddenly the information clicks into place. The restaurant. Dellart. Restaurant. Tonight. "Right right. Oh yes I'd love to. Yes." She nods with inspired enthusiasm.

Now she knows who he is. He's a big time contractor, owns the hotel—the biggest, tallest, and finest in Cambridge. He took over the restaurant in the hotel from the old subcontractor. Dellart. D'Ellarte. That's right. His grandfather started out in the produce business, his father grew it into a grocery store. The farm up in Grando County was one of their…they owned that produce supply farm. Own the grocery store, grow the produce, own the farm. Smart.

"Say what name did you finally decide on for the restaurant?" Anna wonders aloud, hoping she hadn't already missed it.

"Oh I just went with Grandpa's name, at least his last name before it was changed, "D'Ellarte's. From my father's father, Carmello D'Ellarte"

"Beautiful." Anna replies. "Well, really, thank you so much," she says offering her hand one more time before turning off her track. "I'd love to see what you've done to the place. Really."

"Well I look forward to hearing your opinion." Carlo says with a nod as he plants his feet to watch Anna disappear.

Anna takes a few steps, then opts to swing up onto the horse to get home faster. She turns to look back, waving to Carlo. He gives her horsemanship a nod of approval and one last wave before she disappears.

CHAPTER SEVEN

EASY AS PIE

As she's putting up her purchases from the market Anna wonders if it really won't be so bad. Obviously, if she can't be around Erik because of his little scam the kids will come stay with her until he clears out of the house. That makes the most sense. Temporarily they can stay here at her mom and dad's, with her. This brilliant insight shines through after her ride in the fresh air. Well, of course, she can't even take the chance of calling Erik—at home, at the office, or even on his cell phone—until she sorts out the little legal bump he's attempted to create. Since she is, for all intents and purposes, exiled from the farm according to his crafty legal maneuvering, the kids would certainly come live with her. Anna assumes Maggie will drop them off after school. After all, why else had Erik given Maggie the car? With Maggie driving them, Anna won't have any reason to go out to the farm and Erik won't need to skulk around here by her parents' home. With Maggie dropping them off, the adults won't even need to see one another. Now it's all beginning to make sense to Anna.

Tonight would be their celebration dinner! No Erik—they'd soon be free! Without his influence, his intrusions, they could all settle in cozily together. When the divorce is finally settled she may even have her restaurant. He is finally going to divorce her. Once this sinks all the way in she beams rays of eminent relief from ear to ear.

She phones her parents in Florida, chatting happily and asking them if they think it's a good idea for the kids to stay at their empty house with her. "Of course…of course…" they reply. "Congratulations. It's finally happening." They knew how desperate Anna was to get out, although the details were blurred. They'd heard rumors about possible infidelity on his part for years. After a few dropped hints and open-ended questions, they let it drop… chose to let Anna bring it up. She never did in so many words, but they supported her divorce if that's what she wanted.

Conscious of the slow sweep of the clock's hands Anna flutters around the house putting sheets on the spare beds, deciding which room for whom. Would Maggie want to come? Would Erik let her? Cross that bridge when we get there.

At one o'clock she takes the precaution of text messaging the kids. That way they'll find the info on their cell phones immediately when they turn them on after school. Her text reads:

"Come straight to Grandmas—

luv, Mom."

By three fifteen she's run out of things to do. The jambalaya's on the stove and everything is as ready as it needs to be. She errs on the side of caution, making up a place for Maggie to help her feel welcome if she dares to buck her father. Anna knows Maggie'd rather be with them. She's picked up and put down her phone three times already, pretending she isn't checking for missed calls.

She stirs the jambalaya and puts more clean towels in the bathrooms. She paces. She picks up her phone to call five more times, but puts it down before really dialing. She walks past the front window four times, looking toward the street for signs of her kids. Another fifteen minutes finally pass.

At four o'clock she breaks down and calls Maggie since she was the one driving. Or so Anna presumes. "...Please leave a message." Maggie doesn't pick up.

"Maggie?" sings Anna into her phone. "Is everything OK? I just want you to know that you're welcome here with us. When you drop off the kids you're as welcome to stay as...well you know. Jambalaya and fresh bread for dinner!" Anna is at odds as to whether to put the loaves in the oven yet. The fresher the better but...maybe they went home to pack some things, planning to stay until the weekend.

At four thirty Anna catches herself wringing her hands in her reflection in the picture window. What could be keeping them? she wonders. Where are they? She breaks down and phones Drew. "... leave a message." Drew doesn't pick up.

"Drew? Its Mom...where are you guys...is everything OK? I'm starting to get worried, but you know me. Just—give me a call let me know when to expect you here at Grandma's."

She dials Betsy less than five minutes later. "Leave a message." Anna can't speak. Cold dread creeps up her spine. Betsy always answers. She especially would today. Anna only hopes Betsy isn't too worried about her. Betsy was perhaps a bit too tied to the apron strings, if anything.

By five o'clock the bread is ready and she's dialed Betsy twenty more times—but let only three of them actually go through. This blackout is infuriating. Would someone just please call her back. "Please. Please. Please..." She mutters through gritted teeth, pounding her fist on the side table with rising velocity. Just call me and let me know what's going on. Please... She feels she can handle anything if she just knows what that is.

The minutes drag on like hours. In the growing lateness of the hour, Anna is finally force to admit to herself that they won't be coming, at least not tonight. In an effort to deny her fear and apprehension that something deeper, more menacing may be going on, Anna sits dry eyed in front of the television. She's oblivious to the dancing light, chewing dry bread, and finishing a bottle of wine to numb her growing sense of dread. Good wine too, that might as well be vinegar as far as she can tell. At six thirty she scrapes the jambalaya into the garbage and washes up.

Next she phones Janet. She's known Janet as long as she's been in the capitol. Anna even brought Janet on her guilt trip...the European tour Erik successfully bribed Anna with to forget about her extramarital liaison, her young and foolish faux pas. Anna and Janet's friendship stretched, faded, and renewed depending on locations, marriages, divorces, and the few years Janet plied her trade on the West Coast. When the competition for cosmetic surgeons got too intense there Janet brought collagen, facial peels, and tattoo eyeliner to the prairie states. Although they hadn't gotten together in months Janet arrives with all due haste, guessing quite rightly the gravity of the situation. She knew it was inevitable.

After settling Anna for a soak in the bathtub, Janet sneaks a look at the pile of suspect documents. Frankly, they frightened her. While Anna is lost in la la land, pragmatic Janet can see the handwriting on the wall. She'd witnessed some ugly things during her years in LA, but this was shaping up to exceed even those. Janet makes a few exploratory phone calls, pulling strings to get some special appointments organized for tomorrow.

In the bathtub Anna focuses only on what could happen tomorrow. Tomorrow the kids will phone or drop by...for sure... maybe even before school. Well, at the very least Drew or Maggie will bring Betsy by in the afternoon. Betsy must certainly be falling to pieces. Tomorrow Anna will make honey braised ribs... and chicken. Maggie won't eat ribs. And what kind of salad, oh a ·wedge salad that's perfect. With that settled in her mind she lies back enjoying the warm water, letting the gentle heat penetrate her head, drawing out the nagging, repetitive thoughts that have haunted her since this morning, since the envelope, since "…call the police. She's beating me about the head and face," Anna floats ever so slightly on the surface tension.

"Hey…prune girl…you planning on returning to the land of the living anytime soon?" Rapping on the door, Janet says, "C'mon lets' get out of here. I'm invited to a…"

"Restaurant opening?" interrupts Anna. "That's right I'd completely forgotten…"

"Exactly. Yes. A restaurant opening? It's totally closed door, hush hush, a pre-run evening to test the staff. And here I thought I was going to whisk you away to some exotic, surprise…and you already know?!" complains Janet.

Opening the bathroom door to a surprised Janet, Anna says, "Not only do I know about it…I was invited by the owner himself, personally." Janet exaggerates her look of mock irritation. Anna laughs a bit before adding, "Didn't I tell you I ran into the new neighbor out at the farm?"

Janet replies, "Uh no, we hadn't gotten around to anything quite that mundane yet."

"Turns out Carlo Dellart scooped up the Crawford's old place. I ran into him when I took Erik's private mount for a spin."

"No you didn't!" Janet asks in exaggerated horror. "You took his horse out…?"

"Yep I certainly did." Anna says nodding resolutely. "Why, what's he going to do if he finds out…divorce me?" This generates Anna's second chuckle of the evening.

"Look at you making jokes and everything…good for you. Go Anna. Now, what are you going to wear?"

With that, the two of them fall into a familiar routine of joking, teasing, and critiquing one another's wardrobe choices. Anna quite forgot what a simple joy such routine banter could be. She feels a bit guilty laughing and having fun while she's involuntarily separated from her children. They weren't in a refugee camp or in danger, really. In fact, they were right where they'd be on any other evening. The one left out was Anna. This gave her pause.

"Any chance he'll show up at the opening?" Janet interrupts.

"Huh? Who? Oh Erik…show up tonight…at the restaurant?" Why hadn't Anna considered this before now? She pauses to do so.

"Well it's his first official night as a single father, so he may feel obligated to stay home. Then again, he might go with the whole 'keep things normal' concept, and his going out on a weeknight, a Thursday no less, is 'normal.'"

She reaches back in her memory to uncover any crossed history between Erik Reinhardt and Carlo Dellart. Nothing immediately registers. The two men apparently operate in different circles. Erik with the lawyers and politicos, Dellart with…who knew?

"OK, so is that a yes or a no…do you think Erik will show up tonight?" Janet asks again.

"No?" Anna replies. "I don't know. No. Probably not. No!"

IN HER ELEMENT AT LAST, Anna takes careful note of the details of the restaurant. There are things he couldn't do anything about; the location and parking…it was in the tower hotel downtown. Because it was built thirty years ago, the glass-enclosed top floor has always been a restaurant in the round. Carlo Dellart took it over when he bought the hotel.

The décor was gorgeous, understated but not corporate. Roomy tables and sturdy chairs. Anna lost count of the number of restaurants that made that very mistake, using aesthetic statements as tables. It takes a few visits for the shiny novelty to wear off, but eventually diners realize they're uncomfortable, that their plate feels precarious on the table. And they stop coming. Even the tables for two here at Dellart's are ample looking.

What Anna didn't expect was the ebullience, the giddy joy spreading throughout the place. It was as though everyone in the room was happy at the same time. Nor did Anna expect to find the enigmatic Mr. Dellart behind the bar filling glasses, chatting amiably. Everyone seems to know him...well, of course, it is his opening after all.

Janet hasn't even made it that far inside yet. She was hijacked at the door by two gossiping acquaintances. Anna takes in the glasses, the place settings, and the linens; generous, sturdy, and understated, respectively. What impresses her most is the lighting. Getting the lighting just right is a balancing act. Anna also understood why the evening started so late...7:30 p.m. The sky...the setting sun bathes them all in the ever-changing rosy and golden hues that fill the western horizon.

The whole room and everyone in it glows ever so faintly in the unusual light. For a while charged conversations grow subdued. At the peak of the sun's performance there is a general intake of breath, a hush that lasts for the final few minutes. When at last the sun rests and the colors are no more, a sheepish round of applause incites laughter and more furious applause.

Anna notes the emergence of secondary lights magically appearing to keep the restaurant bright enough. "Beautiful... lovely," she murmurs to herself as she scans the ceiling for their source.

"Why thank you..." Carlo says, extending a small glass of champagne toward her. She accepts with a gracious nod and a genuine smile.

"How long in advance did you have to book that command performance?" Anna asks him.

"You know," he says..."as soon as I was old enough to understand what they were saying both my grandmothers told me over and over again, 'I'm praying for you Carmello.' I thought they must have been praying I'd survive childhood…I was a mischief maker. But after that incredible sunset I think that was my grandmothers' prayers for me." He holds up his glass for her to join him in a toast.

"Ohh and the good stuff too," Anna notes after her initial sip. Carl only laughs. "Did you pick out a seat," he asks as they stroll between tables,

"Where are you sitting? Here, let's set you up here. Who are you with? Introduce me to your friends." He says this gesturing at the waving Janet and company.

Although Erik would have been offended, she loves that Carlo Dellart planted Anna, Janet, and two or three friends in view of the kitchen. While she thought he was giving her a peek behind the curtain, he'd really seated her in his serving area. Although everything appears to be operating smoothly Carlo obviously still delights in rushing in and out of the swinging kitchen doors with platters and trays. He strolls from table to table like a bridegroom encouraging a celebratory air.

Anna is almost too overstimulated to register the wafting scent of the edibles taking shape in the kitchen. She hadn't even considered the menu yet. She's enjoying herself too much to stay in her head too long. In fact, that realization has her determined to turn off her analytic thoughts, sit back, and enjoy the ride.

Anna can't remember the last time she'd been waited on with such genuine interest in her comfort and pleasure as she was in the care of Carlo and his staff. Maybe it was the special mood carrying over from the magic of the sky show earlier. Perhaps, she thought, this is what it feels like to be among truly happy people. She could breathe. She didn't have to analyze every glance, every gesture. She can't remember the last time she had more than a single glass of wine or champagne. It was her unspoken responsibility to counterbalance Erik's voluminous consumption with her own sobriety. Someone had to be levelheaded enough to keep the peace, to get them home in one piece.

Anna realizes it's been forever since the madness crossed her mind. She's gone at least, well longer than she can remember not thinking about Erik, the kids, the problems. Probably even an entire half an hour. Determined to keep such things at bay, she throws herself into the conversation ongoing among the nearby tables. She's introduced to Brian and his wife Debbie, Carl's accountant if she's keeping up. Janet surprise, surprise, already knows them or at least Mrs. Accountant that is. Plates are exchanged, entrees tasted all around.

At some point as the meal draws to a close there's a mass exodus of 'those who.' Those who: must call it a night, that have to get home to the babysitter, that need to be at the airport or train station early…after all, it is a weeknight. Those who don't…linger on gladly as the dessert trays are unveiled.

Across the aisle Anna spots Carlo at long last sprawled out, legs akimbo with a towel thrown over his shoulder, and a full glass in his hand. Those still on their way out parade by offering Carlo one last salut! He hoists his glass in response so often he barely has the opportunity to wet his whistle.

Janet, Anna, and company are thoroughly enraptured by their dessert choices asking the inevitable questions…'does it have nuts,' 'is that real whipped cream,' 'did you say strawberry and chocolate?'

As Anna deliberates, Carlo sweeps in saying, "Wait a minute… wait, wait… I've got just the one for you Anna." He chooses a neat triangle of some kind of pie, a la mode, placing it before her inviting himself to sit down.

"Apple?" She asks.

"The best apple…" he replies nodding. He hands her a fork and takes one from the cart for himself. Just as she is about to launch into the concoction, Carlo holds up a hand. Anna freezes. Carl reaches over and nips off the very tip of the point from her pie and gulps it down with strange resolve. He even makes a face as if to say 'ta da.'

Looking bewildered Anna raises the whole plate offering it to him...she doesn't have to have the pie...if he wants it.

"No, no. I don't want any. Go right ahead. It's for you."

Bemused Anna turns the plate around and starts tasting from the back crust. Carlo looks at her oddly.

"Oh no," she laughs embarrassed. "It not that. This is how I always eat my pie. Oh no. Really Carlo," and she laughs some more when he laughs too.

"I'm not surprised," he adds in low tones.

"What? Why? Why what does that mean? Eating from the wrong end of the pie...? Janet. Janet, does that means something? Eating the crust first?" Anna asks, appealing to the others for clarification. They all shrug, either because they had no idea or they didn't want to stop eating in order to answer.

Carlo leans in closer to Anna and says, "I'm not surprised you can't eat your pie right way around. Shall I tell you where we've met?"

"No, really, I've done this since I was a kid." She insists. "I've always eaten my..."

"Shhh!" he says putting his finger to her lips.

She nods to his finger but says, "Ok yes...tell me where we met."

"You really don't remember..." he asks.

"Not off the top of my head," she answers.

"The university's 10th anniversary gala..." he says, "...about twelve, fourteen years ago." He pauses. "Big donor's dinner...we sat at the same table. He adds "...my former wife and your former husband I hear?"

Anna was beginning to get embarrassed she couldn't remember.

"No I—sorry. I can't believe I can't remember…anything," she murmurs.

"Well let's see, you were quite pregnant at the time. If I'm not mistaken there was talk about this being your first. You were incredibly young. I must have seemed like an old man to you then."

"That would have been Drew…he'll be fifteen soon." Anna adds. Carlo nods.

"And you were rather quiet, you didn't say much. But your ex-husband, on the other hand, he was quite the entertainer. He told one yarn I found particularly…revealing."

Carlo pauses for a few beats to see if Anna will say anything, anything at all.

"He told a story about his college fraternity—the Phi Gamma, somethings."

Anna nods unconsciously. Yes that sounds like him yapping about his frat boy days, crossing the line, inappropriate context. That's Erik in a nutshell.

"He told a gory tale about a murderous and cruel Fijian king who so couldn't trust his house staff he always had someone else eat the first bite of his meals. Most conveniently he assigned the task to his wife, or should I say wives, for before long he was a serial widower."

"Anyway somehow this tradition came down through his fraternity that the Phi whatever house never eat the point of their pie lest they should be poisoned. They always have their wives or girlfriends, or whoever they can get to take the first bite…for tradition."

Anna knew the old Phi Gamma tradition, of course. That still didn't help her narrow down the evening. Erik still tries trotting out that old song and dance number at dinner parties.

"That night he acted as if he were going to break the tradition, as though he were going to risk his own neck for a change. Then at the last instant he gave it to you and you ate it without so much as batting an eye."

Anna nodded. Of course she remembered that stupid old story. On one of their weekend getaways she met some of Erik's fraternity brothers or other and their wives. Where was that, Florida? She couldn't remember.

The first time they did that shtick Anna was tipsy. They were just dating and the other couples were in on the joke. The first time he'd done it in other company she'd been embarrassed. She felt like a trick dog. She tried ignoring or deflecting his attempts to bring it up or to depart unnoticed before dessert, but it was inevitable.

"What bothered me," says Carlo "is that you were pregnant. Visibly, I mean, pregnant and all and here he was metaphorically feeding you the poison off his plate to save his own skin. It just displayed the true color of the man, his doing something like that. It gave me the chills for a moment that night. And I've never forgotten about it. I've never once been able to do business with that man, for any reason."

Anna sits stunned in a bit of a daze. Hearing her gut reaction about Erik mirrored by someone else was rare and precious. She'd despised that insipid passive-aggressive little trick since the very first time he'd done it. But she went along with him at first, never realizing it would become a way of life. 'Go along to get along' Anna—look what she'd gotten herself into.

Just hearing someone acknowledge that it was icky behavior, tasteless and crass, made her feel lighter, less wrong.

"That's why I took it off for you. So you could enjoy this fine apple pie made by the world's greatest baker...Sue" he called out. "Sue come on over here and rest your weary bones...come have a drink with us." Sue was only too happy to oblige.

Once again Anna was naturally swept up in the friendly banter. At last, though, even Janet was done in by the growing hour and carted Anna away and home.

Chapter Eight

HOPE AND LOSS

Anna had thought Janet was only joking or making a kind gesture when she promised last night to cancel all appointments to help her sort some things out. Anna's shocked to see Janet's car wheeling into the driveway a few minutes past nine in the morning. For the first time in ages Anna managed to sleep all the way through until seven that morning. But by nine, she was up and anxious and starting to pace and mutter. Janet's car pulling in the driveway floods her with relief.

Anna made a choice to organize her energy around fending off situations that would get her feeling bad today. After yesterday's insanity, feeling bad was 'bad' and to be avoided at all costs. Anger, resentment, and self-pity were all bad. Better to steer away from such emotions. It was a bit like living in a mine field. She's gradually developing a map of the hotspots and learning to avoid explosions. At least she's no longer being prodded blindly through Erik's emotional landscape. She has an image of herself, eyes bound by a dirty cloth as he pokes her between the shoulder blades, using her as a kind of human shield. She tears the image from her mind as if destroying a billboard.

At some moment as she relaxed before sleep that night Anna recognized that allowing her feelings to get away from her, to be urged into anger, depression, fear, or anxiety on account of Erik was akin to being yanked around on a leash. She wants independence and will not settle for anything less. Not interdependence, not reaction, and not remaining enmeshed in Erik's twisted games.

She's o-u-t out of his crazy minefield. She needs all her resources to learn to navigate her own emotional landscape.

Always efficient, Janet went straight to the top. She arranged a meeting with a well-informed committee member of the State Bar Association. Who better to offer recommendations for representation against the head of the heavily advertised Personal Injury Enforcer; Reinhardt & Associates? His local media presence saturated the airwaves during local broadcasts of shows like, "Cops," "Judge Judy," "Montel," "Real Life Mysteries," even "Dr. Phil." The Enforcer ads were imitated by morning shock jocks in the big cities where Erik advertised heavily; Chicago and St. Louis.

As she ticks off the agenda for the day Janet's upbeat tone rings a bit hollow to Anna's ears. Janet is far too preoccupied by the charges, or whatever they are, associated with what Anna has come to think of as, 'the office theatre incident.' Janet just doesn't understand what a farce it was, what a lie. Betsy was there for goodness sake, and two of her school friends Anna had known for years. Those charges would disappear instantly under the most cursory of scrutiny. Anna was sure of it. All Anna cares about is securing a divorce…once and for all.

Even the affable attorney Dennis Stanhope looks rattled as he peruses the packet of papers Anna produced after some who-we-know-in-common chit chat.

"Anna you're clear on the fact that you will not be receiving any maintenance or financial support from Erik for the foreseeable future…that is, until this whole mess is sorted out, which frankly could take months. Years if he puts his back into it."

Anna nods, struggling to swallow that.

"So…do you have other resources you'll be using to fund you're legal battle?" he asks point blank.

Anna opens her mouth to speak, but nothing comes out. Tears well up as she struggles to find an answer. Janet interrupts with, "Well that's just it Dennis. That's the crux of our problem. Erik has tied everything up for the time being. We're looking for someone smart and aggressive, and maybe even hungry enough to work on contingency, collecting his…or her fees once Anna receives her settlement."

Dennis falls back in his executive leather chair. "Whoa…this could take years you realize? Especially with Erik's resources. There are few reputable—I don't know how…" As Dennis looks at Anna a rainbow of emotions flutter behind his poker face.

Janet interrupts again. "But Dennis, certainly there must be an endless line of attorneys Erik has pissed off, beaten using questionable means…there must be a long list of lawyers eager to 'get back at the 'Enforcer'."

"I'm certain that there are," he assures her, "dozens if not hundreds of attorneys who'd give their eyeteeth to take down the Enforcer in what promises to be…if you'll excuse me Anna…a volatile and messy divorce. But remember, lawyers are practical people. Not likely to volunteer to work, in essence, for free in hopes of a lottery-sized end payout…even for revenge."

"Well first of all," says Anna at last, "his holdings are, I'm guessing, at least three times larger then he lets on. So the payout will be potentially bigger than presumed." As she talks Anna rises to pace. "He's got property in six states that I know of. Heaven knows how many title loan stores and currency exchanges he owns across the country. So…one." She holds up a finger. "The payout will be a bigger jackpot for the willing candidate. What was the other fear…the other objection? Oh the delay…"

"Right," Dennis replies, "not a lot of independent attorneys can operate for a year or more without a monthly stipend for fees, filings, paperwork, motions, and whatnot."

Anna goes on, "So we're looking for someone who's made it. A lawyer who's established, set up, maybe part of a larger firm so the cost of pursuing Erik is absorbed up front…"

Janet adds, "Oh, or someone who's nearly retired, who has lots of assistants and can use the ultimate windfall to bankroll an even better retirement than he hoped."

"Right, right…" Anna nods, her eyes glowing. Even Dennis seems to be getting the hang of it now, adding, "Well certainly there must be someone who meets those qualifications, that the Enforcer just screwed at--- oh pardon me."

"No go on…you've got it." Anna says. "How about someone he hit early on, years ago. One of his earliest splashy headline cases maybe?"

There's a rapping at his office door. "Yes" he answers. "Your lunch Mr. Stanhope, you're due at the country club in ten minutes."

"Right, thanks Jean. I'm…yes. On my way." Dennis turns grinning to Anna and Janet.

"Actually this works out rather well. If you don't mind my making a few discreet inquiries among colleagues that is."

Anna's eyebrows raise.

"This is a committee lunch. A lot of lawyers who meet our first criteria. Let me ask around about the early days of the Enforcer to see if I come up with any names. In the meantime let me keep these," he said indicating the piles of papers, "get them sorted and see if and when any responses are required." he says as he slips into his suit jacket. A very nice, well-cut suit jacket Anna thinks automatically.

Anna lets out a deep sigh of relief as he walks them to the door. "Exactly Dennis, right. Yes, ask around, drop hints, fish for volunteers. Just see what you can discover."

"Will do," he nods. As Janet turns to leave, Anna takes a second to put her hand on Dennis's forearm. She wants his attention to say…"Thank you so much," before nodding deeply in gratitude.

They were off.

Once back in the car Anna checks her phone for messages from the kids. Nothing.

Janet is almost giddy with relief that they are hot on the trail of the perfect attorney. "Dennis will find someone great, Anna. You know. We've been friends for years…If you need money, I'm here. If you need me to pay lawyers, I'm here. I mean, certainly I'm no Erik but Anna…I'm doing OK and I can help if you need it."

Anna is crying again, but it's only the first time…today, which is good. And this time for a good reason. "Oh Janet. I figured that was the case but this is better, don't you see. This way we get some really motivated lawyer."

Janet interrupts, "I don't mean just that…"

Anna reassures her, "No I know you don't and I am grateful. And if it comes down to it I'll keep your offer in mind. But you know as well as I do that nothing spoils a friendship faster."

They both choke out a hard laugh as they had seen time and again people in their circles ruin friendships, wreck families over money. Over business deals gone bad, over inheritances misplaced, lending…borrowing, you name it. Neither of the women were anxious to tempt that fateful pattern…but if it came down to it, who knew what they'd do?

That's the irony of living among people who have a lot of money. They have a proportional number of money problems. More money; more problems, at least from where Anna stood next to Erik. Erik was for years utterly preoccupied with making more, investing, spending, buying huge tracts of land. She didn't mind all that much—his distractions, his preoccupations kept him out of her hair...for the most part.

Anna can hardly remember how, or even if, money affected her childhood family. She attributed that to the fact that they grew up in the country, on the farm. Anna didn't even realize they were 'well off' until the other girls in high school took to calling her 'rich bitch' because her family had their own house in Florida. Their jealousy was one of the many reasons Anna pushed to graduate early, to get out of that stifling town and off to college early. Anna was a college freshman at sixteen.

"Where to now?" Anna finally thinks to ask Janet.

"Well since it's too early for lunch...how about...shoes?" Anna laughs as Janet points the car in the direction of the luxury mall. "The Governor's Ball is tomorrow. And since Steve is in Honolulu...you're my date," Janet adds.

As the hours creep by the ladies' small talk dwindles. As they linger over lunch Janet watches Anna grow more and more physically restless and jittery. Janet tries to distract her. "Hey did you read the paper about the new intergovernmental harmony between the city and the state? There was a full-color photo of the mayor and the governor making a big display of unity in front of the spot where the Presidential Library is going to be built."

Anna guffaws, "Those two...together? Oh please, did hell freeze over or something? Oh now wait, it must be money. The tie that binds all good politicians together. They must have found a way for both of them to make a fortune off the construction of the Presidential Library."

"Yeah, it was pretty funny seeing them trying to fake smile. They looked like they were grimacing," Janet adds.

She watches Anna register the time and waits for her to say something.

All Anna says is, "I need to get home now Janet. Please?"

This is the moment Janet dreaded. "Why Anna, where do you have to be?"

"Well it's time I get ready for the kids. They'll be coming home from school soon." Anna replies.

"Anna honey," Janet says reaching out to her friend. "The kids aren't coming home."

"Well I know…I know they're not…you know coming home, but surely they'll come stay with me today for the weekend. It is Friday. I'm the weekend parent for the time being I guess…even though it doesn't make any sense." Anna says, gathering herself to go.

"Anna," Janet asks, "have you heard from the kids? Have you spoken to any of them since…the office incident?"

"Well no but…" Anna freezes wondering how long it's been since then. How many days have gone by? She wonders.

"Yesterday you waited for them for hours Anna. Right?"

Anna nods…OK, so that was yesterday…that means the incident was only the day before yesterday…two days ago. If today is Friday then it happened on Wednesday. Anna goes on… "and now it's the weekend so…they should come stay with me. And when they do I doubt they'll want to go back. Certainly their opinions, what they want, will take precedence over anything else? Right? What's best for them?"

Janet nods and decides to finish this conversation not in a restaurant in the middle of downtown on a Friday. Honestly, they were lucky they hadn't crossed paths with Erik already. Janet didn't want Anna to fall apart sitting here in the restaurant. "C'mon Anna let's get out of here."

As they pull out of the lot Anna asks, "Can you take us past the school? Let's at least check the parking lot, see if Maggie drove to school, if they even went to school. For all I know…"

"Argh, Anna this is exactly why I didn't want to take you home…I knew you would have gotten in your car and done exactly that…go by the school. It's not healthy. It's not smart to you know…stalk the kids right now. Not under the circumstances." Janet argues.

"But Janet…" Anna croons, "you're here…that's the difference. You're here so I can't do anything, you know, crazy," she says bulging out her eyes and waggling her tongue.

"Are you kidding me? Like I could stop you," says Janet.

"No I'm not going to…I just want to see them." Anna says. "I just need to see that they're alright, reassure myself. Watch them walk to the car, get in, and go home. I just want to see them Janet. I need to. I have to. I'm worried…"

"Gah stop stop stop. I'll do it. But you have to promise. No funny business. No jumping out of the car, no shouting across the parking lot, no nothing…promise?" Janet says at the stoplight.

"Janet…honestly what am I going to do? All I can do is look at them," Anna assures her.

"I just need to make sure you understand the gravity of the situation. Anything you do at this point only has the potential to make this thing worse, more complicated," Janet adds. "As long as you understand that. We're fine."

"I understand," Anna nods.

In just a few blocks Janet sidles into a 'pickup' parking spot along the street in front of the school campus. The women have a prime view of the pouring forth of the students when the bell rings as well as of the parking lot exit. This is, of course, the private school campus, one of the academy schools. The whole operation is run by the church; that is, the Temple Academy operated by the Christian Temple Fellowship Center.

For just a minute there Anna marvels at the magnitude of what the Temple Fellowship has managed to accomplish. Both her stepchildren attended the Temple Academy but back then it was one simple building. Now the entire campus compound has tripled in size. The so-called 'new' classroom building was in fact, eight years old. Then there's the even more recent monumental state-of-the-art new worship center, the first of its kind in the area. Anna remembers the competitive spirit of the fundraising committees for both operations. Who had the better, more generous community connections? Who could bring more to the table was the gist of it. It was like a political fundraising effort, which Anna knew well from her father's career (and perhaps why she excelled at the game as well).

As Anna sits in Janet's car looking in from the outside she no longer remembers why she struggled so hard, why the game even mattered to her back then. It must have been back when she still believed that if she made Erik look good, if she was accomplished and successful at whatever she put her hand to, she would somehow win him over. From the outside looking in the whole Temple Fellowship can appear like a writhing showcase for petty jealousies played out in competitive one-upmanship.

Years ago Anna stopped counting the divorced couples that remarried others from within the church, creating more divorced couples. How very Christian. Keeping score of who married up, who humiliated themselves, who got cuckolded, and who won the settlement eventually became too burdensome. Like everything else surrounding Erik, the Temple Fellowship was only the appearance of what it was supposed to be. Beneath the very Christian surface was a teeming mass of acting out the seven deadlies—greed, lust, gluttony, pride, envy, wrath, and sloth. She could name a fellowship member that embodied each. But Erik topped them all by breathing life into so many deadlies at once. So Anna took refuge in the boring school committees. There was too much work to do there what with accreditation, enrollment, and hiring for there to be room for much jockeying for position.

Janet keeps her eyes on Anna as the bell rings. She's tempted to engage the safety locks on the car but is afraid Anna would hear the telltale clunk. Anna lights up for an instant.

Janet swivels her head to find out why. A Betsy lookalike, well a girl with the right size and coloring appears to be heading toward Janet's car. Anna realizes it's not her. The girl veers off to the car three spots behind.

Janet reminds her, "They won't recognize or think to look for my car Anna…right? They won't know to look for you here."

Anna nods. But Janet can see the warning does no good. She regrets allowing Anna to talk her into this. No, that's not true. Janet knew all day she'd do this for Anna. Planned it, in fact, so Anna wouldn't have to do this alone.

Anna catches sight first of Drew horsing around with a crew of other boys, throwing and catching a mini football through the crowd. Oh, how many times had Anna told him not to…sigh. Drew looks normal…or the same at least.

Janet elbows Anna as a giant black Escalade noses up to the horseshoe pickup lane. But the driver has white hair, it's not Maggie. Besides, there were a handful of such vehicles associated with school families.

Anna keeps her eye on Drew, taking in his physical grace and ease, the careless carriage of his long lean shape. The height he gets from both sides; Erik and Anna's father. Anna shifts her focus when something attracts Drew's attention. There she is. Betsy.

Unlike Drew, Betsy looks wretched, pale and blotchy, stiff and ungainly. Not at all like her usual self. Anna is pleased to see that Drew recognizes this, although there is little he can do beyond hover in Betsy's periphery. He even puts a protective arm around Betsy when she's unnerved by a pack of screaming fifth graders running by.

"Here she comes," Janet says at last pointing to Maggie. This confirms for Anna the sign Drew just gave Betsy to head for the car. As they get in the car, Maggie rolls up her driver's window and all three of the children are lost behind the smoky glass as the car pulls away.

Within what feels like minutes, the entire street and parking lots are relatively deserted. The whole school departure routine has been choreographed down to a fifteen-minute interlude over the years. Janet and Anna find themselves sitting and staring out at a veritable ghost town.

Only then does Anna turn to her friend, overflowing with emotion, tears spilling over.

CHAPTER NINE

CARRYING ON THE DANCE

Usually immune to the lights and noise Anna feels especially raw and sensitive tonight entering the Grand Ballroom of the Executive Mansion. Her Friday night and Saturday afternoon were particularly desolate without the kids, but she soldiered on doing all she could to ignore the void in her heart. After all the quiet, the ball is a sensory overload. She almost chokes on the air, heavy as it is with anticipation.

The bonus of being Janet's date instead of Erik's is that Anna slips around the publicity line. Erik always demanded they have their couples photo taken in hopes of ending up in the back pages of the Society magazine. The first time this happened was at the Governor's Ball right after their honeymoon, her first gala. The flattery rag always ran a 'who's who' page of stills from local charity events, galas, and whatnot. "Mr. and Mrs. Erik Reinhardt at the Capitol Association for the Arts Denim and Diamonds fundraiser." Erik was disappointed every month at not finding himself featured there. Tonight Anna escapes the obligation to nod and smile for the cameras and at the uninterested governor and his even less involved wife.

The diminutive governor gave Anna the creeps from the get-go. Although he was fresh and trying hard to play the Kennedy youth card, the fact that he talked only in circles spoiled the effect. Though he'd only been in office two short years, he allegedly already had three illegitimate children with three different twenty-something girls in the capitol city. That Anna had heard of mind you. From a cocktail waitress at the martini and cigar bar to the police chief's daughter...the new governor seemed to be making new friends everywhere he went. Anna couldn't understand what these girls thought they were doing, couldn't understand why no one seemed to use protection anymore?! But that thinking just made her feel old and she refused to waste time doing that.

As if reading her mind a masculine voice at her elbow says, "Anna please let me get you a cocktail...let us walk you to the bar." Anna startles at finding Carlo Dellart offering her his other arm. On his left hangs a leggy bottle blonde, an obvious fan of Janet's more expensive augmentation procedures. Nevertheless Anna is relieved to be obscured by companions and that much closer to a drink. This affair is going to be more complicated than she bargained for.

She does all she can to disguise how her head swivels toward the entrance every time a new group shuffles in. Anna does not want to be caught off guard by Erik's appearance. Unlike the restaurant opening, Erik will never forgo the Governor's Ball no matter how distraught he is as a recent victim of 'domestic battery.' Anna wonders if his gigantic ego will allow him to show up donning fake bandages around his head and face. Probably not, he's far too vain she decides as Carlo hands her a gin and tonic.

Carlo's Barbie attempts conversation, "So how do you know Carlo here?"

"Anna," offers Anna.

"Oh, hahaha. Anna, how quaint. That was my grandmother's

name. I think. Funny you don't hear it much now do you?" Barbie says with a straight face.

"Well, actually I hear it everyday," Anna replies. Barbie's face contorts in confusion. Carlo whispers in Anna's ear, "Be nice now, it's not her fault God shorted in one department and shall we say he compensated her with other assets instead." Anna nearly spews her drink all over Barbie attempting to suppress her guffaw.

Anna meets Carlo's keen blue eyes with even greater curiosity. OK, so he's not fooled by the act as so many of them are, but still she wonders, is this his type of woman? Carlo seems so much more, so much more. Oh, she doesn't know what the heck she's thinking. Anna hardly knows the man after all. She has no idea one way or the other what his 'type' is. Nor does she wonder why it matters to her what kind of woman Carlo Dellart prefers.

Anna finds herself suddenly invisible to innumerable acquaintances and associates of Erik's. Rather than being relieved Anna catches herself laughing longer and talking louder in hopes of catching their attention. She's enjoying this after all those years of nodding and smiling and going to the trouble to remember people's names, filing something away for making polite conversation. Yes, so nice to see you again Mrs. Bannockburn. Carol, yes, how is your son Bradley doing at Tech this year? In spite of her disdain for Erik's friends, Anna finds herself annoyed by her apparent anonymity.

As Janet arrives with a new entourage Anna rasps in her ear. "I feel like I'm invisible Janet. Am I? Am I losing my mind? Look there's Bill Delaney and his wife, Karl Hover and his wife, Mike Gallinga and his husband, and...and...what's his name, the chamber of commerce guy! Not one of them has even acknowledged my existence."

"Well good, saves you the trouble of small talking a bunch of Erik's bootlickers. Lighten up lady! Meet my new friends, Abby and

her husband Carson. They just moved here from Oregon where
Carson here was recruited to join our Inspector General's office.
He's a prosecutor, you know…um…the people who stamped out
the license for bribe scandal a few years ago."

Anna smiles, nods, and extends her hand to welcome the
stunned and nervous Carson and Abby from Oregon. The seating
is, of course, arranged but conventionally flouted by everyone.
People sit with those they can stand in order to choke down the
rubbery catered food.

Sitting at a function with Janet is dizzying. Waves of chatty
social climbers crash at Janet's feet in hopes of overhearing or
confirming the latest gossip. The ever-wise Janet diverts them with
the newcomers.

After waifish Abby from Oregon is whisked away to the dance
floor, Carson invites Anna to join him.

Gliding in circles among the crowd in an old-fashioned waltz,
Anna lets the sense of motion take her as the familiar strains echo
in her head. Her ease makes Erik's looming presence closing in
on her all the more shocking. She stiffens and steps back out of
rhythm generating a chain reaction of bumped shoulders and
trampled toes. It takes another instant to register that Erik too
is only dancing, not coming straight for her as she imagined. His
partner is hidden from Anna's view behind the affable Carson
from Oregon. Carson takes Anna's stopping short as a signal to
break for the table or for the bar.

Anna can't resist looking over her shoulder to identify her
husband's dance partner. Erik of course catches her in the act, and
she jerks her head away from his gloating mug. She takes some
satisfaction in knowing the affable Carson is a complete unknown
to Erik. Anna's presence will annoy him, having no idea who she's
with will infuriate him.

Anna's feels a pang of pity for whoever his companion tonight is until she sees its Maggie. Then icy dread slips through her bones. He wouldn't dare be one-eighth as obnoxious, confrontational, and reckless as he was with Anna with his own daughter in tow, would he? From where she is now there is little Anna can do to soften Maggie's fate. Erik's anger and indignation will take its own course. Besides, it was Anna who was his designated scapegoat anyway. According to him it was Anna that ticked him off, Anna that raised his blood pressure, Anna that provoked him. So anyone who is 'not Anna' should theoretically be fine. Right?

'Ugh' thinks Anna, 'why couldn't he have brought an innocuous Barbie like Carlo Dellart?' That way, she wouldn't have to worry.

Speak of the Devil, Anna adds a little hustle to her trek back to the table when she notices Carlo chatting with Janet sans Barbie.

"Speak of the Devil," says Janet as Anna approaches. A smooth grin spreading over his face further charges Carlo's charisma.

"Why here she is…" says Carlo, "here she is. Anna, Janet here claims you have impeccable taste in furniture, design, and decor."

"Well," Anna says trying in vain to read their faces for what was going on. "I like mixing colors and textures, yeah, sure…?"

"Hmm hm, Janet was just describing the wonders you achieved in that old farmhouse," adds Carlo.

Still wary Anna nods slowly… "uh huh…yes. The farm house. I decorated the farmhouse."

"Oh Carlo, out with it for goodness sake." Janet says. After a few more beats of silence Janet declares. "Anna, Carlo has not one but two houses that need top-to-bottom furnishings, the farm house out by…well you know where that is. And, oh you'll never guess what else he bought. Tell her Carlo." Janet urges him with a nod of the head.

"You're familiar with the old Waterston house? Janet here seems to think you are. Anyway, I just hired the contractors. They should be finished with the interior updates in six weeks or so. If you'd be so kind, I'd be delighted if you'd extend your expertise to help me?"

With her mouth agape, Anna finally sits herself down. Janet and Carlo follow her lead. "What?" She murmurs. "You bought the Waterston place across from the old country club? I've always loved that place." Her voice softens and Anna gets a faraway look in her eyes as her head swims with memories of her dreams of that place. "Wow? Wow! Carlo, that's great someone is finally putting it to good use again. Watching that place sit empty year after year always made me a little sad. Congratulations!" she adds with a more appropriate level of enthusiasm. "That's great! Good for you! That's a terrific place. What did you decide to do about the kitchen? Oh, how about the carriage house? What are you... you didn't knock out any walls did you?" Conversation gets easier as the big band takes its break.

Carlo and Janet laugh as Carlo launches into a vivid description of the improvements he's having done. Anna volleys question after question at him. He greets each interruption with more enthusiasm, eager to have involved and thoughtful input at last.

A rumbling static mixed with feedback comes over the sound system. All the formal introductions had gone down before dinner during cocktails, so they thought. Rather than standing on stage behind the podium, the diminutive governor grapples the microphone free from the riser to stand in front of the dance floor for what appears to be a little impromptu chat with the crowd. Anna slumps and rolls her eyes. The three of them give up continuing their conversation as the governor 'would like to thank' people.

"Hello ladies and gentlemen. Thank you for joining my wife Joy and me for this lovely annual event for the Arts Guild." Break for applause. Nodding and flipping the mike cord around like Tony Bennett, "That's right ladies and gentlemen, give yourselves a big round of applause for helping keep arts programs alive in our state schools." Another smattering of applause. "Ladies and gentlemen, as you know, my good friend and long-term advisor Ed Royson has just stepped down from his post as head of my reelection campaign. And I know you all join me in giving Ed a big thanks for all he's managed to pull together for us. Sorry to see you go Ed…Ed…where's Ed, ah there he is. Sorry to see you go Ed. Look what you've accomplished." At this the governor simply gestures to himself in his tuxedo as if to say. 'Look at me now Ma…Top of the world.' As if Ed Royson single-handedly plunked the little governor down in the ballroom of the Executive Mansion with the mike in his hand. Then he bowed deeply in Ed's general direction.

"What I'd like to take a moment to do right now ladies and gentlemen. What I'd like to do right now is introduce you all to the man who's going to keep us here next term…my new campaign manager. You may know him from his work on the senator's behalf, that is before our senator was selected to run for president! Yes, that's right ladies and gentleman, none other than—Tony Roscoe." The governor busts all ear drums by tucking the mike under his arms and clapping directly into to it. Feedback screeches and Tony Roscoe jogs out onto the floor, snagging the mike from the governor to make the noise stop.

Janet, Carlo, and Anna exchange questioning looks and raised eyebrows as if wondering, 'Did you know about this?' 'No. Did you?' Roscoe was kind of a big deal in federal campaign fundraising. Renowned for his ability to bring in the big money, but infamous enough to move along when the star state senator was drafted up to the big leagues to run for president. Why he was joining the governor's team was anybody's guess.

"Thank you everybody. Thank you Governor, and of course thank you Ed Royson for all you've done for this great, great leader who I intend to keep right here for another four years." Smattering of expected applause.

"I just wanted to introduce myself and say hello, and let you know I'm the new guy here on the governor's team. I'm sure I'll get to know each and every one of you well over the next twenty months. Just wanted to invite you to stop by my office over the next couple of weeks, to let you know my door is always open. Now I just wanted to quickly to thank the one man most responsible for bringing me to this fine state's capitol, Erik Reinhardt. Erik? If it wasn't for the persuasive skills of this man here, ladies and gentlemen, I wouldn't be lucky enough to be here taking part in the solidifying of this great state's government." Erik appears, looming behind the governor—stiff and pale compared to the two professionals. Roscoe takes Erik's hand in his, puts his other hand on the governor's shoulder, and poses for the cameras. As the flashes diminish the 'celebrities' are engulfed by well-wishers and the room returns to normal conversation.

Anna and Janet exchange exaggerated open-mouth gapes. "Did you know he was getting involved with Roscoe? Or knew the governor that well?" Janet asks quietly.

"Are you kidding me? NO! No way. I have no idea how or why he had the audacity to get involved with Roscoe. I know nothing!" Anna replies. "Have you met this Roscoe?" Anna asks Carlo. Carlo simply shrugs holding his hands up blocking the very idea, shaking his head as if to say 'no way, not me. I know nothing.'

Anna opens her mouth to say something hateful about Erik, about his incessant social climbing, his vanity, his obsessive need to have tendrils of involvement in every nook and cranny. And if she and Janet were alone the night would have devolved into a mutual Erik defamation society meeting. But Anna closes her mouth, swallows hard all the rising reactions before speaking.

When she does she directs more questions about the Waterston house to Carlo. Janet breathes a sigh of relief that her friend isn't going to get swept away in a sea of misery at the moment. Not that she hasn't earned the right to, with what she's put up with, considering what she's gone through in a matter of days. Janet offers a silent thanks and beams a proud smile at Anna. The last Janet hears as she finally abandons the two of them to their fun is Anna suggesting, "Oh you know what would look great in the front there…"

Carlo responds, "I was thinking pear trees? Yes?"

After they finish comparing plans for the outside, Carlo jaunts off to the bar for fresh cocktails to support their discussion of the inside of the Waterston house. Much to her own surprise, Anna finds herself smiling. She's actually enjoying herself at one of the year's most obligatory social events. She rests back in her chair, taking a deep breath and savoring the moment only to find herself face to belt buckle with Erik glaring down at her, now alone at the table.

"It won't work," he hisses. Anna is tempted to jump up and confront him on her feet until she realizes how uncomfortable he is hunching over her. Instead she folds her hands, setting them calmly on the table and saying, "Oh it's lovely to see you too Erik. Maggie looks lovely by the way. Is she enjoying herself?" She punctuates her jab with a vacuous smile.

Ultimately Erik crouches down to meet her in the eye, saying, "It won't work Anna. You won't get what you want by going through with this divorce."

"Oh really and why is that Erik?" Anna asks with mock sweetness.

"Because I'm going to make you regret ever crossing me, make you regret ever even knowing me. I'm going to make you…" he blusters on and on and on. Anna only blinks and smiles as if he discusses nothing more than the results of the company golf outing.

After his subverted tirade finally winds down Erik is red in the face and his right hand twitches for a drink. Anna realizes he's stuck there in his awkward squatting crouch position. His frame is folded uncomfortably to blast her directly in the eye with his fury, and now he's stuck and can't get up. He's so unhealthy and out of shape he's stuck.

Anna swings her legs around the other side of her chair and skips away, leaving Erik hulking over and empty chair, at an empty table, across the vast sea of white linen.

CHAPTER TEN

NIGHTMARE

Anna is running across a destroyed landscape; the aftermath of some horrible catastrophe. She is barefoot and the howling gale scatters debris everywhere. A flying clothes washer crash lands to her right, sending her reeling in the other direction. Sirens blare, the wind roars. She spies Betsy and Drew cowering beneath a picnic table up ahead. They are not twelve and fourteen as they should be, but Anna guesses more like four and six.

Anna ducks to just miss being blindsided by a flying vacuum cleaner. The kids are pointing at something behind her. She turns and finds their father in a tuxedo crouching on his knees in the center of the maelstrom, howling in rage and panic. The land immediately surrounding him is stripped bare, decimated, but Erik is fully intact. Only his hair ruffles a bit in the wind.

Now Anna is torn. She was heading toward the children, running to rescue them, to take them to safety. But now she realizes she can stop the storm, stop the destruction, eliminate the danger if she can just knock Erik over. All she has to do is knock him down and the whole tornado ceases.

Should she grab the kids and run? Or try to stop the madness by knocking him over, jarring him, knocking him loose from his power?

Anna turns and turns again, looking at the kids and then at Erik, the kids…Erik. Jerking her head back and forth and—her own flailing wakes her in midair as she tumbles out of bed.

'Not again,' she thinks, 'Not another one, not again and again.' Anna wakes every morning, or rather 'comes to' as 'wakes' implies she gets any actual rest, which she doesn't. Rest is something that's eluded Anna for weeks now. More accurate to say Anna surfaces every morning from a black sucking sea of dark fear and worry. All day again today her head will echo and buzz with fatigue and confusion. Which is bad, today of all days.

"Shoot! What time is it?" Anna says aloud in an effort to shock herself into reality.

Court today.

When she realizes she has fifteen minutes until she must be standing before the judge, Anna resumes flailing in an effort to do six things at once. Not fifteen minutes until she meets Stanhope—yes, Stanhope—deigned to maneuver to help Anna legally himself. Not fifteen minutes until they enter the courthouse. But fifteen minutes before the gavel bangs at nine am and Anna is standing next to Stanhope to put an end to the domestic violence charges and schedule her time with the kids…at last, at long long last. Anna is zipping her skirt while stepping into her shoes with a toothbrush sticking out of her mouth. She spits and rinses at the kitchen sink as she grabs her purse, phone, and keys. The phone, of course, is throbbing from neglect. Ringing and vibrating beeps and dashes of various lengths and pitches, all of which Anna ignores as she races for the car.

'Marvelous. Judges so love tardy defendants,' Anna frets as she winds her way toward downtown.

SHE'S SO LUCKY. As she sidles in the courtroom the judge has some other couple engaged in discussion at the bench. Her lawyer sits in what she considers the batter's box, mouthing, 'Thank God' at her as she slips into the bench behind him. Closing her eyes for an instant, taking a deep breath, she tries to consciously shed the physical tension, the muscular tightening, the cramped facial expression brought on by her fear of being late.

The whispering from the other side of the aisle draws her attention. No wonder the whispering and muttering sounds familiar. Not only is Erik there with an array of impeccably dressed gents from his firm. Betsy and her two best friends are there in the gallery as well. So is Erik's assistant, Marge.

"Should the girls really be here for this? Is that allowed?" Anna whispers to Stanhope. "That's Betsy," she says indicating her daughter and her school friends.

"I can request that they wait outside when our turn comes? Would you like me to?" asks Stanhope. Anna shrugs baffled as to why the kids are even here, out of school for the morning.

To distract herself Anna focuses on her daughter. Betsy looks pale and weepy, as if she's been crying off and on. Anna takes her in for the first time in three and a half weeks. The longest Anna had ever been away from either of her own children, or even her stepchildren, until Greg went off to college that is. 'Is it possible for a twelve-year old to shrink in three weeks?' Anna wonders to herself. Betsy looks smaller somehow, or cowed.

Anna tries catching Betsy's eye, tries to get Betsy to acknowledge her, look at her. Anna expects Betsy to give her a wink or a nod— some signal that she understood Anna was doing everything she could. Anna hoped for some indication that Betsy understood that order would soon be restored and everything would be OK. Things would eventually be even better than before, probably. Anna could hardly wait until the hearing or trial, or whatever the hell it was, was over so she could put her arms around her daughter, comfort and shield her from anymore nonsense. Anna wonders again why she didn't do this sooner. Then the judge calls Erik's name and her own. She watches him rise decked out in his suit and boots as if he is some kind of English manor lord dragged away from his hunting dogs and horses for the day.

The feeling that ran through her nervous system when he took his full height, her conditioned chemical response to his size and the force of his personality: fear. Anna recognizes for perhaps the first time that the complex reactionary emotion she had for Erik underneath everything else was and always had been naked fear. She never left him before—seven years ago she buckled to the pseudodivorce, caved in to 'remarrying' him—because she was afraid, plain and simple. FEAR.

How she could have not recognized this? How this bare fact could have been obscured from her own rational mind baffles Anna. She's tempted to follow the thought to explore this new realization, make room for this new truth, until she hears the judge ask, "How do you plea?" Stanhope turns expectantly to Anna. She missed the charges or whatever went before but, well rehearsed, replies, "Not guilty."

It was a family and not criminal court so the atmosphere is a bit less threatening, but because Anna had never been to the county building to do anything beyond pay property taxes the whole scenario rankles her. The first thing she notes is how obvious it is that everyone knows one another: the lawyers, the clerk, the judge, and bailiff. Cambridge is an incestuous little place after all, not much bigger than a decent-sized university town. For them this is routine, for them this is normal, sitting in this room deciding people's lives.

The judge requests that Mr. Reinhardt's lawyer explain what happened. He states that Anna came to pick up her daughter after school, but because she was drunk Mr. Reinhardt declined to allow Mrs. Reinhardt to take the girl. Mrs. Reinhardt, then enraged, attacked Mr. Reinhardt in an attempt to get to his office to claim her daughter. Of course, Erik's version of the story.

"And we have noted here as witnesses to this, uh…Ms. Obelik, Marjorie Obelik, Mr. Reinhardt's executive assistant." The judge simply speaks directly to Marge where she sits in the gallery, "And, uh, you were there Ms. Obelik?"

"Your honor I was at work just…" she begins.

"A simple yes or no will suffice please ma'am." The judge interrupts.

"Yes…sir. I was there." Marge responds.

"And is this account you've heard accurate. Mrs. Reinhardt took violent initiative against her husband?" The judge asked.

"Yes," she replied nodding.

"And how long have you worked for Mr. Reinhardt Ms. Obelik?" the judge asked.

"Twenty-five years your honor sir. Since right after he…" she stops herself when the judge lifts his gaze from the papers in front of him.

"And which one of you ladies is Betsy?" The judge asks the girls. The two friends on either side lean away and Betsy half stands up, unsure of what's required of her.

"And you were there that afternoon Betsy?" The judge asks.

"Yes." she whispers, then clears her throat ineffectively. Again says, "Yes."

"And these are your friends Betsy?" The judge asked.

"Yes," Betsy replies nodding first right and then left.

"And is this your normal routine Betsy? I mean does your Mom often pick you up from your Dad's office after school like that?" the judge asked.

Betsy is taken aback, looks confused, and searches first her father then the other attorneys' faces for clues.

"I mean is that how it normally goes after school? You and

your friends go to your Dad's office and wait for your mom? And she picks you up later?" the judge offers.

"Uh…no…no, not usually." Betsy answers.

"Special day was it then?" the judge asks. "Father daughter luncheon, special outing planned? Or was Mom out of town or something?" the judge asks.

"Uh…no…uh. I don't. I mean Maggie drove us to school that morning so I don't know." Betsy answers.

"Hm hm" says the judge. Flipping pages and skimming.

He sets aside the pages and directs his request to the lawyers, "Gentlemen, I'd like to invite the young ladies up to the bench so we can chat a bit more. You're both welcome to stand by." He nods and the attorneys rise. Erik indicates to Betsy as the judge says. "OK now ladies, Betsy….uh…and Karen," he flips pages searching, "and…uh. All of you," he says giving up on the third girl's name.

Anna turns on her super mom hearing powers. All she hears is "…there that afternoon?" Some nodding on the girls' part. "Bzzz bzbz bzzz…mom act like that before?" A murmur of indistinct answers on the girls' part. "Blah blah blah bzbzb since then?" Betsy shakes her head no and sniffles a little bit, looking at her toes.

"Describe the incident for me if you will, ladies." She hears quite clearly.

"Your honor," intercepts one of Erik's boys, "…bzbzb bbb blah."

Anna can tell by the judge's body language the guy is pissing him off. "Blahs blahs bzbz bzbzb bbb for themselves. I'd like to hear their version."

Anna's heart leaps with joy, 'at last at last,' she thinks, hugging herself.

Ann is shocked when one of the other girls, that little butinski Sara Lockhart, begins.

"Maggie dropped us off there. She's the one who picked us up after school. We were supposed to be working on our language arts project as a team and…" Sara Lockhart went on.

"And Maggie is? The nanny, a friend of the family?" the judge interjects.

Even though he obviously directed the question at Betsy, Sara Lockhart answers for her. "No Maggie is her older sister, well-l-l her stepsister, she's a senior…" Her voice shifts a bit lower as she grows accustomed talking and becoming more difficult to hear.

The shining instant Anna waits for is not coming. Why doesn't Betsy just step forward and say, 'It was nothing. My father is blowing this way out of proportion. Nothing happened. He just started yelling and thrashing around. My mom just left.' But instead Betsy stands mute, barely answering questions, not turning to look at Anna. Nothing.

When Anna refocuses she hears the judge asking, "…afraid? Safe spending time…bzbzbzbzzz?"

"Blah." Betsy answers. Anna can't tell yet if it was a one-syllable yes or no.

"We can arrange bzbzbzbzzz." He says nodding.

Betsy nods.

"Great…anything else you'd like to add? Any of you?" he finally asks. "OK then," he responds to their negative head shakes, "Take your seats and we'll figure something out."

After a few minutes the judge clears his throat.

"OK Mr. Reinhardt, due to the gravity of your assertions and the fact that none of the witnesses disclaimed them I am going to grant you your restraining order. Do you understand what this means Mrs. Reinhardt? I'm sure your lawyer will explain the details, but your job is to steer clear of Mr. Reinhardt. Don't call him, don't talk to him, don't go where he is. If you end up somewhere he is… leave. You understand me?"

Anna nods swallowing hard, tears burning behind her eyes. Every fiber inside her screams 'jump up and straighten him out. No no no your honor sir, you've got it all wrong'. She senses that to do so would shatter a very delicate balance. Besides, she had no issue, no problem at all staying away from Erik. But what about…

"The children," he said. "Andrew and Rebecca. Let's see fourteen and twelve, for now will stay where they are. If I understand correctly there is a divorce pending, the couple is not cohabitating at the moment?"

Stanhope nods as does the crew at Erik's table as well as Erik . "Yes," "sir," and "your honor," flutter through the air.

"Let them stay where they are, in the family home, but Mrs. Reinhardt is to have equal access. The restraining order doesn't affect her seeing the children. So…let's start this weekend with every other weekend with Mom at her place." The judge says writing notes and filling in forms.

At last he looks up and says. "Everybody on board. Everybody agree?"

Anna has to consciously restrain herself from lunging at Stanhope to urge him to speak up…the whole thing's a mistake, the kids belong with her…in the family home…he should be out, Erik should be out. But she doesn't. She sees that unlike her, Erik can't control himself. He in fact leaps at his lawyers, hissing and spitting in their ears with a vein popping out of his neck.

The lawyers do the shhh, shhh, shhh thing at him. Talking very softly and showing their palms, trying to hypnotize Erik into submission before he blows it. He got his restraining order, not all he hoped for certainly. He probably wanted Anna in jail. But mission accomplished as far as they are concerned. They don't really catch the gist of Erik's larger agenda. And the fact that Anna is OK with today's outcome, is smiling in some degree of relief at being assured access to the kids, that gets under his skin more than anything. He wants her annihilated, not merely subdued.

The same thing chafes Anna's sense of integrity and dignity. She should stand up and fight for the truth, defend herself. Nothing happened, it's all invented. But she compromises based on the second half of the agreement: access to the kids, spending time with the kids, getting back to being their mom again.

The past three weeks were enough to drive her insane. Sure, every other weekend sucks utterly and completely and is totally unfair and wrong, but it's better than the past three weeks, the past month. Plus, a bird in the hand…guaranteed. If Erik keeps the kids from her, he'll be in violation of a court order. She's protected in some way now too. So she accepts the compromise for now. For the time being.

CHAPTER ELEVEN

FULFILLMENT AVERTED

Anna doesn't hunker down behind the steering wheel this Friday afternoon, two days later. She parked in front of the school extra early. Her weekend has finally arrived.

Her cell phone rings as she waits for her kids. "Hello?" Anna doesn't recognize the number. "Hello," the male voice says, "Anna? This is Carlo. Carlo Dellart." Taken off guard she answers, "Oh Hi. Hello. Carlo nice to hear from you." It is amazing how the sound of his voice, the sound of his name even, makes her smile. She smiles speaking to him now. She can't seem to help it. She was so nervous, so keyed up a second ago, and now she's grinning like a fool.

"Well Anna," Carlo goes on, "I have a proposition for you."

"Oh? So soon Mr. Dellart?" Anna feels silly even saying it but she's admittedly still smiling. The bell rings so loudly it startles Carlo at the other end of the line.

"Ohh...uh oh. I'm so sorry Carlo but I really have to go. I—I... can I call you back later?" she says.

"Well sure that'd be fine. But between now and then think about this. What do you say to giving me a hand with interiors of Waterston house up at the Chicago home show this weekend?

Lots of distributors, how about helping me pick out furniture and drapes?"

"Oh Carlo, that's sounds perfect. So great...but I. I can't get away this weekend. I have the kids and I..."

"Say no more. Understood. I'll let you go, but if anything changes you give me a call and we'll be back on in an instant. OK?" He asks.

Anna feels relief. How easy. How kind. He sounded genuinely disappointed but also genuinely OK with it, too. This is shocking to her. She said 'I'm sorry no.' And he said 'ah too bad maybe next time.' He did not try to argue with her. Or force her to change her mind. Or try to convince her she was wrong. Or worse yet, passive-aggressively manipulate her into changing her plans. Or still worse yet, aggressively manipulate her into his way.

During her marriage it got so she prepared for argument, for controversy, over seemingly every single statement out of habit—as a reaction. She had to keep an eye on that. That habit hadn't exactly worked out all that great for her so far. The last month or more, totally away from Erik for the first time, granted the past three months commuting to the farmhouse everyday had been some improvement. These past weeks absolutely without him allowed Anna to realize how much of a drain, how much of a depletion being in his limelight truly was. It was like she'd been let out of the cellar. She could breathe again. She went days and days without screaming or crying. With him, she was lucky to make it hours there at the bitter end. Hmph. Miraculous.

Still smiling at Carlo's much different, much more flexible and easygoing attitude she says, "Sure Carlo. I will. I'm actually disappointed I can't come. Don't have too much fun without me. Hey, and thanks so much for thinking of me. That's nice. I appreciate it." She hangs up, hoping he can hear the smile in her voice.

She's got even more to grin about as the waves of children pour out school doors. Anna likes to watch and see if she can spot her own kids as quickly as possible the instant they set foot outside, no matter how crowded it is. It's a game she's always played. She's gotten really good at it. She thinks she does it by recognizing something in the way they move. Something she can sense. But today she's struggling.

The bulk of the crowd is beginning to dissipate and Anna still can't see Drew or Betsy. Everyone was clear that today was the day. Anna's lawyer even talked to Erik informing him that, as per judge's order, Anna would be picking up the kids from school on Friday. There was no argument from him. So where are they?

Anna finally catches sight of Betsy encircled by three or four friends at the foot of the stairs. Anna leans over the passenger side and sticks her head out waving her arm. She expects Betsy to come running. She doesn't.

Instead the tight circle of girls gradually moves closer to the car, inch by inch. They seem to be dragging her. Anna knows all these girls, has known them since they were in kindergarten, and of course immediately recognizes the two who were at court, Betsy's best and closest friends among the clutch surrounding her now. The giant many-footed and ponytailed organism finally makes it to Anna's car window.

Anna is rather proud of how cool she's managing to be. Not leaping from the car to embrace and embarrass Betsy.

"Hi girls," Anna says to the group.

Betsy is expelled in front. She leans her head down to speak to Anna. "Uh. Hi. Uh, I'm going to be spending the night with Sara tonight so I can go with you now for a little bit…but…I have to be home to get my stuff for the sleepover by like six o'clock tonight. OK?"

Anna is confused. "Well. Betsy I don't think so. I mean I haven't even seen you in like what, over month? I'd kind of like to, you know, make these decisions together like we usually do," Anna says searching Betsy's face. Betsy immediately turns her back to consult the cluster on how to respond.

Anna leans over and reaches out to touch Betsy's arm, gets Betsy to look her in the face for the first time and says, "Please Bets, let's discuss all this somewhere else together. Just come with me honey, we'll figure it out. C'mon." She clicks the door open a few inches.

Betsy rolls her eyes from her neck up, looping her whole head and shoulders around. She even stamps her foot a tiny bit, but she also reaches for the handle and yanks the door open and throws herself in the seat. She slams the door behind her crosses her arms over her chest and barks "BYE!" at her friends.

Anna keeps one eye on her daughter as she turns over the engine, checks the mirrors, and turns away from the curb. "Wait," Anna says at last. "Where's your brother? Isn't Drew coming?"

"Why are you asking me?" Betsy flares. "Like how the hell am I supposed to know?"

Anna automatically snaps, "Watch it! Language."

"He didn't say anything to you? One way or the other?" Anna asks.

Betsy just makes an explosive noise of exasperation, throws her hands in the air, and rolls her eyes again.

Anna slides the car back into her parking spot and dials Drew's phone.

"Yeah...?" he answers.

"I'm here aren't you coming?" Anna asks.

"Uh...oh yeah. Uh, well right now I'm on my way to tee off with Jake and his brother. Then I was going to go to the soccer game with Brandon and the other guys so...Why don't I just call you later? Huh? OK?" he drawls.

"No," Anna retorts. "Where are you? You're not here even? Wait who are you with?"

"Jake and his brother. I golf with them all the time, like every weekend, Mother. Don't tell me you've forgotten already. I have a life remember." And he hangs up. Click. Dead air space. Anna shakes with repressed fury. The audacity! To tell her what's wh-- but he was right. Through most of the sports-related weather Anna hardly sees Drew with baseball, soccer, golf, and friends, and training camps and his rounds of golf with his father, and their dinners. But this still comes as a shock.

She stares open mouthed at the phone, making a little choking sign of disbelief. Anna half shouts in frustration. Then she turns to Betsy and demands, "Do you mind telling me what exactly is going on around here?" Then Anna guns the engine to life and yanks the steering wheel around pulling into the street. Betsy responds by slouching further into her seat covering her chest with crossed arms.

"I mean I don't really get it! You just... I... It's just..." Anna slams her mouth shut before she blurts out anything else. She actually has to bite her lip to remind herself to stop. Normally she'd never tolerate this kind of bossy, petulant snarkiness on the part of either of her kids. Not that they each didn't have their moments, but these moments would certainly not go unchallenged. But things are not...normal...not at all. The kids are behaving in unconscionable ways, unexpected and baffling ways, but Anna can't flip out, can't react as if things are normal. The world has shifted.

Anna drives and takes a few deep breaths calming herself. She tries a new angle. "So obviously your Dad and I are finally getting that divorce. Right? You're not real surprised about that are you? You're not like in shock or anything. Right?"

"Obviously," is all Betsy says. "And why do you think I care? However you and Dad intend to screw up your lives has nothing to do with me. It's not like you consulted me or anything now is it? If I didn't like it, there's not a whole lot you can do about it now is there? We're all pretty much stuck thanks to you!" Betsy's lip starts to quiver and her nose turns pink as silent tears overrun the cups of her eyes.

Anna is fit to start blubbering, too. She makes the mistake of cooing softly and reaching out to touch her daughter who recoils as if a rattlesnake sprung at her. Betsy grabs her cell phone with shaking hands while Anna is trying to find a way out of traffic for a place to pull over and wipe her daughter's tears. Betsy dials while Anna tries changing lanes.

She gets through. "Dad!" she shouts. "You have to come get me. Get me away from her. I can't stand it. Come get me now!"

There is a deep buzz coming from the other end. Betsy grows more hysterical as what Anna assumes is Erik goes on and on.

"Dad's office!" Betsy shouts over to Anna. "Take me to Dad's office NOW!"

Anna, finally pulling over into the park says, "Whoa whoa who…relax honey. You don't have to go. Dad can't make you go." Anna says in as reassuring a voice as she can muster. "Just call him back and tell him everything's OK? Alright?"

Betsy whips out her phone and starts dialing still, heaving and face flushed, eyes hard and defiant.

"Dad. You have to come to the park and get me…Bailey Park! Mom won't take me to your office. You have to come get me here, that's where we are now."

Anna makes the mistake of grabbing the phone from Betsy before her mind registers it's a bad idea. She flips it closed and based on the betrayal on her daughter's face drops it back in Betsy's lap. "Betsy…what's going on? Calm down honey. You don't have to leave with Dad. Everything's fine…"

Betsy starts fumbling for the door handle, the lock. She's out of the car shouting, screaming, hysterical, "You don't know. You don't know! I'm, stuck I'm trapped. And you have no IDEA! All you can think about is yourself. Mother…" At that she slams the door, but Anna is already out and around the car trying to reach Betsy.

Betsy whirls around to deflect Anna with icy eyes glaring. In low tones she says much more calmly now, "If you couldn't handle it…we live there now. We LIVE there now. You bailed. You don't even know. He's out of control and there's nothing…" At this Betsy crumples and collapses into full on tears. She falters as if she's going to sink to the ground but only hesitates and takes a breath to gather her forces before running off. Anna begins to follow her as quickly as she can.

As she runs away Betsy yells back over her shoulder, "There's nothing, there's nothing you or anyone can do! This just makes it worse. I can't stand to have to see you ever! I won't! I promise!"

Anna gradually slows her pace, thinking to herself, 'If I keep chasing her she's just going to keep running'. Fear courses through her bones at what Betsy implied. 'What did she say exactly?' Anna wonders. She gropes in the car, rifles through her bag for a paper and pen, or in this case a stumpy sticky pencil nub and big receipt. She should write this down. She wishes she had had the presence of mind to record it, so she could try making sense now without the emotions and the shock and pain in her face.

She notes the date and time. Writes 'Betsy ran away—Bailey Park.' She writes 'Live there now…nothing anyone can do.' What else, what else…Anna writes, 'he's out of control,' and 'You abandoned us.' Damn, none of it's specific, none of it's incriminating. Even though what she said was oblique, shaded, Anna knew precisely what Betsy meant.

From where she sits in the driver's seat she can still see Betsy stomping over the center green of the park toward the main road,

Patton Avenue. Despite the fact that traffic's heavy and the street is busy Erik's big SUV stops in the right-hand lane and flips on his hazard lights. She can see Betsy heading toward him across the lawn as he just waits there holding up traffic in the right-hand lane. Anna's car is shielded from him by the shrubs and trees at the entrance. As she watches her daughter pull away in the big dark vehicle Anna drops her face in her hands and gives in to her worst fears. They are happening.

She picks up her phone to call someone. To call Erik and yell at him for whatever it is he's doing to the kids. To call Betsy to convince her to come back…that Anna can make it all better if Betsy would just come back, tell the truth. To call her lawyer and tell him he's not doing a good enough job, that she's through compromising the truth to catch crumbs. But since she's not technically paying him she doesn't feel she has any right to complain, let alone tell him how to do his job. Anna stares at the phone wondering who to call now.

She jumps from the shock of the ring. She actually loses her grip on the phone and bobbles it around like soap in the shower. Number; unknown. Hmmm, it could be Stanhope. Did she ever get around to programming him in? Surely she must have. On the off chance it may be her attorney, she picks up.

"Hello?"

"Anna hi, it's Carlo again."

"Oh Carlo," she says quietly, "I'm so glad you called," she chokes out before bursting into tears. And much to her shock and surprise she is relieved to hear his voice. She doesn't want to unload her misery on him and tries to suppress her cries, but none too successfully. But Carlo is a constant surprise.

His voice softens, "Hey," he says gently, "have I caught you at a bad time?"

"Ummm" Anna replies stalling, "Umm no actually…no it's no

longer a bad time. You've rescued me." She says breathing through her hiccupy, teary voice to make it smooth again.

"Then…is there anything I can do?" he wants to know.

"Umm there might be," Anna suggests. "What time is it? Four o'clock? You available for a Friday happy hour Mr. Dellart? I could use at least one strong drink this afternoon, how about you? You fancy a tension tamer?"

"I—I…I'd love one, but I'm afraid. I'm afraid…well. I'm at the airport I was going to take off for Chicago, get there tonight, arrive early at the home show…"

"Airport?" Anna asks. "Flying to Chicago? Well what time does your flight leave? Is there time for a drink first? I'll zip out that way real quick."

"Well let me make a suggestion first…" he says. "Why don't you swing by your house, grab what you'll need for the weekend and then come to the airport and go with me? Really, it's the perfect opportunity. I was calling to ask about what kind of shutters I should be on the lookout for, but if your plans have changed. If you're…available why not let me whisk you away?"

"Oh Carlo," Anna's heart leaps, both at the flattery of the invitation and the relief of checking out for a day or two—to be somewhere else where her problems aren't up in her face, constantly confronting her at every turn. Boy, would that ever be a relief. "But Carlo…what time is the flight. There's no way I can make it out there that fast…is there?"

Carlo laughs. "Oh Anna, the flight takes off whenever you can get here, you just give me a time. Say six o'clock? Does that give you enough leeway?"

"Oh that's plenty of time. If there's a six o'clock flight I'll even be there early to check in and everything. That's plenty of time." This time Carlo can hear the smile in her voice.

CHAPTER TWELVE

FLIGHT

L iterally as soon as she crosses the airport threshold she's met by an attendant who insists on handling her carry-on as he leads her directly to Carlo. Carlo and several others are rising from their seats, reorganizing themselves for action as Anna is swept into the private lounge.

Carlo offers her his arm asking, "Now, if it's alright with you we're going to board and prepare for takeoff right away?" He brings her straight out into the evening gloam and onto the plane. Apparently his plane. The others who sat with him in the lounge; his crew.

Anna is speechless at the idea that Carlo owns his own plane. She marvels at the efficiency and apparent routine of the crew getting his jet ready for takeoff. This is his normal life. This is not even remotely unusual for him, she reminds herself.

He keeps an eye on her, finding her silence through boarding and takeoff a bit out of character. "Should I even ask what prompted this terrific surprise?" he prods.

"That depends," she replies "How melodramatic a story are you interested in hearing tonight?"

"Whatever it is, Anna, I'm sure I've seen or heard worse," Carlo reassures her. Anna presses her head and shoulders into the cushy deluxe seat with a deep sigh. They haven't quite leveled off from takeoff. Anna senses the imbalance inside her head. She thinks, 'as soon as we level off…'.

Despite the overlong pause Carlo remains silent and attentive. Anna rewards him with a wan smile and asks, "What about you Mr. Dellart? You are an utter mystery to me and here I am allowing myself to be whisked away at your command. Is there anything I should know? For example…are you good friends with the Sultan of Brunei or anything?"

Carlo's laughter is the antidote to the disarray inside her head. The resonance of his voice smooths the rough spots, making it easier for her to breathe, to think, and to laugh.

"You've found me out," he says. "I was just about to tell the pilot to change course for the Middle East. That is how I make my money; selling Midwestern pageant queens to the Sultan. How did you find me out?" He continues laughing.

"Oh, they'd demand their money back if you dropped me off with them," Anna says. "I never entered any pageants, let alone won one."

This initial burst of laughter sets the tone for the trip. Anna's confusion and discomfort dissipates entirely.

"Say, was that the governor I saw on my way in? Do you ever let him fly with you?" Anna asked.

"After that huge flap in all the papers about the cost of his flights to Chicago, three, four, even six times a week? I wouldn't get near that mess with a ten-foot pole," answers Carlo.

"Oh, afraid of a little controversy there mister I-own-my-own-plane." Anna jibed.

"Me afraid of controversy? Not in the least. Me not willing to stick my neck out and look like a patronage stooge? Yes. Definitely. Absolutely. I really have no desire to be associated with this regime.

I was surprised your ex was so willing to stand up and be counted among his good friends and backers. You do know what's bubbling under the surface there, don't you?"

From the blank look on Anna's face, her ignorance is obvious.

"Well, our governor is going to be in for one hell of a party in the coming months. There's rumors of federal investigations into his hiring and firing practices, among other things alluded to," Carlo says conspiratorially.

She realizes as he's talking that she's stopped second-guessing her judgment; about Carlo, about running away from her dismal reality. She's stopped the creeping self-doubt she's been experiencing, recognizing it as just a habit; a trained reaction from living with Erik. Erik's brand of crazy succeeded in undermining her sense of self. With him, no decision was safe because the sands were always shifting.

Enveloped in buttery leather, caressed by Carlo's infectious laugh, Anna shifts into an easygoing feeling of normalcy that's been severely lacking in her life. She acknowledges that it just feels good to be at ease in the company of an interesting man.

After they land and arrive at the hotel Anna buzzes with an electric excitement pulsing just below her skin. She knows she must have a ridiculous grin plastered on her face, but she can't help it. She keeps wanting to laugh.

She thought the electric buzz in her body was a result of the flight but because it's still kicking now, two hours later as they sat over the ruins of a lovely dinner, Anna begins to reassess this assumption.

For a moment Anna sits back in her chair, taking a long breath in and gazing around her. She takes in Carlo as he shares with her what he hopes to experience in this new house they were here to bring to life, to animate, to decorate. "I want it to feel like a real home, not a showcase. When I walk in I want to smell the aroma of all the meals I want to make and share in that house, hear the laughter that just belongs there. Oh, I must sound goofy now," He says, embarrassed.

At that moment Anna catches the breadth of longing in his blue eyes. Carlo comes into a new perspective for her. She shakes her head no and wonders to herself if the wine has gone to her head.

"Are we losing you Anna? It is getting late." He draws two key envelopes from his breast pocket. "Looks like you're in 1059 and I'm across the hall in 1060," he says, smiling as he slides her key envelope toward her. Anna isn't sure why she flushes so as he slips the envelope into her grasp. Of course she wasn't going to sleep with him, of course not. She hardly…well of course he'd gotten her her own room. How respectable, how thoughtful, how, how inconvenient.

Anna shakes her head again, this time more vehemently. How did that pop into her mind, she wonders? "Whew I guess I am a bit more tired than I expected," she says reaching for her water (lots of ice), something to subdue the warmth spreading through her body. She tosses back the full glass and in a single gesture rises from her seat, picks up her key from the table and bends to kiss his cheek.

But Carlo turns ever so slightly tantalizing her sensitive lips with his. His wide hand supports her as she leans awkwardly sideways. Despite the picture she must make and the discomfort, Anna is unwilling to shift a single inch. She can feel herself being swept in by that single kiss. He finally releases her, searching her face and penetrating her with his blue blue eyes. "Good night sweet Anna." He whispers barely audible and then adds more loudly, "Shall we meet for breakfast around seven thirty? The convention center opens at eight."

Anna can only nod dumbly. It takes all her dignity to straighten herself and decamp the restaurant. What she wants to do is collapse breathless in his lap and squeal with delight. She would much rather have slipped back into the ocean of his kiss. But she doesn't. Instead, she rambles out on what must be obviously unsteady legs. In her mind she is fleeing, at least that's what she tells herself on the elevator heading upstairs, alone.

She washes up and stands looking at her case. Was it an oversight or a suppressed wish that caused her to completely forget to pack her night slip? She settles for a t-shirt and underwear. Yet, she still finds herself rummaging through her things. Looking for something nicer, something pretty or at least passable. Just in case.

She pulls her hand back as if it were on fire. In case. Her mind echoes. In case what? She wonders, slamming the case shut.

As she locks herself in the hotel room and settles into bed she notices the racing sensation under her skin has diminished, is not as obvious and noticeable as it was at dinner. She wonders what it was. It wasn't necessarily unpleasant, or uncomfortable, it was just-- noticeable. It must have been a little pleasant because as she ponders it she realizes she misses the zinging sensation a little bit. Like the scent of a flower or the burst of a summer sun shower, unexpected but enlivening. She senses that the subtle hum of electricity she experienced is somehow related to him, to Carlo.

She caresses her forearm, testing the energetic tingle she senses inside her. She feels nothing unusual to the touch of her hand. She closes her eyes and her hand slips to her lips as she remembers the solid and tender touch of his kiss. His kiss. She replays that instant over and over and over. Letting herself get swept away by her imagination she drifts into some kind of half sleep. Much to her own surprise she finds herself barely repressing the urge to get up and go knock on his door. Within minutes the debate raging in her head has her standing with her hand on the doorknob, wondering if she should unlock her fortress, tiptoe across the hall, and rap lightly on door 1060.

She scrambles back under the covers. As she drifts toward sleep again she purposely encourages her mind to pursue what it might be like to cross that threshold, hoping to encourage the scene to play out in her dream.

ANNA UNFORTUNATELY HAS NO IDEA of what she was dreaming when the blare of the wake-up call blazes across her consciousness. She surfaces reluctantly, only to be reminded where she is by the fineness of the sheets and, of course, the requisite showers spraying next to, above, and below her island of dreams. 'That's right Carlo…the home show…what time is it?'

With invigorated animation she prepares herself for the complete unknown with equal amounts of nerves and excitement. Anna tries to calibrate what Carlo might expect her to be wearing only so she can put a twist on it to make him comfortable, but with a little something unexpected. These calculations go on for a long matter of minutes before Anna catches herself in the mirror, sees the look on her face as she's thinking those thoughts. 'Is he interested in me? What does he like? Am I his type? How can I keep his attention?'

"Hold on a minute there lady," she says to her reflection. "You don't know a thing about this man aside from the fact that he's rich, attractive, and a smooth operator…what was the deal with that kiss last night anyway? Huh? Just what did Mr. Carlo Dellart think he was doing?"

"Yeah…that's right…" her reflection throws back to her. "This time let's wait and see if you're interested in him. Can he capture your attention? Is he a strong man? A good man? A worthy man?" her reflection demands.

"OK…I get it," Anna relents to the woman in the glass. "Watch and learn. Watch and learn what he's about, who he really is." This resolve, however, doesn't stop her from wearing her 'good' bra and keeping her look simple and classy, just in case.

The day quickly turns into a whirlwind with the mass of consumers flooding the center and the retail reps putting on their best convention grins. 'Buy it today for over 30% below regular retail.' 'Guaranteed delivery in 3 business days.' 'If you purchase an entire suite delivery is free.'

Anna lost track of the innumerable variant shades of brown, cocoa, and mocha couches she laid eyes on. This phenomenon, in fact, became their first 'inside' joke as Carlo took to asking all the floor salespeople for a settee the color of Italian espresso. Not French espresso, or Turkish, or—heaven forbid—American espresso. No, it had to be Italian espresso or nothing. The poor obliging sap would lead them from one brown couch to another while Carlo appeared to hem and haw over the miniscule shades of difference. At one point he proposed testing the color match by pouring some of his steaming coffee onto the couch in question. The game finally came to a halt when Anna could no longer hold a straight face as he started in on them. She laughed and laughed. So much so that her odd behavior actually drove the final would-be-commission-earner away.

"Boy I just can't take you anywhere," Carlo said as he gave the impression of dragging her away by the elbow. However, he was actually using her to shield his potential victim from his own guffaws.

Anna found out that unlike her ex Erik and even her father, Carlo was a self-made man. The number of cell phone calls he fielded that Saturday gave her some insight into the differences between those like her father—who'd made his fortune selling the steel mills he inherited at precisely the right moment—and those like Erik who made his the 'easy' way, by gouging accident victims with exorbitant commissions and fees. Erik rationalized early on that a certain percentage of his clients were liars and con artists. He felt no remorse for shaking them down. When Anna dared to ask him, "What about the others? The ones who are real victims of terrible circumstances trying to make the best of shattered lives and diminished hopes?"

"How am I supposed to tell the difference?" Erik asked her. When Anna didn't have a ready answer, he told her his secret. His way was to assume all his clients were on the make, trying to pull a fast one, looking for the personal injury pot of gold at the end of the rainbow. That way his processing fees, incredible commissions, and hourly rates were justifiable. "Punish them all and let God sort out the guilty. Besides," Erik rationalized, "after I get through with them they're always better off than they would have been without me. There's nothing wrong with me taking my piece of the pie."

Carlo, on the other hand, was legitimately busy. His calls were from construction foremen, business managers, and from what Anna could overhear, two or three times back and forth with the chef at D'Ellarte's about the quality of the seafood that was delivered. During all these interruptions Carlo was polite to the callers and to her by being incredibly quick. He made decisions fast and stated his intentions with full certainty that his instructions would be followed to the 't.'

It was obvious he respected those on the other end of the line. "No, no don't worry about it Mick," she overheard him say, "when in doubt...call. Don't apologize. I'd rather be in on the decision making when something comes up than find out too late." This made Anna smile and shake her head at the vast difference between how Carlo operated compared to what she'd become used to during her years of marriage.

They managed to find several key pieces from which to start building the interior of Waterston house. Something for the formal living room. It was unusual in that it was constructed with unconventional curves married to traditional textures on the upholstery. Discovered purely by accident. She in fact tripped over an ill-conceived and even more poorly placed glass coffee table, landing gratefully on the couch albeit head first. It almost seemed to her that that was why Carlo liked the piece; because it cushioned her fall. He was immediately as attached to it as if it were a stray dog that had retrieved his lost wallet. He bought it on the spot.

Then, of course, there was the kitchen. The home show offered the widest possible variety of luxury kitchen equipment for the connoisseur. Anna discovered to her delight that Carlo was as informed and quite as snobby as she about fancy kitchenware. This became apparent when he wisely snubbed the Subzero display in favor of the top-of-the-line Whirlpool. "They all use the same innards," he reasoned. "Same cooling mechanisms from the same manufacturers. And you can actually get a Whirlpool repaired in the confines of the Cambridge."

Carlo told her stories about growing up on the wrong side of the tracks. Although it was his grandparents, not his parents, who immigrated, the family as a whole was as isolated and detached from the locals as possible while running their grocery business. Everyone who worked for them was family. Uncle Vic drove and eventually came to oversee what grew to a veritable fleet of delivery trucks. Vic's sister-in-law and brother originally owned and operated the farm up in Grando County where Anna grew up. They supplied the grocery with everything from chickens and eggs to specially blended Italian pork sausages. Then there was the lettuce, strawberries, and peaches. Some summers there were peas, carrots, and sweet corn from the farm as well.

The shop itself was manned by the women. Whatever sisters, daughters, or cousins weren't pregnant or nursing took care of the shop in their turn. The youngest Carlo admits he was doted on by the endless stream of sisters, aunts, and cousins. But that didn't stop them from teasing him.

Over dinner that evening Carlo regaled her with anecdotes about his time working at the grocery. By the time he was old enough to follow directions, Carlo was drafted as the delivery boy. Most of the customers he'd known for years. There was a real buzz, real excitement when someone new moved into the area or they attracted a new customer.

"When I was about twelve or so," he started, "we got a call from a new customer, a Mrs. Lively. The address she gave was right across the street from the fairgrounds. Well I knew the area like the back of my hand, yet I had no idea what place she could mean. So I load up her cabbage and potatoes, the poor man's selection by the way, and head in that direction."

"The address ended up being up a flight of stairs at the back end of the biggest tavern across the street from the entrance to the fairgrounds. I would have never found it only Mrs. Lively was on the lookout, standing on the landing smoking in nothing but a silk robe. As I got closer she called me upstairs and hustled me inside where lo and behold a veritable bevy of scandalously underclad 'ladies' lounged about. 'Sit down young man' one of them invited. And believe me I did. I sat down to gawk open mouthed at more skin than I'd ever seen. I was overcome you might say. Of course, they thought I was adorable. They cooed and doted over me. One of them handed me a cold beer to drink. So I sat in somewhat of a daze, listening to them fawn over me. 'Isn't he just adorable.' 'Oh he's going to be a ladykiller that one...'"

"It was the ringing phone that finally roused me from my living fantasy. I jumped up and muttered something about having to get back, more deliveries to be made. And I backed out, taking in every delicious flash of flesh my young mind could absorb. When I finally made it back to the store I ended up taking a good cuffing.

I'd forgotten to collect the cash for the groceries. I'd given them away free."

"Being the kind of boy I was I snuck around there once a day, sometimes more. It only took me a day or two to figure it out. Manny's Tavern had imported a burlesque show from Indianapolis to try and beef up their revenue during the months the fair was shut down. The 'ladies' apparently pulled the same trick with every grocery in town. I'd seen at least two other delivery boys being sucked in only to wander out a few minutes later dazed and dazzled."

"Eventually I started making myself known to them, bringing gifts of a few head of cabbage or a small bag of potatoes. In exchange they'd sneak me backstage so I could watch them perform their risqué songs and dances. Huh, they even had one of the girls doing a fan dance with skimpy molted feathers," Carlo finished, laughing into his glass. "I don't know how my family never caught on. My cousin Vic must have covered for me."

They were both reluctant to leave the table, to end the evening. Anna felt like a human being for the first time in such a long time. It dawned on her as she readied herself for bed that night that she wasn't broken. What she had endured did not break her. In fact it was her depth the attracted Carlo. Too many women he knew live superficial lives of little substance, unlike Anna who earned her wealth of experience the hard way.

It wasn't until they were comfortably ensconced in the cushy leather seats on the flight home Sunday that Carlo broached the subject of Anna's divorce.

"We're still only separated," she told him. "I just found a lawyer who'd work for a slice of the settlement a few weeks ago. Not surprisingly, Erik's being evasive about the full extent of his assets. The lawyer says discovery may take longer than anticipated. So I don't know when it will finally be official," she added.

"And the children?" Carlo prompted.

With that Anna's face fell. The weekend had helped her to put the pain of separation on the back burner for a short time. For that she would be eternally grateful to her new friend Carlo.

"He's...he's...I'm not..." she took a deep breath. "It looks like he's going to try to keep them from me." Anna tried to remain dignified and serene but her lip quivered and a few stray tears escaped, collapsing her resolve and opening the floodgates.

Before a single tear dropped from her cheek Carlo was at her side offering a shoulder. "Why would he do such a thing? Is the man insane?"

Between stifled sobs and choked apologies, Anna bared her soul to him. "Honestly Carlo...I only hope it's his doing. The reason I came with you. The reason I was suddenly free and available is because neither of my own children would come with me for my visitation weekend. Neither of them would see me. Maybe they just hate me? I don't really know for sure what's going on."

She explained how Betsy'd thrown down her accusations and fled from Anna's very presence.

"And your relationship before this? Was it rocky and tempestuous?" he asked.

"Well, no better or no worse than any mother and teenage, well almost teenage daughter. I thought we were doing pretty good. I thought we were still close," was all she got out before reverting to silent tears once more.

"Oh Anna. I'm so sorry." Carlo murmured in her ear as he continued to hold her while she spent her agony.

CHAPTER THIRTEEN

COMMITTEE OF ONE

After weeks of utter silence, Anna's cell phone is suddenly ringing off the hook Monday morning. Clara from the Jaycees: "Just wondering if you plan to participate in the annual rummage sale Anna?" The sale wasn't scheduled for another three months. Bernice from the Temple Academy Mother's group: "Anna were you planning on selling raffle tickets as usual?" On and on, almost a dozen such calls on such pretexts fill her voice mail.

The only call Anna answers for the moment is from Janet; "Hey girl…you disappeared off the grid. Everything OK? Have anything you want to share with your best and oldest friend about your weekend?"

Truth was Anna wanted information about Carlo, and she knew Janet would know or could track it down in a short order. "Exactly how old is he Janet? Is he involved with anyone?"

"Wait, wait a minute," Janet stops her. "Why don't you tell me what happened this weekend? It's all over town that you ran off with Carlo you know."

"Ahhh," answers Anna. "That explains the sudden resurgence of interest in my well-being from among my good friends. You know the ones who ignored me at the Governor's Ball."

"What do you mean?" asks Janet.

"I mean suddenly I'm popular again. I got almost a dozen messages from women I thought were my friends, despite the fact that they ignored me for the past three months. Now all of a sudden I'm a hot commodity."

"Yeah, I guess the word is out," Janet adds. "Everyone wants to know the skinny. Maybe they just want to know if they can take aim at Erik for themselves. Some of them, at least. You'd think they could manage to be just slightly less obvious though."

"Well I don't have time for them just now," Anna assures Janet. "I'm going to talk to Stanhope. He should be able to do something about the kids not coming for visitation. Shouldn't he?"

"You go get 'em girl. If anyone will know, it will be him. Let's get together later to…"

"OK. OK great, you come here for dinner will you? Do you know how long it's been since I had anyone to cook for?" Anna insists.

"Oh Anna!" Anna can just see Janet rolling her eyes. "Fine, but don't let it be too fattening," Janet chides her. "I won't escape this office until about six this evening. But by then I'll be armed with the information you've requested madam."

ACCORDING TO STANHOPE THERE IS little he can do legally to enforce her visitation rights under the circumstances. "If Erik had blocked your access, if he had simply refused outright to allow the kids to go with you, that would have been a simple matter. But under the circumstances there is little I can offer."

"Call them. Write e-mails. Text them. Do whatever you can to reestablish communication and find out what's going on," he advises. "No, wait, let me get back to you after I review the documents to be sure those aren't off limits to you during nonvisitation times." 'Call, write, text' thinks Anna horrified. These mean nothing to her.

"I'm their mother Dennis, their mother damn it! You had a mother did you not? How well would you have managed at twelve if she just apparently disappeared off the planet. For all intents and purposes was banished from your presence?" she demands.

Stanhope says in his calmest and most palliative professional tone, "Anna I understand, believe me. I adored my mother as a matter of fact. At that age I was still under her wing had to be home from the park before the street lights came on. But honestly, we don't have a legal leg to stand on."

All he hears on the other end is Anna breathing fire. He can almost hear her biting her tongue. "Anna?" he asks tentatively "you still with me?"

After a longer than bearable pause Anna finally answers. "Look Dennis. I fully realize that you're working pro bono such as it is... until the settlement shakes out. Then it will all be worth your while. But tell me...do you expect to do less, to be less than aggressive because of this arrangement we made? Because I have to tell you, I must do something. Dennis, I have to get my kids back. I have to. I'm their mother for..."

She breaks down again, much to her embarrassment. She's so furious and so ashamed she hangs up. He rings back immediately, of course. But Anna knows better than to try to continue talking about this with him, at least for the moment. She needs to think, to figure out what's happening and fix it. Fix it for good so she'll never be separated from her children for weeks like this ever, ever again.

She spent weeks living on the thread of hope that the hearing would have straightened everything out, that Erik's ploys would be exposed, that Betsy or Drew, or both of them, would stand up and explain. When that thread snapped she clung to the consolation that they would be with her at least that weekend. Of course, she had all the confidence in the world that once under her protection they would of their own free will and desire stay with her and the court could just deal with that!

But if she can't even see them, can't even talk to them, how can she ever solve the mystery of this growing rift?

To purge the toxic anger and shame welling up in her body, threatening to overwhelm her, Anna laces up her runners and stomps down the front steps heading toward the park. The movement does her good.

The fact that the world outside is unchanged, showing no ill effects from the destruction of her life, is a paradox. On one hand she's relieved to feel the breeze, see the sun, and take in the number of dog walkers and stroller pushers that become her company as she makes her second lap around the park green. On the other hand, the fact that the cold unfeeling world continues going on, that the sun continues to rise and set, that dogs frolic and toddlers giggle on the slide is a slap in the face. Anna feels a bit as if she's losing her mind.

She recognizes that from minute to minute she can be filled with seemingly opposite feelings. At times she's awash in gratitude for the beautiful feel of the sun on her cheek and the next instant she might find herself grinding her teeth, stomping, and choking back screams of agony, defeat, and dismay. She'll have to watch that, keep tabs on her sanity. Considering the tempest she's facing, she recognizes she'll need all her wits about her, need every ounce of strength and will she can muster. She can't afford to slip off the deep end. Not now.

Her walk ended up being long, long; in fact, she watched the shadows shift as she made lap after lap around the park green guessing how much time was slipping by. Once at home Anna takes out a legal pad and starts writing. What ostensibly started as a letter to Betsy trying to remind her of their bond, trying to understand what could be happening, becomes something completely different.

Anna ends up pouring her heart out on paper. All the fears, all the terrible things Erik had done to her and to the children spill out onto the page. So many things she managed to remember. Once opened, the doors to the experiences and events she repressed simply flow...like the time he locked her in Mother Reinhardt's basement.

These negative repressed memories come out like pulling fishhooks free. These truths lacerate her self-esteem, her self-respect. Seeing them all scrawled in black and white...well, blue and yellow...makes her second-guess her own sanity, again. How could she have sat by and allowed these things to happen? How could she have rationalized, excused, and explained away all those painful episodes? How could she have failed to recognize the danger, the neurosis, the psychosis she exposed her children to, never mind herself? And now her children are trapped, stuck in the world of his insanity, as a result of her own stupidity, her own selfishness, her own weakness.

"Damn," she catches sight of the time and realizes most of the day has slipped by. She stomps to the shower to get cleaned up for a trip to the grocery store. She promised Janet dinner and Anna knew that doing something, anything might help her out of the emotional quicksand she seems to be sinking in.

The running water, however, has the opposite of the desired effect. Instead of washing her cares away, the flowing water brings on the tears. Worse yet, she can't seem to stop herself. She covers her mouth to hold back the sobs. That doesn't work. She bites her tongue to hold back the tears. That doesn't work. She's afraid she's going to hyperventilate and props herself up in the corner. She can feel panic rising through her body, threatening to swallow her whole.

Just as all women do in childbirth, Anna calls for her mother, she longs for that all-encompassing embrace from childhood that pushes all the fears away, holds them all at bay. That in turn makes her think of the hundreds of times she comforted her own children. 'That's right honey, you just go right ahead and cry, get it all out. Don't try to hold it in, let it out, Mommy's here. I won't let anything bad happen to you...'

At long last Anna takes her own advice. Instead of trying to hold it all in, keep it contained, she lets loose. The overwhelming power of her rage and fear comes out in horrific wracking yowls and screams. She's thankful she's alone in the house and that the houses in her parent's neighborhood are spread far apart as she clutches at the walls, doubles over, and curls in a heap on the tiles. The hot water runs out of steam before Anna does, so she simply shuts off the tap and ignores the chill. When at last she is fully spent Anna bundles herself in fluffy towels and shuffles into her room, where she proceeds to fall onto the bed.

IT TAKES HER A FEW BEATS TO IDENTIFY the source of the buzzing that draws her back to consciousness. 'Not phone, not fire alarm...doorbell. And something else, what's that humming buzz?' She finally identifies her cell phone vibrating on the glass table. An additional improvisational element quickly adds to this cacophonous duet—insistent banging. Janet.

Once Anna finally makes it to the front door Janet can't hide her exaggerated relief. "Anna? Are you alright?"

"A mess, yes, but all intact..." Anna nods drawing Janet inside. "Sorry Janet, sorry. Have you been waiting long? I—I think I must have fallen asleep."

After taking a good look at her old friend, Janet breathes a deep sigh of relief that her friend is OK, then can't help but laugh at the state of Anna's poor hair and the pink creases on her face. Although she managed to pull on some clothes, obvious remnants of sleep still cling to Anna. "What, were you sleeping on a pile of dirty laundry or something? Here," Janet says drawing her to the hallway mirror. "Take a look at your hair."

Anna throws her hands up in despair and then smooths her hair back into a ponytail as she apologizes for her lack of preparation for Janet's arrival.

"Please Anna," says Janet, pushing away Anna's apologies. "I'm just glad you were only asleep!"

"Janet what are you saying?" Anna demands.

"Well honey I know you think you're capable of anything," Janet says as she leads Anna to a comfortable couch. "And you are. But no one. I mean no one could withstand the hits you've taken over the past weeks without…"

"Without what?"

"Without crashing Anna. Frankly your infernal optimism and certainty was beginning to worry me. After all that's been piled on you, Erik, Drew and Betsy, living here." Janet says, indicating Anna's parent's living room. "Breaking down a little bit, crashing, it's expected that you're going to, you know, feel low or a little lost."

"Is it that obvious?" Anna asks, grateful not to have to put on her mask for a change.

"Well, you want the truth?" Janet asks. "Yes. Yes it's obvious. But only to me. Any other human being would look at you and not be aware of your misery. It would be completely undetectable. But as I said, I'm glad to see it finally. I was afraid you were going to get stuck in denial, that this was all somehow not really happening." Janet kicks off her shoes and cozies up next to her friend, putting a reassuring arm around Anna's shoulder.

Anna groans, covering her face with her hands and shaking her head. "You know what's ironic?" she asks Janet. "I think for the first time since I met Erik…I'm finally escaping from delusion…slowly waking back up to sanity, to reality. I think I'm finally breaking through to truth. For years and years I was living in denial. As I became inured to his thoughts and habits I fell under some kind of spell." Anna could tell by the look on Janet's face she isn't making herself clear. She settles more comfortably to look Janet straight in the eyes and takes a deep breath.

"OK as I lived with him and his, what I chalked up as idiosyncrasies, two competing truths developed. One truth was that he was just not a good person, not nice, not really loving from the very start. The other truth was that I was an intelligent compassionate woman who married a difficult man. I fed this truth by rationalizing his petty cruelties. I fed this truth by absolutely refusing to acknowledge that I could have made such a drastic mistake. And of course he fed this truth by playing the pity card, 'Boo hoo I had a terrible childhood.' He fed this truth by offering excuses, apologies, and promises. 'It'll never happen again. I swear Anna.' 'I didn't mean it, I'm just under so much pressure, you understand that. You know I'm doing all this, working all these hours for you, for us, for our family.'"

"Two conflicting truths existed. And I chose the one that was easiest for my ego, for my comfort, and even to some degree... for the sake of appearances. I chose based on what looked right. Between my own pride and his manipulation I gave up on the truth that he was just a bad seed. Instead, I spent all my focus and energy trying desperately to fabricate a life, build a sustainable truth out of nothing but empty promises and denial of the facts. I mean he evolved into a full-fledged alcoholic for heaven's sake. And I just got used to it."

Janet mulls this over silently, watching Anna with care. At last she whispers "Anna, if things were so bad why didn't you tell me. Why didn't you say something?"

"What and shatter my carefully constructed illusion? Sure I bitched and complained about marriage, about the burdens of being a wife and mother, but I was never totally frank. I always held back the worst of it. I didn't want anyone to know what kind of gnarly dysfunction I really put up with or they would have thought I was…well…crazy."

"Well how do you feel now? I mean about the separation, the divorce," Janet asks.

"About the divorce? I'm ecstatic! This is something I should have done decades ago. Tried to and failed to do years ago. Getting free of him is the best possible thing that could happen to my life. I'm free!"

"Or will be," Janet interjects. "If you can get him to declare his assets and not contest the divorce."

"Oh Janet," Anna says with new grit in her voice. "Now that I understand that I was responsible for letting myself get trapped in that illusion, you have no idea the strength and determination I suddenly have to fight for my freedom if necessary. And with Erik a fight is always necessary."

"Vive le resistance!" Janet shouts. "Well that's a relief Anna. I'm so glad you're finally willing to fight for what you want."

"Yeah, great, now that I finally know what it is I want…years and years too late." Anna adds with a chagrined shrug. "And once I get myself free, I'm going to break the kids out of that sick delusional world of his as well."

"Yahoo," Janet offers. "You know what they say—admitting the truth is the first step to recovery. You know what's another truth?"

"You're starving," Anna says laughing.

"Oh you're getting psychic now, too?"

"Yes, watch this," Anna says closing her eyes and putting her fingertips to her temple. "I see you are hungry. I see that you want…Thai noodles…wait, no, Chinese noodles."

Janet laughs as she rises from their cocoon. "Take-out or delivery?"

CHAPTER FOURTEEN

FIRST OFFENSIVE

Once Anna decided to come out swinging, willing to fight for her freedom, she starts where the big boys start: with a public relations campaign. She returns all the phone calls from the 'ladies who lunch.'

She met Bernice of the Temple Fellowship Mother's committee the very next day at the school's volunteer office. "You know Bernice," Anna responded to her subtle queries. "After years of living a lie I'm all about the truth now. Ask me anything you want and I'll tell you the truth." Bernice learned all about the first 'secret' divorce for the first time in the fifteen years she'd known Anna.

"And he had…women. He had affairs right in front of you then?" she asked.

"Well it's not an affair if you're divorced, now is it?" Anna answered.

"Sure, but no one else knew you two were divorced. You know, I saw him out with one of his 'lady friends' I guess you'd call them all those years ago but I didn't know if it was my place to tell you. I'm so sorry Anna. I'm so sorry you went through all this, that you're going through all this."

Anna met Clara of the Jaycees for lunch.

"No, Anna tell me you're making it up," Clara said with alarm. "He really called you by his first wife's name...during...you know...?"

She went down the list, dropping bombs of truth everywhere she went. Her story was so scandalous, so juicy and melodramatic that she became more popular in her former circle than she had ever been.

This wasn't the only branch of her first offensive. She also took that outpouring of misery, the document that started out as a letter that she spent almost a whole day drafting over to Stanhope. Rather than going for a no-fault mutual divorce, she wanted to change her plea to include the examples of emotional abuse, manipulation, and outright blackmail. She wanted the truth to be known in every corner of town. She wanted it filed forever in the court documents; the truth of what really happened. It was time to set the record straight.

Simultaneously, she started her campaign to reconnect with the kids. She phoned them at the same times every day, what would be on the way to school and what used to be homework time. "Hi honey...it's mom. I just wanted to wish you a good day. You know I love you and I miss you very much. I'm always right here if you need me, all you have to do is reach out."

Sure it was challenging to keep her voice light and cheery, but she was a warrior. Or would that be warrior-ess, now. This meant she had to fight against her own disappointment four times—well, six times a day since Anna included her step-daughter Maggie in the calls. She never really thought Maggie would pick up, but Anna didn't want to exclude her.

She sent e-mails with pictures from each child's infancy and toddlerhood. She searched for images of her with each of the kids, but working from her mother's collection she was shocked to find so few photos with her in them. Then it came to her. That's because

she was always behind the camera…taken for granted. Capturing
the isolated moments of 'fatherhood' camaraderie for posterity;
otherwise, the kids certainly wouldn't have remembered them.

She was glad to have her days full again, to be in social demand
even if it wasn't for the most wholesome of reasons. Besides Janet,
the one she most looked forward to having on her schedule was
Carlo. He invited her to review the items that were delivered a
week after their trip. And since she was going to be there, he took
her on a tour of the improvements and renovations going on at
Waterston House. The construction foreman tagged along to fill in
the details and answer her questions.

Carlo wanted to officially hire her to be the decorator and
make decisions about paint colors, and tile, and wallpaper, and light
fixtures, and, and, and. In Carlo's mind, the list of minute details
was seemingly endless. Frankly he didn't have time for them all.
"Please Anna you'd be doing me a favor. I just don't have the time
to manage all these details with the demands of business bearing
down on me."

"I'm happy to do it Carlo." She reassured him. "I'm enjoying
it. This helps keep my mind off my troubles and on something
creative and productive. I probably should be paying you. This is
therapy for me. Retail therapy, but therapy nonetheless."

"How is it, Anna, that your taste is so right on the money. How
is it that you know me so well? Know what I'll like? Know what
makes me feel homey and comfortable?" He wondered aloud.

"Uh…are you forgetting how I 'picked out' the couch that was
delivered? I just stumbled across it…literally."

Janet had come up with the information Anna wanted and
then some. But by that time the memory of that single kiss had
cooled and Anna and Carlo's friendship was growing…platonic…
she guessed. Although there was still some kind of extra charge in
the room whenever the two of them were together, she learned

from Janet that his Barbie from the Governor's Ball lived in his hotel. She was only employed as the hostess at his restaurant, no way could she afford the penthouse on her own income. Between Janet and herself, they surmised that he must be footing her bills. And they both knew what that meant.

He was married, twice, but he'd been divorced for more than ten years. Also, he was a few years older than Erik, who was ten years Anna's senior. Maybe he thought Anna was too young? Maybe he thought Anna's life was too screwed up for him to get involved with? Either way, he clearly hadn't put the moves on Anna and she was just fine with that. She enjoyed his company no matter the excuse for seeing him. If he wanted to be friends, great, she could use a few of those right now.

Aside from the biggest hotel, the acres near the farm, and the Waterston house, he also owned: a local bank chain, a construction firm that specialized in building research laboratories, an electric contracting firm, and a significant share of the local power company. And that's what they knew of. No wonder he's so busy, Anna thought to herself.

When she found out about all the demands and responsibilities that shadowed him she was even more honored he chose to spend some of his precious free time in her company.

DESPITE ALL SHE HAD ON HER AGENDA, her next visitation weekend took far too long to arrive. The disaster that befell her last time was not going to happen again. Anna was determined. Certainly all the phone messages and e-mails must be making some dent in whatever armor the kids were hiding behind.

That Friday morning Anna leaves her daily messages for Drew and Betsy saying, "I'll see you after school today...don't make other plans or leave with anyone else please." Just to remind them. That way, they couldn't claim they'd forgotten.

Anna pulls up outside the school far earlier than any other mothers just to be sure to secure a good spot, one that allows her a full view of the exit doors. She intends to be on guard for any funny business, but not knowing what form that might take makes her a bit paranoid. The book she pretends to be engrossed in is actually upside down if anyone were to take notice.

As the clamor of release shakes the air Anna's anxiety ratchets up yet another notch. In the sudden splash of color and movement Anna swears she recognizes her own flesh and blood instantly by the way they move, by their shapes, even from far away. Drew stands on the edge of a circle with a few other boys brainstorming for anything 'not boring' to do that weekend. He is turned toward her. He picks her out, sees her watching him and nods ever so slightly as if to indicate he's coming, he knows, he's just getting the final update on who to call when.

Betsy is once again insulated by a clutch of girls. But she seems to be hugging them each in turn as if she's saying 'Bye, see you Monday. Wish me luck.'

'Good, good,' thinks Anna. She struggles to knock away fears that demand to know exactly what she thinks she's going to do if either or both of them suddenly turn and walk away. Chase them? Scream after them? Tail them in her car? "They're coming, saying goodbye…they see me…" she intones under her breath as if the words have some power to make her desires come to life.

At last Drew is jiggling the back door handle. Anna clicks unlock. 'Why is he getting in the back…where's the big 'shotgun' contest to decide who gets to sit in front? Drew has no problem taking the best for himself most of the time. Is he suddenly getting solicitous of his sister?' Anna wonders.

Betsy follows close on his heels reopening his door almost before it shut.

"Move…over…Drew," she grunts trying to push him. Instead

of fighting for the sake of fighting Drew slides over, making room for his sister. Anna tries not to let her jaw hang open. Her teenage son was being…considerate? 'Hey…wait a minute why are they both in the back? Are they trying to punish me, make me feel bad?' Probably but Anna is determined not to let them get to her.

She turns around bodily to get a good look at both of them, looking them each point blank in the eye when she says, "Hey hello, you have no idea how happy I am to see you." Then she sighs turns around and starts up the engine.

"She's crying. See I told you!" She hears whispered in the rear along with a lot of scuffling and wiggling around. "She is not!" the other one murmurs.

Drew asks her directly, "You're not like, crying or anything? Are you?"

"Who me?" Anna answers. "What would I have to cry about?"

More silence.

"So you guys want to tell me what's been happening? What's been going on in your lives?" Anna says with as much light in her voice as she can muster.

More silence, then whispering and muttering in anger, more animated this time. Anna just keeps her eyes on the road, glancing occasionally in her rearview mirror for clues.

"Oh yeah," Betsy finally bursts out enraged. "Well yeah sure why don't you tell us what you've been doing MOM? Huh? You totally dump us, wreck our whole family to run off and be the mistress of some old guy?" Drew is shushing her, rolling his eyes, and getting as far away from her as he can. He's punching her thigh murmuring, "Shut up, shut up…stupid. Shut up."

But Betsy's on a roll. "You just leave? You just up and walk out and start shacking up, start traveling the world with some guy we've never even heard of? Ohh I'm, Mom, 'screw you guys I'm busy flying off in our private jet…'"

When she's finally spent, Betsy throws herself back hard against the seat. "This sucks! I don't even know why we have to go with you." Then there is dialing- beep-beep-boop-boop-beep. "Hello…Daddy? Do I have to? No! No, no that's so not fair…no. I hate this. I just wanna come home. No. No. FINE!" Then the ironically benign click of her phone shutting. She pushes back into the seat, grinding her teeth, breathing like a bull, tears streaming down her face. Drew is shoved into the opposite corner staring blankly out the window, facial muscle clenching and releasing his jaw in rhythm.

In as quiet and calm a tone as she can muster Anna carefully begins. "Betsy…honey…it's not like that. It's not like that at all. I live at Grandma's house. I'm sleeping in the room Aunt Katherine usually stays in, you know the blue bedroom." Anna stops, leaving room for she's not sure what. A rebuttal or perhaps questions.

"I'm not involved with any man at all in any way. The trip you're referring to was only as far as Chicago and if you remember correctly it was time I should have been spending with you," Anna halts again. Betsy glares at her in the mirror. 'Oops,' Anna thinks realizing too late she might have gone too far, sounded accusatory, petty. She holds her breath.

More silence.

"A friend did something nice for me to try and cheer me up, that's all," She adds after a few beats.

"Drew, do you want to tell me who's filling your sister's head with all this nonsense?" Anna asks. Drew remains silent.

"See, here we are," She says pulling into the driveway, "Grandma and Grandpa's house. Betsy I made up the yellow bedroom for you. Drew you're in Grandpa's study. Lucky you, you get your own TV," she adds with emphasis. There is a sudden uptick in the muttering and whispered arguing between Drew and Betsy. Betsy ends loudly with, "No YOU!" as she elbows him.

"Come on," she says shepherding them into the house. "Now, I haven't decided what's for dinner exactly, although I narrowed it down."

"Uhh. Wait a minute. Uh Mom?" Drew begins as he drops his backpack in the foyer.

"What honey?" Anna asks smiling...he called her Mom for the first time today.

"No one. I mean NO ONE said anything to either of us about spending the night. Nothing. I mean, I for one have plans. I can't. And ummm Betsy. I mean, Mom, no one told us. We thought we'd be home around like nine o'clock tonight, like at the latest." Despite the uncertainty in his words Drew stands stock still, one hand grasping his pack's strap.

In a flash Betsy disappears into the bathroom where Anna assumes she's back on the phone. Anna and Drew can hear Betsy arguing. "NO way. No way! Nu uh. You never said anything about us having to spend the night, to stay here with her. That wasn't part of the deal."

Drew makes a 'see I told you so' sign with his hands and face. They both are stuck staring at the door waiting for a verdict.

"You said! You promised. You said you'd only be five minutes away, no matter what. And you said if I didn't like it, if something went wrong, no. No. No, no one even told us." Silence while Erik responds.

"Well if you don't...I'm just going to walk out of here on my own. She can't stop me! I'm old enough to decide for myself, that's what you said the judge said. I get to decide. Well then I'm just going to walk out the front door. If you don't show up I'll just call Karen's mom and tell her it's an emergency."

Silence.

Betsy appears in the doorway, leering at her eavesdroppers. She passes Anna and Drew in the hallway outside the bathroom, intentionally pushing herself as far away from Anna as she can. She marches straight back out to the foyer, picks up her backpack and opens the front door. With her hand on the knob she turns to stare at Anna, in turn searching Drew's face to see if he's on her side. Drew shrugs his shoulders, walking toward Betsy at an even pace. When he catches up with Betsy they both turn to stare at Anna, both daring her to do something to just try and stop them.

Anna jogs to the door in a few long strides, slamming it shut, squeezing herself between the stunned children and the door.

"Don't do this. You guys…please. Don't," she says panting. "It's not right--"

Drew interrupts, "What's not right? Huh? What exactly?"

"Nothing," Anna answers honestly. "None of this, not one of the things that are happening to you, to me, to all of us is right. None of this is OK." Anna falters. "This isn't how it's supposed to be. You two don't understand. I mean obviously your dad has been telling you things…making up things to tell you about---"

"Oh right," Betsy throws out. "Are you kidding me? I know Dad's the one who's finally telling us the truth. He's being completely and totally honest. He's vowed never to keep secrets from us again."

"And you believe him?" Anna says unable to retract the bitterness rising in her throat.

With that Drew reaches around his mother for the front door handle and yanks it open, jarring her to the right, out of the way.

He gestures for Betsy to slip out before him and she does, refusing to even look back at Anna. Drew, on the other hand, stares at her. "If Dad's the one who's lying how come you're the one who moved out? Huh?" His eyebrows raise, challenging her to offer some argument but letting her know in no uncertain terms arguing will be pointless. He doesn't even shut the door as he pushes his way out. He trots up to Betsy.

Anna too plunges out the door. Raises her hand and opens her mouth to yell, 'Wait. Hold on!' But nothing happens. No sound escapes her. What can she say? How can she stop them?

They are two houses away, three houses away, four. Where will they…

A big black luxury SUV comes roaring around the corner, pulling over to pick up the kids at the curb. "Erik," escapes her lips. He cruises by rolling up his tinted window as he passes, obscuring himself with impeccable timing. Rather than dodging back inside and cowering Anna crosses her arms over her chest, drops her shoulders back, and fixes him with a detached stare. It doesn't matter whether she can see him. She knows he's watching her. She holds his eyes until the very end of the turn at the far intersection. She knows he saw in her something completely new and unaccountable. A factor he hadn't considered in plotting his calculations.

Anna's silent assurance as the evening breeze riffles her hair about, the stillness with which she stands…watching. All these strange and foreign attributes alarm Erik, as they are unrecognizable; thus slipping more than a few wild cards back in the deck.

CHAPTER FIFTEEN

THE NAKED TRUTH

Anna's hand shakes as she writes up her 'report.' She doesn't know who will look at it, or if or when she can bring it to the judge. But logging all the twists and turns of events helps her feel somehow less powerless. The task makes her believe, even if temporarily, that what she's enduring now has some importance, will one day be accounted for. Perhaps somehow her experience will be equally counterbalanced by good turns at some unknown time in the future.

Anna laces up her running shoes and heads out the door. Dusk descends. She's walking toward Carlo's house, toward the Waterston house. She wonders if she's blowing their friendship, their acquaintanceship really, out of proportion. Maybe he's just a really nice, open-hearted guy. She thinks of him at the restaurant opening and smiles. No doubt about it, from what she's seen Carlo is a truly kind and thoughtful person. As she pounds the pavement she wonders how she must appear in his eyes, through his perspective.

Dark descends faster than she anticipates, and the walk takes longer than she estimated. A bright moon peeks through the ancient arching old trees that line the charming boulevard. Early

shrubs are starting to fill out. Anna picks out rhododendrons that
will bloom soon and stripling clusters that will soon be bushy lilac
greens.

The house looks neutered by the missing lawn and garden. The
colorless dirt makes this house the odd one out. The construction
equipment and materials are arranged in neat intervals across the
dirt expanse, giving the place an aristocratic air. Order suits the
house.

Anna always had a soft spot for the Waterston house. One
evening she drove by…probably dropping or picking up one of
the kids somewhere. But the obvious vacancy of the house stood
out against the sky. No curtains, broken glass, collapsed former
boards up over the windows. It made her inexplicably sad and it
stuck with her so that she thought of it every time she went by.

Then one Christmas as she watched "It's a Wonderful Life"
for what must have been the eightieth time, Anna recognized her
sadness in Mary's attachment to the old Granville house. "Oh
George don't throw that rock…I love that old house. Someday
I'd like to live in it." The old Granville was the spot that ingenious
Mary Bailey, Mrs. Bailey if you don't mind, set up housekeeping
after the run on the building and loan, where Burt and Ernie sing
their duet in the rain.

That summed up Anna's affection for the 'old' Waterston
House. Anna imagined herself as Mary Bailey. As she takes in
the rebuilding of the dilapidated dream, a new hope glimmers in
Anna. Seeing this house being tenderly brought back to life after
all the neglect it endured gives Anna hope. That small sliver of
hope wedges open the portals of her imagination to what might be
out there, for what could be possible. She is surprised to hear her
phone ring. Carlo? What timing.

Just as she answers she sees a truck on the other side of the
house come to life and draw slowly out into the boulevard.

"No I'm not psychic," Carlo says into her ear. "That's Mick in the truck." He laughs. "He saw you daydreaming out there and called me to tell you to get home missy. It's getting dark out."

They both laugh. Anna waves as Mick cruises past, sticking his head out the open window and waving.

"I asked him to make sure you turn around and head home," Carlo says only half joking.

Anna does turn and head in the direction of home and Mick purrs off into the night.

"Well I am sorry I'm not there to escort you home safely myself. I'm in Pensacola," Carlo says.

"In Pensacola?" Anna replies momentarily confused.

"Checking out the plans for a lab nearby," Carlo explains.

"Ah." Anna nods. "Then it's even more remarkable you mysteriously knew I was here at the house. Considering how far away you are and all."

Carlo chuckles, then says, "Tell me what you think about the front. It's getting close to time to put in the shrubs and trees," Carlo asks getting down to business.

"Well what do you know. I was just thinking about that," Anna sighed as she strolls home.

CARLO PICKED HER UP EARLY SUNDAY and they ate a breakfast picnic on the front porch of Waterston house. This way they could pace out the property to figure the number of plants they'd need to order or decide how many of what kind, of what colors will go where. Today's big event involved driving out to the nursery in the country to choose the plants for the yards.

"What do you think of hydrangeas?" Anna asks, obviously thinking of Mary Bailey again, 'Over here in the hydrangeas.'

"I can see that. I can easily picture that. But are they sensitive to sun?" Carlo asks.

The list Anna's scrawling with a carpenter's pencil on a scrap of board is growing crowded. But the back provides a convenient place to map the lot and include all the major plantings. Anna feels for the historic scribes, who chipped at stone tablets with chisels and mallets, for the first time in her life. She is shocked back into the present when her pocket buzzes.

When she see who's calling, 'home'-- Erik, the kids, she accidentally drops the board making a loud clatter that catches Carlo's attention. She hurries, afraid they'll hang up before she gets on.

"Hello," Anna yells into the phone.

"Hello?" says an unfamiliar voice on the other end.

"Hello?" repeats Anna. "Who is this?"

"Is this...I'm, I'm sorry I don't know your name. Are you uh, Drew and Betsy's mother?" the voice asks.

"Yes. That's me. I am. I am their mother. Is everything OK? Is anything wrong? What is it?" Anna demands.

"Uh. This is LaShay. I'm the uh...the housekeeper here at Mr. Reinhardt's home ma'am."

"Yes? Yes? What's the matter?" Anna presses.

"I'm new here and I don't know if I'm supposed to call the police or what?" LaShay hedges.

"What's going on?" Anna practically screams, squeezing the phone.

"Um Mr. Reinhardt, uh he's running around the house buck naked chasing them kids. He's got a belt in his hand and he keeps slapping it against the walls and the furniture. He's screaming and shouting, cursing those kids like crazy. I want to know if I'm supposed to call the police or what? I found you on one of the kids' bedroom phones on speed dial marked 'Mom' so I figured you'll know if this kind of things is normal around here or what?"

"What?" shouts Anna. "He's what?"

"Yeah he and his—uh lady friend. They must have passed out sometime last night right there in the living room. When the girls woke up and came down I guess they—uh discovered the mister and his- uh lady friend laying here stark naked on the living room carpet."

"What?!" Anna screams yet again before biting her hand to shush herself from interrupting the story.

"Uh I guess those girls started taking flash photos with their fancy camera phones…uh I guess the flashes woke those two up. And Mr. Reinhardt, he took to chasing all three girls but they scattered off in every direction. He'll never catch em. He's still blind drunk by the looks of him," she finishes, falling silent at last.

"Girls…? What girls, who, how many, which ones are they?" Anna demands.

"A little black girl and a chubby dark-haired girl, but she's real tall. I can't remember their names at all. I don't know," mumbles LaShay.

Anna retrieves her fallen pencil and writes down who she thinks they must be; Michelle, the only black girl in Betsy's grade at the Temple Fellowship, and Karen who's been Betsy's friend since the second grade.

"Is he still, you know chasing them? I don't hear anything?" Anna asks.

LaShay answers cautiously, "I-- I'm upstairs ma'am in the boy's bedroom."

"And where are the girls?" Anna asks.

"Like I said, they scattered off real fast as soon as he started shouting…."

"And where is he?" Anna asks.

"Oops hang on. I'm looking out the window…the lady friend she just got out to her car and pulled away. Now Mr. Reinhardt he's yelling at her, running after her car," says LaShay.

"OK...LaShay? I'm going to put you on hold and use the other line to call the police. Will you just hang on for a few minutes while I do that?" Anna says.

Anna presses the hold button and tries to spill the elaborate story out to Carlo while dialing and redialing 911...how could 911 be busy?

As the pieces came together and Carlo makes sense of what's going on, he holds up his hand to stop Anna.

"Wait," He says. "Hang on a second. Should you be calling the police? You're not even an eyewitness. It'll be hearsay. You could get in trouble if no one else is willing to attest to what happened. You said you didn't even hear anything right?"

Anna nods. "I couldn't hear anything."

"And why did she say you couldn't hear anything?" He asks.

"Uh...because she was upstairs in Drew's-- or I guess it could have been Greg's room-- and Erik was outside at that moment, chasing his lady friend's car," Anna rationalizes.

"And what's going to happen when the police arrive?" Carlo asks.

Anna's shoulder's fall, her head droops. "What do you mean?"

"I mean the police, the county guys right?" He asks. Anna nods.

"The county guys pull up and they're just going to what? Find Erik running around naked in the front yard waving his belt around?" Carlo says. Anna thinks for a minute.

"Hang on. Let me just" she indicates the phone as she clicks back over to LaShay's line. But the line is dead. "LaShay?" Anna yells. "LaShay?"

Anna returns the call, pressing redial again and again and again, willing her to pick up. But nothing happens.

Anna wants nothing more than to hop in the car and ride out to the rescue. Carlo is cautious and wary. He loads her into his truck and they head out to his house. This way it will be in Carlo's truck, not her recognizable vehicle. They can take the long way around and pass Erik's farm to see for themselves if anything is still going on—if anything was indeed going on and it wasn't some ploy on Erik's part as Carlo suspects.

As they head out and the traffic dies away, Carlo turns and asks her the question she'd been dreading.

"Is this possible Anna? I mean is this the kind of thing Erik has ever done before?" he asks her.

"Um, yes," she blusters, hurrying to add, "but not the way it sounds. I mean yes, he has chased the kids around the house yelling if he was drunk or hung over. Yes he has in the history of their existence threatened them with a belt."

Carlo sees the look on her face and simply places his hand gently over hers, resting limp on the bench seat between them. She looks at him and he says almost without sound, "Anna I'm so sorry. So sorry."

When Anna's phone buzzes again she's on it in an instant. "Hello?" She didn't even bother to check the caller ID, has no idea who it is.

"Hello Anna?" the stranger says.

"Bernice? Is that you?" Anna asks.

"Uh yes. Uh Anna I know, uh I know you're under a lot of pressure right now…and I hate to add to that…but there's something I think you should see," Bernice says. "I mean it's on the Internet, but it's on Betsy's MySpace. Lindy was disturbed by what she saw and was concerned for Betsy so—I. I'm sorry Anna."

"On the Internet…couldn't I see that on any, oh yeah, that's right Betsy's MySpace is closed…invite only," Anna wonders out loud. "You're right Bernice I'll have to see it from your house unless Lindy wants to give me her account log in. Can you tell me what you've found? I'm just on the edge of town but I can make it to your house in a few minutes. Hang on, I just have to turn around."

Anna covers the mouthpiece of her phone, explaining that Bernice has something…something that must be related to this morning. Although Carlo doesn't understand exactly why they can only see this from Bernice's daughter's computer, he obligingly turns around to follow Anna's directions to the house.

Anna asks Bernice again. "Tell me what it is Bernice. I'm pretty sure I already know. The housekeeper called me this morning from the house."

"Are you driving? I don't want you to get in a wreck when I tell you," Bernice cautions.

"No, I'm in the passenger seat. Someone else is driving. I'll be fine. Go ahead," she urges Bernice.

"Well Anna. It looks like two people are sprawled across your living room floor completely naked," Bernice adds hastily. "Oh, but don't worry it's not Betsy or Drew or any of the kids. I believe. I- I'm pretty sure it's their father and um—some strange woman?" Bernice says tentatively.

"Yes," Anna mouths to the sky. Then, covering the mouthpiece again, she says to Carlo "Thank you God…evidence. Bernice saw naked photos of Erik and some woman posted on Betsy's MySpace. "

Carlo only raises his eyebrows and lets out an exhale of relief. He also pushes the gas pedal just a little bit harder.

"Ok Bernice do you know how to save an image from the web?" Anna asks, knowing full well Bernice has no idea. "Let me walk you through the process."

CHAPTER SIXTEEN

MIRROR IMAGE

Bernice's turned out to be wild goose chase. Bernice couldn't be talked through the process of saving a picture. She'd never 'right-clicked' before in her life. At one point the screen went blank and Anna was sure Bernice just closed out of MySpace by accident.

When they got there they couldn't reload Betsy's MySpace profile. It seemed as if it had simply disappeared. They even called poor Lindy back in to log on three, four, five times. Anna was even suspicious that Lindy or even Bernice had done it on purpose. She needed that evidence that could get her kids back. That evidence could solve the biggest and most heartbreaking problem she ever faced in her life. She urged Lindy to "try again…please."

After over a dozen attempts to reconnect, a message that Betsy's personal profile was no longer available came up. Lindy tried linking through from the friends sections of other girls' profiles and nothing worked. Anna even had her phone two girls to be certain that Betsy's profile was blocked to everyone…not somehow just mysteriously Lindy? Although she knew it was unlikely. That's what it took for her to finally give up.

Anna asked Bernice over and over again…"What exactly could you see. You say you know it was Erik? How could you tell?"

Bernice was obviously flustered and so sorry she hadn't known what to do to save the pictures before they disappeared into the abyss. Bernice didn't even realize it was possible for such things to happen, for things on the web to just vanish inexplicably.

It wasn't inexplicable, though. Obviously someone or someone's kid saw it and told their parents who in turn called Erik. Once he found out, he made Betsy delete her MySpace. Maybe he bribed Drew to do it for him in secret; that is, if Drew knew or could guess Betsy's username and password. Either way, the evidence she wanted, the information she needed, managed to slip through her fingers.

Even though it was only noon, Anna was spent. She wanted to go home and add this latest to her report before she lost any pertinent information that might help Stanhope. Carlo, however, was gently insistent and convinced her to let him take her out to his farm to relax, to get away from this such as she could. It would do her good, he argued, to stare at four different walls for a change.

CARLO INSTALLED HER IN A COZY WINDOW seat overlooking the woods. Anna caught sight of the clouds scudding by in the insistent Midwestern winds. She makes an effort to let all the compacted emotions she's experienced that day float away like the clouds. Carlo returns after a few minutes with a nice glass of wine. "Yeah, it's a little early but…you've had a hell of a day."

Anna doesn't hesitate. She accepts the glass with a, "thank you," then takes in the scent appreciatively.

"OK. I'll be right back," he says, then disappears again. Anna returns to her clouds.

A few minutes later he returns with a tray bearing a yummy looking antipasto platter, small plates, napkins, his glass, and (of course) the rest of the bottle of wine. Olives, pepperoni sliced thin, two kinds of cheese—Anna guesses mozzarella and provolone—

and lovely crisp bruschetta. Anna's only response is, "ummmm" as she digs in.

"Great," he says as he makes himself comfortable. "I can see I don't have to prod you to eat," he says laughing.

"Oh," Anna says startled. "Am I embarrassing myself?" Even though her mouth was only half full, Carlo still had to work to understand her.

"Good God no! I appreciate that kind of honesty. If you're hungry, for heaven's sake eat, eat," he answers, encouraging her further by digging in himself.

After doing significant damage to the contents of the platter and making a serious dent in the wine, Carlo leans back to get more comfortable and says, "So Anna, tell me more about you. What are your hopes…what are your dreams…what are your plans for your new, wide-open future?"

"Well…I—I don't really know. I--" Anna blusters. "I mean, I had plans once upon a time."

"Well, if 'plans' is too loaded of a word, tell me what you enjoy. What do you like or dislike. Given your druthers, how would you spend your time?"

Anna takes this in, thinks, but remains pensive.

"OK, think of it like this. What would you do with yourself if the world were your oyster…because it is," he adds under his breath. More loudly he proposes, "If you could do anything at all in the whole world? What would you do? How would you spend your time from day to day? Would you golf? Play tennis? Or do that pilot-e exercise thing I keep reading about everywhere?"

That gives Anna a good laugh. "Pilates," she says.

Carlo gives her a quizzical look.

"The name of that kind of exercise class…it's Pilates" Anna says.

"Oh, so that's what you'd do?" Carlo says.

"No. Not me. No. Not anything like that, or yoga. I need to really be doing something. I like to keep busy, stay on my toes," Anna explains.

"So how do you like to keep busy?" Carlo asks. "What's your favorite thing to do? How about this…What makes time disappear? I mean what do you enjoy doing so much that once you start, once you get going, time disappears, the world disappears, and you get finished and it could be hours later and you don't even notice?"

Anna thinks about this. She considers the things she does now to fill her days. Not walking or running or anything like that. She did those things, but mostly because she was driven to, not because she really wanted to, or particularly enjoyed them.

"What makes time disappear?" Anna repeats aloud as Carlo sips his wine watching her.

Then it hit her…of course! "The kitchen! I've been known to fritter away entire days puttering around in my kitchen if given half the opportunity. Flipping through recipe books and glossy cooking magazines, blending ideas, tweaking the details, and coming up with my own variation of things. That's one thing I love to do!" Anna says with real excitement in her voice.

"Huh? Wait a minute, let me get this straight. Not only do you cook, rather well from what I gather…but you're willing to say it loud and proud?"

"Well, of course?" Anna answers, "Why wouldn't I?"

"Well I haven't heard a woman admit to enjoying being in the kitchen since the mid-nineteen seventies," Carlo says with a laugh.

"Well I do," Anna asserts. "In fact, I was this close to opening my own restaurant," Anna says with pride.

"Really?" Carlo says. "How come I didn't hear about this?"

"Because like everything in my life it was only a dream. I came close, but in the end it was no dice," Anna says in defeat.

"OK, out with it. Tell me the whole story," Carlo insists.

As they polish off the wine Anna tells Carlo all about her dream of Coco's Café. She tells him about the building and the delays and the renovations, and the permit problems. She tells him about her ideas for the seating and the design. She tells him her top three entrees and how she planned on preparing them. Anna finds herself reclaiming the excitement and anticipation of picking out her place settings and glassware, of finding just the right comfortable chairs and booths. For the first time Anna shares the pain of having her dream torn away at the last instant by Erik's inconsistency. Once again what began in a flurry of excitement ends in blazing disappointment.

Seeing the look on Anna's face, realizing his prodding led her back to yet another bad memory, Carlo rises to his feet. "OK...I've got an idea. Hang on," he says as he clears the plates and glasses. He disappears for what feels like an extra long time to Anna.

Not doing the clearing was difficult enough, but to just sit there lounging while he does it is almost unbearable. But what's she going to do grab the dirty dishes from him? After all, it is his house.

When he returns holding out her jacket, he says, "Let's take a little ride...shall we?"

They hop in his farm truck, the antique D'Ellarte delivery truck, and he drives her to the ragged edge of the woods. From where he parks Anna can see a makeshift target range and wonders if they're going to have a rock-throwing contest. She gets out as he pulls a big locking case toward the end of the truck bed, which he folds down. He clicks open the large case.

"This ought to help you vent some of that pent-up frustration," he says cocking the hunting rifle and holding it out to her.

Flabbergasted, Anna can only laugh. She's not sure if he's joking, or nuts, or what. "You've got to be kidding me."

"I promise you there's nothing better for throwing off anger...

and after all, that's happened to you today, and from what I gather, for far too many previous days. You've probably got a lot of bottled-up frustration and pent up anger."

Anna only laughs and looks embarrassed.

"I'm telling you...there's nothing better. Here watch." Carlo says as he takes a few paces and sets his sights. He stops mid aim and returns to Anna and the truck where he extracts two sets of headphones for noise protection. He hands her a pair and puts the other set on.

Once again he takes his stance, sets his sights. He gives a slight nod to warn her, then blam...a series of sharp concussions rip the air.

Watching him closely Anna is surprised to discover that watching him absorb the recoil...gave her a warm rush of lust or longing, she wasn't sure. She hadn't expected that! He looked particularly 'manly,' of all things.

Suddenly she is all for the experiment. She steps up to the imaginary line next to him and shrugs. "OK, show me what I'm supposed to do," she challenges.

He comes around behind her, using his feet, knees, and hands to set the angle and distance of her stance, to guide the angle of her hips. He indicates where on her shoulder the rifle butt should be. He aligns her elbows and demonstrates where she should line her gaze. Then he closes in tight behind her to support her grip, her stance. Anna is delighted at the concentrated focus she feels emanating from him. It is as though she is the only thing in his universe at that instant.

Her first shot felt like jumping in an icy river. She shakes off the impact, takes a long look at Carlo, and returns to the stance he taught her, ready to try again, and again, and again.

They keep at it until it starts to get too dark to see—not that they were actually all that concerned with aiming and hitting the bottles, cans, and planters set in a drunken line at a distance. But the descending dusk is a good enough signal that they've done all they can for today.

As they drive back to the house Anna suggests it's time for him to take her back to town, drop her off at home. She's probably in the way she hedges. He probably has someone waiting for him after all.

"Now just what do you mean by that?" he asks her.

"Well," she answers. "It has come to my attention that there is a young, shall we say, buxom lady who resides in the penthouse suite of your hotel, at your expense. I figured she might have something to say about all the time we've been spending together…I believe I had the pleasure of meeting her at the Governor's Ball?"

Carlo is laughing so hard he has to get out of the truck and double over. She's afraid she's induced a heart attack or something. He eventually straightens up to look at her through the open window.

"Oh Anna," he begins still interrupted by chuckles and guffaws. "That young lady is my stepdaughter, Amber. She belonged to my second wife. Amber was in high school when I married Kathy, and we didn't last long. But Amber is a good, if silly, girl."

"Last year after her mother died of cancer I took over trying to get Amber on track. I had her try nursing school, beauty school… nothing took. Eventually I just gave up and put her to work at the restaurant. I was at a loss as to what else to do with her."

"Oh NO!" Anna cries covering her face. "I'm so embarrassed. Oh Carlo, I'm so sorry to assume that was the kind of woman you…" Anna let the implication of her assumption drift into oblivion.

Carlo opens the truck door and extends his hand to lead her out. Once she's on her feet, Carlo takes her fully in his arms, "Oh Anna, are you telling me I haven't yet made myself clear?" He draws her closer. "If you want to know what kind of woman I'm interested...look in the mirror."

Anna blushes and looks down. It takes just a few seconds for her to digest his compliment, to make sense of what is happening. But as soon as she does she raises her face to his. It is Anna who closes the small gap between them, kissing him full on the lips.

That is all the cue he needs. He picks her up and carries her back in the house. He makes it as far as the living room before she wriggles free. For a moment they break free to drink in the sight on each other. They move to sit stiff and unnatural on the couch, staring, breathless.

She makes the smallest effort not to lunge at him leaping and bounding like an ecstatic Labrador but fails abysmally. She plops herself just shy of her target with a graceless thunk. She's relieved she lands next to him. After all, she might have broken something necessary in her enthusiasm. She sidles next to him and lays across his chest.

He breathes in the scent of outdoors and gun smoke from her hair with a relish profound enough to stop time. Anna throws off heat like a live coal. For an instant he wonders if they might actually fuse together before he concentrates on simply absorbing every essence of her there in his arms.

She murmurs, wordlessly into the sensitive flesh of his throat, her lips and breath fluttering like so many butterfly wings. And when she recognizes gooseflesh rising at the back of his neck, she responds. He feels it before he hears her laugh deep in her throat. To his surprise that mischievous laugh urges him to throw her on her back, arms overhead. The urge passes, leaving an ache in its wake. Her heart beats directly over his.

With almost excruciating slowness she slides one ankle across his lap, straddling him most impertinently. She shifts just a bit so she can look him in the eye. She takes his face in both her hands, presses her cheek against first one then the other. She presses her forehead to his lips and withdraws to see his face. Her hands creep around, caressing the tender skin behind his ear and gently massaging his neck and shoulders.

He catches himself as he succumbs to her touch. Forcing his eyes open, he looks directly at her. He presses his chest against her, guiding her back and back. He wraps his arms around her shoulders still shifting her back and back. She flows like water, backwards, yielding laughing, throwing her hands above her head as she lands on her back with Carlo over her.

He puts his lips to her ear and whispers "Sure, I let you have our first kiss but if you think I'm going to sit passively by, you're nuts." Pinned such as she is with her knees over his hips she kicks up her heels, fully aware of the effects her rocking hips have on his thighs. He draws her earlobe in his teeth. He floats warm breath into her ear slow and steady, subduing her as intended. She succumbs completely. He takes a moment to look into her face and into her eyes, to remember forever this sweetest first.

Anna casts herself adrift in his embrace, in his kiss, his warmth, his touch. At some point she stops being surprised by his kindness, his wit, and his charm, and simply shifts to receiving.

CHAPTER SEVENTEEN

TAKING CHARGE

Carlo is an even earlier riser than Anna. He has to be in a meeting in Boulder at two p.m. local time. Quick coffee and toast standing in the kitchen, no regrets, just knowing smiles. Anna and Carlo know better than to prod or poke each other too much about last night. Their slow easy smiles speak volumes.

By ten a.m. Anna is in Stanhope's office with Bernice in tow. Bernice offered to come speak to the lawyer, or the judge for that matter, should it come to that. Bernice knows what she saw, even if it's not there anymore. Those kids shouldn't be exposed to that kind of behavior. What Bernice saw just wasn't right. She was appalled to have had her Lindy see it first.

"Anna. Without something more than just your story about the phone call and Bernice's story about Betsy's MySpace, this is never going to fly," Stanhope says rubbing his brow. He keeps hoping his secretary will come in to tell him he has a meeting to be at. "Unless we can get the housekeeper."

"Well Dennis, that should be easy. Track her down. Ask her. I mean if she bothered to call me, right? She'd do the right thing, right? Talk to the judge, tell him what happened?" Anna says. "I mean, for God's sake Dennis, Erik passed out drunk, naked in the living room while the kids were hopefully asleep…and he was not alone!"

"I know, I get that Anna. I'm not diminishing the wretchedness of what Erik's done but…just—just. There has to be proof. It can't just be you, Anna the soon to be ex-wife telling this story." He searches the women's faces for some ripple of understanding.

Anna and Bernice remain stone. "OK, OK, let me see if I can track her down," he says throwing his hands in the air. "Worst I can do is ask her, right? What did you say her name was?" Dennis asks, searching his desk for a pen.

WITH BUSINESS UNDERWAY, Anna takes some time to address the more juicy aspect of yesterday. Janet's first opening wasn't until three thirty in the afternoon. They agreed to meet for a late, late lunch. Anna, of course, was early.

"Anywhere you like," the hostess tells her.

Anna didn't notice the newspaper as she slid into the booth. She gathered it up and laid it on the table. She'd give it to the busboy to throw away when he came with the—wait a minute. The front page picture catches her attention as she folds it up. Who's that with the governor? The headline says. 'New Agriculture Director Appointed.' Why does he look familiar? The caption says: 'New Ag Director Art Newbold (r) with Governor Kasovitz (l) cutting the ribbon on the new department headquarters groundbreaking.'

Art Newbold where does she know that name? Anna starts laughing out loud when it comes to her. Art Newbold was Erik's most recent disastrous farm manager. Even with prices on everything being up, up, up Newbold managed to lose Erik money two years running. And now he was in charge of the state's Agriculture department. Anna doubted he even knew how to send or receive an e-mail. He'd certainly make a hash of the job, likely costing the tax payers endless dollars.

"OK!" Janet says as she slides in across from Anna, "what's so funny."

"Look," on second glance Anna notices something even more interesting. She points to the third man on the right behind the podium.

"Is that Erik?" Janet asks.

"I think it must be. See this guy," she says pointing out the new Ag director.

"Yeah," Janet nods. "What about him?"

"That's Erik's I guess, former farm manager. Newbold. He's practically managed to run Erik's crops and livestock into the ground. Newbold turned a perfectly functioning operation into a losing prospect in less than three seasons."

"So Erik pawns him off on the Ag department? How's that happen?" Janet wonders aloud.

"Remember the Governor's Ball? Erik was responsible for convincing Roscoe to come work for Kasovitz's campaign. This is the way the big boys show each other their love...nepotism," Anna says shrugging.

"Don't tell me you dragged me out of the office to talk politics?" Janet says wagging her eyebrows. "There must be more to this urgent, urgent meeting than that..."

"Are you ready to order?" the waitress interrupts.

They both decide and place their order, and once she's gone Anna leans far forward over the table so she can speak as softly as humanly possible and Janet will still hear her.

"It's Carlo," Anna whispers.

"What's Carlo," Janet says in a normal voice.

"Shhhh!" Anna reacts.

"Anna...look around will you. There's exactly five people in this restaurant and I doubt three of them understand more English than the menu items." Janet says leaning back and crossing her arms.

"Fine, you're right," Anna says in her normal tone. "OK. It's Carlo. He--- I—we. Carlo…then…uh."

"Do you want me to guess?" Janet asks, "Is this charades?" She puts her chin in her hand and says. "Uh let's see. You…and Carlo. You and Carlo. The two of you. Uh let's see. You finally had sex."

"Shhhhhhh! Please. Janet." Anna warns.

"Why what's the big secret? You like him right? He's nice. You enjoy spending time with him?"

"Well yeah. So far. I mean, I've only known him for a few weeks, only seen him a few---"

"Anna," Janet interrupts, "We're not seventeen anymore. You know whether you like someone or not. I mean he doesn't rub you the wrong way or anything does he?"

"Huh..uh. NO. In fact…that's…he rubs me exactly the right way," Anna blushes.

Janet's squeals echo in the empty room. "Ah ha…I thought so. Now explain to me why being rubbed the right way, as you so colorfully put it, is a bad thing?"

"Janet! I'm not divorced yet. I've only been away from hell husband for a few months and…" Janet interrupts.

"Anna. Hang on a minute. Take a breath here. You're worried about this being too soon, happening too quickly?" Janet says.

Anna nods.

"I want you to think about something long and hard before you go messing this up for yourself. What were the last years of your marriage like, the last two, the last three? Really, how have things been since you agreed to get remarried? Better or worse than they were while you were 'super-secret' divorced? Anna you have been living like a nun in a loveless hell for ages now. You're finally free, right?"

Anna nods.

"You're free and you're gorgeous and you're alive. You like

Carlo right? You had fun I can tell…I see it in your eyes. Can't you see that you of all people deserve a little of this kind of happiness, a little bit of this kind of good luck? Anna honey, you've been doing without anyone to care for you, or anyone to look out for you, or anyone even to laugh with you. You've done without so much for so long." Janet reached out to clasp Anna's hand lying in the table. "I know this must seem a bit scary, or overwhelming, or unfamiliar. But honey, if it feels GOOD then you have nothing to feel guilty about or be afraid of."

"But what will people say. Will this complicate the divorce?" Anna says.

"Who cares what people say? And how can it complicate the divorce any worse than it is already? Huh. Relax. This is the part of life you've been missing out on all these years. Just take it in. Enjoy the attention, the attraction…the sex. Enjoy it! Who knows when you'll get a chance like this again? We're not getting any younger and they don't come much better than Carlo. He's a good man Anna. You don't have to rely on your own judgment here. I'm reassuring you. He's a good man," Janet says reaching out to grab Anna's hand. "You deserve to be happy Anna."

The arrival of their waitress with the food breaks up the welling tears; tears of relief for Anna, sentimental tears for Janet. Janet remembers the incredible blessing of falling in love and wonders if she'll ever get that lucky again. They certainly weren't getting any younger. Janet wonders if Anna even realizes what's going on. She decides to hold her peace and let Anna discover the truth on her own.

CHAPTER EIGHTEEN

ALIEN ANXIETY

Anna decides to take Janet's advice regarding Carlo; in fact, she can't wait to enjoy his attention. She greets him eagerly when he returns later that week and is surprised by the sadness she feels when he jets off again in the middle of the next week. She's especially worried because he won't be back until Sunday. That means she'll have to face a visitation weekend, which usually means heartache and chaos, alone.

That Friday afternoon Anna spends an hour and a half staring at her silent son on the couch as he texts his friends. She was relieved that they showed up at least, got in the car. The previous Tuesday Erik apparently changed the kids' cell phone numbers. Anna got the dreaded, 'this number has been…' recording. So she'd lost even that one-sided sense of connection.

Yes they did at least show, but it's devolving into yet another debacle, Anna admits to herself. Betsy has been hiding in the bathroom since the instant they walked in, claiming she's sick. Anna isn't surprised when a car horn outside draws Betsy out of the bathroom and Drew out of his stupor. Betsy mutters, "I'm too sick," on her way to the door. The kids walk out her door without turning around.

Anna learns to keep time according to these thwarted 'visitation weekends.' Five more such disastrous visits come and go. It's been four full months since Anna's seen her children in any meaningful way. A whole summer and then some wasted.

She feels almost as if she's being torn in half. One part of her life, the part involving Carlo, grows stronger and more exciting by the day. The other part, missing her children, inspires no end of gnawing anxiety. There is no way to block out the idea that something very, very wrong is happening to her children that Anna not only can't understand but, no matter how hard she tries, can't seem to stop either.

She did manage to force Stanhope into complaining to the judge about the situation. All the judge had to recommend (as Stanhope had warned her) was that she request court appointed monitor to supervise her visits, to observe and keep track on what was going on. Of course, the last thing Anna wanted to do was involve yet another layer of bureaucracy into her life. She can barely tolerate the legal invasion she's already experiencing into her life, let alone apply for a visitation supervisor from the Department of Children and Family Services.

After that recommendation she gave up shouting at Stanhope. It was obvious there wasn't anything useful he could do regarding the children. So Anna started her own research. Whenever she wasn't at the Waterston house or with Carlo, or working on her usual committees, she searched the web and the library, scoured newspapers and magazines. She worked so furiously to come up with some sort of plan to rescue her children she almost felt as if she were back in college. Doing nothing and seeing no results was shredding her.

From what she'd witnessed, something was obviously not right at home with Erik. Betsy'd first said, "we live there now," insinuating Anna had abandoned ship and left them at the mercy of their ruthless captain. Then there was Erik's passing out naked in the living room. He must be going nuts, absolutely bonsai honking crazy to be that far gone. Before, she'd always been there to buffer the kids when he went on one of his tears—shouting, accusing, chastising, just venting every evil thought that crossed his mind since that last episode. The kids didn't have her there to diminish the impact, to take the brunt of his moods. They were getting the full force of his mania; not a fate she'd wish on her worst enemy, let alone her own offspring.

No wonder they might be convinced to hate her. If they think she abandoned them to their fate thinking only of herself, why wouldn't they hate her? That wasn't the case of course, but he must be telling them such things.

Anna found a way that might earn her access to her own kids, a way that might reveal the truth. She's gathering material and information Stanhope will use to convince the judge to require psychological evaluations of the kids. This is a move Stanhope intends to slip in amidst a bevy of other requests. But maybe, Anna thinks, he should lead with it, take a hard edge, make it an issue? Exploring the web, Anna discovered there is a name for what's happening to her and her kids: parental alienation. Just realizing that she wasn't alone was a vast relief.

In those early years when Erik criticized or chastised her for some hitherto unnoticed fault, it was always her fault, her responsibility, her problem that needed to be solved. If she was hurt because he chose to go out with the boys over spending time with her, it was because she had unrealistic expectations, she wasn't appealing enough to keep him at home. If Erik didn't like the meal she prepared, it was because she didn't think enough about what he likes or wants. If he found fault with her clothes or how she presented herself, it was because she was being selfish, oblivious, childish, naïve—she wasn't following the rules…his rules, which of course were in an ever-changing state of flux.

As she read the information about parental alienation, she had an epiphany! She realized that when the whole thing turned ugly, when Betsy and Drew pulled away from her, she immediately assumed it was because she was doing something wrong, that she was at fault, that she had to do something to fix it. She was trained to think that way, trained to believe it was always her responsibility to resolve all rifts and fix all hurt feelings. If Betsy was anxious around her and wouldn't be with her, Anna immediately concluded that there was something wrong with herself.

But the few professionals who wrote on the subject clearly state that 'a decline like this can't possibly happen on its own.' This rift she's experiencing with her kids is a direct result of Erik's interference. Anna recognizes her situation as a textbook case. She realizes that her conditioned response to feel guilty, to feel responsible, has been a liability in this situation.

A few child and family psychologists around the country write about how, in some divorce cases, the children's relationship with the outside parent collapses. Anna most absolutely, without question had what would be termed as a positive relationship with both her children prior to that fateful day in Erik's office when Anna 'tried to kill him.' But after that, all hell broke loose or, according to psychologists, endured a substantial deterioration. The mysterious one hundred and eighty degree turn in the kids' attitudes toward their mother is evidence of parental alienation, not some mystic karmic signal that Anna is bad or wrong.

Without a doubt something or someone incited the changes in the kids' attitudes toward her. Clearly Anna is trying to maintain or reestablish her former relationship by doggedly keeping after her visitation rights. Her rights, because Anna does in fact share joint custody of the children with Erik. Not that the paper ruling has done her any good, of course.

Until the phones were cut off, she maintained her daily calls.

Even though they never answered, she hoped they heard the messages she left. She's still doggedly trying to sustain her visitation rights, even though she's getting sick and tired of being lied to and rejected. Anna just wishes that whatever it was the Erik was holding over them, whatever he was threatening or bribing them with... she wishes they'd just come clean, just tell her so she can help. Instead, they're locking her out, just like she used to lock everyone out of her life when she was trying to live in denial, pretending to herself that living with Erik was not toxic and dangerous. The kids are doing exactly what she did back when she was still rationalizing his behavior and taking the blame for his outbursts.

In the worst parental alienation cases one parent, usually the mother (who gains custody nearly ninety percent of the time) aims accusations of alcoholism, drug abuse, or sexual assault at the other parent that later prove false. But in the interim the damage is done. One parent's goal is to destroy the other parent's relationship with their children. It starts by interrupting their access to the children out of spite, anger, and resentment. Erik, of course, accomplished this through his 'office theater' incident, his false accusation of drunkenness and battery long before Anna had any idea what was happening.

Every article she read is clear about this. Certainly the judge will recognize the pattern. Pure and simple, the healthy and well-established relationship she had with her kids could not have crumbled naturally of its own accord. Her once strong and normal relationship with her kids must have been attacked.

One of the important indicators of this form of child abuse, defined by doctors and therapists, is an "obvious fear reaction" by the children. This is exactly what Betsy has been doing. All her extreme behavior fits—fighting and arguing with Anna over phantom issues or, conversely, refusing to even acknowledge Anna's presence. Betsy's rage and anger, her outbursts and accusations, reveal the kind of surreptitious undermining Erik has been up to: filling Betsy and Drew's minds with lies and misinformation.

Drew, on the other hand, has managed to detach himself entirely, insulate himself from the whole ugly mess. He looks through Anna, accepts her presence like a rock or a fallen log. He approaches their visits with a distant stoicism. He rarely argues or fights, but matter-of-factly ignores everything going on around him when Anna's present. He relies on Betsy's melodrama to get him out of the visits—when he bothers to show up, that is.

More and more often Drew simply stands at the meeting spot talking on his phone, ignoring the growing conflict of the day that Betsy incites. Drew just waits for the inevitable crescendo then lopes away, shadowing Betsy as she stomps away screaming into her phone, "DAD! Dad--."

Anna thinks back to the time Erik actually moved Maggie and her older brother Greg—his own kids—in with his mother during the first weeks of the 'super-secret divorce.' He never explained or rationalized his actions to any of the kids. He just did whatever came into his head and everyone ducked, hoping they weren't in his line of fire.

During those weeks he spat threats and accusations at Anna about how he wanted to keep 'his kids' clear of her 'unchristian thinking.' For a few weeks there Anna was a 'poison,' threatening the wellbeing of his flesh and blood children. Anna never pressed him for answers about what he thought of his 'other' children, the ones that were also hers.

The whole episode only lasted until it became inconvenient for Erik…until his mother started complaining about all the driving around, taking the kids to and from school. They weren't little kids; they were in junior high and high school. But catering to them was interfering with Mother Reinhardt's routine, which made her edgy and even more vocal than usual. And although normally anything that would anguish or irritate Anna she was all for, taking care of her real grandchildren was more trouble than she could tolerate.

Anna considered this irrational act on Erik's part when she considered pushing for divorce yet again. But she figured since she was Betsy and Drew's mother she was safe from him trying to use them against her the way he'd used Maggie and Greg so long ago. She rationalized that Erik was using Maggie and Greg to try and hurt her, to remind her that she wasn't really their mother—as if Erik had ever let her forget!

She mistakenly taken his partisan attitude toward his two tribes of children as a signal that he considered Greg and Maggie his while Drew and Betsy were hers. This was just fine with her, as long as he was going to leave her kids out of his insanity.

According to the books, "the attacking parent demands the kid's cooperation in creating chaos." "In some extreme examples," she reads, "the custodial parent instills destructive negative beliefs about the missing parent." Which of course is the only explanation for what's been happening with her kids. Obviously Erik has been pounding his version of the story into their heads. Betsy was a perfect mimic. Anna could almost hear Erik's voice when Betsy accused, "You just abandoned us. You don't even care what happens to us as long as you can do what you want Mother," her voice dripping with the icy sarcasm only a teenage girl can muster.

Anna knows. In fact, she is now living the consequences of going against Erik's agenda. She wonders if her kids are savvy enough to catch on. Do they know that her fate is their potential fate if they dare to cross his agenda? After all, they see what he's done to her for crossing him…and Anna has to be honest with herself—it took her years, decades even, to screw up the courage to demand her freedom.

She knew the divorce would be uncomfortable and potentially messy, but she took her cue on his attitude towards the kids and divorce from the first time. The fact that he only removed his kids from her last time had lulled her into believing that they were all he cared about. She'd thought he would continue to overlook Drew and Betsy by virtue of her blood in their veins.

She never suspected Erik was capable of such treachery against his own children. Certainly the kids must see her exile and his poisonous attitude toward her and realize instinctually that their fate would be the same if…if they cross him…if they go against his wishes. And in this case his obvious wish is to exile Anna from all their lives, for good. But he's not going to get his way. Not on this.

Knowing Erik, he's probably threatened to pack them off to boarding school, or military school.

The most obvious symptom she can point to in a court of law as evidence is the sudden changes in visitation plans for no apparent reason. Hmmm…Anna thinks, score one for our team. There's plenty of evidence of that, sixteen weeks worth in fact.

Other possible effects of parental alienation can be "developing false memories, depression, thoughts of suicide, and always a profound loss of self-esteem." From Anna's new perspective, after being out of Erik's reach for these months, she realizes she suffered from almost all of these simply by being his wife.

He brainwashed and manipulated, bribed and threatened her into allowing herself to be completely at his mercy for years and years. If he was able to do that to her, his wife, an adult—well no not quite exactly. When Anna married him she was only nineteen, five years older than Drew. An 'adult' on paper, but obviously she wasn't truly an adult then.

The point is, she reminds herself, if he was able to control her using those tactics, controlling the kids would be a cakewalk for him.

The courts, the experts warn, can be easily fooled into thinking the current turmoil represents the 'true' parent-child relationship. Once a court ruling is made, reversing it is nigh on impossible. This, of course, is what Anna is up against. She only hopes it's not too late for her. The clock is ticking and moths are piling up, but the wheels of bureaucracy turn excruciatingly slow.

Of course, her case is even more problematic than the cases explained in the books and articles. Not one of them involved a high-profile attorney. Anna and her children are in an even tighter spot than most victims because of Erik's position as one of the most recognizable attorneys in the state.

CHAPTER NINETEEN

SPLITTING HAIRS

Waterston house, after the normal delays, is expected to be completed once and for all within the next few days. Anna stands in the center of each room reviewing the impact of her decorating choices—well, her collaboration with Carlo on decorating. She would never have gone with drapes that dark on her own, but Carlo's take was right on. The darker drapes give the den an old-fashioned elegance that sheers and chiffon just can't muster. As she surveys her work she's pleased at how their contrasting ideas manage to harmonize, creating a rich, comfortable, inviting home.

Now that summer is in full swing Anna stands in the midst of her endlessly blossoming yard—well no, not hers, but Carlo's yard...that she helped create. Amid the growing plants she feels utter delight. She's especially pleased by the curving row of hydrangeas that shift almost imperceptibly, beginning with deep purple, shifting through shades of robin's egg blue, then ending in delicate pinks.

Carlo dragged Anna away from her garden, anxious to have her look at a newly arrived catalog of furniture for the porch and deck. For the moment, they are perched uncomfortably on saw horses and piled crates.

Over their four months of togetherness, Carlo and Anna have developed a harmonious rhythm. Maybe it was his constant leaving and Anna's growing joy at his returns? Maybe it was the relief Anna's body experienced as a result of enjoying sex with someone she actually liked for a change? With someone who liked her for a change? Maybe, too, it was how smoothly they worked together. Disagreeing with humor, finding resolution in discussion. The comfort Carlo's presence gave her combined with the heady hormone cocktail of all the fantastic sex had been growing into something more, something greater than the sum of its parts.

For Carlo, Anna was the antidote to all his prior relationships with women. He came to recognize that compared to Anna, his previous relationships were with overgrown girls—selfish, irresponsible, moody, truculent girls disguised as women. His whole life he looked for women he could admire, strong smart women like his mother, his sister, and the cousins he grew up with. But somehow he ended up tying himself to a string of needy little girls passing themselves of as full-grown women. He longed for the comfort of a home that neither of his wives ever provided, the scent of dinner on the stove, the warmth of family and friends gathering around. Instead, he was worn down by houses full of chaos that he was required to tamp down.

He should thank those overgrown girls, though. It was because home was so unhappy that he was literally driven from the hearth to work so hard, become so successful. What he lacked in love in those days he made up for in cold hard cash. After a decade alone he pretty much gave up. Sure, he dabbled in superficial affairs just to feel alive. But none were serious, none were real in the way that Anna felt to him now. In her he recognized a worthy counterpoint to himself, someone who'd graduated from the school of hard knocks wiser, more resilient, and aware. Just like him.

"Anna," he says as she browses the catalog. "How many rooms does the Waterston house have again?"

Anna laughs. "Are you losing your mind Carlo? You know perfectly well it will have sixteen rooms when all is said and done."

"And how many square feet is it?" he prods.

"Almost five thousand square feet. Why?" she asks giving him a suspicious squinty-eyed glance.

"Well, what exactly am I going to do to fill up sixteen rooms and five thousand square feet...all by myself? Especially considering I'm only around three or four days out of every seven, and that's if I'm lucky?" he wonders aloud. Trying to figure out what's going on in his mind, Anna remains silent in an effort to draw him out.

"Well it's really almost a sin for such a beautiful space like this," he gestures into the picture window behind them, "to be empty and abandoned like that. After all the trouble and expense we went to, to make it perfect..." he says. Anna waits.

"What would you say to...to...to moving in here with me?" Unlike the uncertainty in his voice, his smile and the power behind his eyes tell Anna that he's certain. He knows hidden deep within that's precisely what she's been longing to hear. If she's honest, Anna can't keep, couldn't keep, from thinking of the place as my, our. Because they both contributed ideas and objects, our living room turned out beautiful. Her gardens will grow to be balanced and abundant...even though in her intellect she knows of course, always knew, never let herself forget in fact...that it's Carlo's house.

Her eyes brim with tears of an unfamiliar kind; tears of joy and surprise and delight spring free before she can form words. "Oh Carlo..." and in a shot he is by her side.

"It's perfect...don't' you see? The house is made for you Anna, it suits you, like you and me. Doesn't it feel like...like we were made for each other?" He is holding her now. She can feel his voice resonating through her head and heart. They've danced around this conversation, dipped a toe in now and again. But both of them, leery and damaged from the past, were reluctant to sound loopy and naïve, to give voice to the effortless balance and peace they'd both experienced since finding one another.

Instead, they expressed this to each other only in gestures, in smiles, or in laughter after coming to agreement after protracted battle. With Carlo, 'battle' meant something entirely different. He listened and discussed her ideas and opinions as if they had value. Every time it happened she wondered at the difference between Carlo and Erik, even though she knows she shouldn't compare. 'So this is what it feels like to be respected,' she thought to herself as he took her opinion and opened it, expanded upon it until she could begin to see the thing, the color of the exterior, the integrity of the old woodwork, whatever it was, in a different light. She wasn't simply ignored, overridden, or distracted by arguing about red herrings.

When he ended up agreeing with her, seeing the issue her way, she thought, 'This is what it's like to be heard and understood.' Anna and Carlo thought things through together as a team, with ease and almost always with lots of laughter and fun.

"It's a perfect idea. A perfect solution Anna," he says. This perks her up. She shifts so she can see his face. He recognizes the confusion in her expression.

"The solution to what exactly?" she asks.

"The solution to how I can't stand to be apart from you. The solution to how much time we waste going here, going there when we both know that we are meant to be together. You make my life better Anna. In every way. In your presence I feel like a better man, more worthy, more intelligent, more…" he stopped short.

"More what?" she presses.

Carlo swallows, pins her directly in the eyes with his and says…
"more loved Anna. In your presence I feel more loved than I ever

have in my life. I know, I know...you've never said. And maybe you don't even. But in your company I feel warmed and comforted and embraced. So, if that's not love I don't know what is," he falters at last dropping his eyes from her gaze.

"Yes..." is all she can get out before covering him in kisses. "Yes. Yes...yes."

They hug and kiss and laugh with delight. 'I love you's drift off the porch, sweetening the air of the font yard. They wallow in the perfect moment and are only interrupted by the beep-beep-beep indicating a truck backing up into the driveway. Looked like a tile delivery if Anna wasn't mistaken. Onc of the inside foremen comcs to sign the receipt. When Carlo has the presence of mind to ask, "Uh...yes to what Anna? Yes you'll live with me here at the Waterston house...yes...'I love you.' Yes what?"

Anna bites her lip. In that moment she understands the full impact of those words Betsy's bitter accusations rise in her memory, clouding her present. 'You abandoned us to run off with some old guy...in his private jet...' She swallows hard, willing herself not to let the tide turn, not to let this beautiful unexpected instant be tainted. But she isn't yet strong enough—the problem of her missing children, the gaping hole in her heart is still to vast to withstand.

"But," she whispers. Carlo senses the uh-oh moment and responds, "It's OK. Just tell me what it is. Just...it's ok, you don't have to do this alone anymore."

"The kids," she answers. Carlo doesn't understand the terror in her eyes.

"That's exactly my point. You can create a room for each of them; after all, how many bedrooms do we have now? I welcome them Anna. You know that. I'd give anything to have them move in tomorrow if I could. When the day finally comes, I'll welcome them with open arms. You know that, right? You get that?" he says.

Anna nods and swallows hard again. "But they'll hate me," she blurts before she can stop herself. She bites her lip again, glancing at Carlo, sure she's said something wrong, that he will feel hurt.

"Why honey?" he asks. "Why will they hate you?" He reaches for her again.

"They'll think I—I mean, they don't know you. They don't have the slightest idea who you are. They'll judge me. They'll accuse me. They'll use you as another excuse to stay away," she murmurs motionless, numb.

"Oh. No Anna. No no no. That's. No they couldn't possibly. No, they'll see how happy you are. They'll see how whole and healed you are. Seeing you in bloom like you are, like you never have been before I'm guessing they'll gravitate more toward you."

Anna only stares at him.

"Anna you know as well as I do that love breeds love. Right? Love multiplies because it is a blessing. Lies breed horror. I lied to myself that I loved and trusted Judy, and those lies bred years of bitterness and emptiness. If we lie now Anna, you and I, knowing the truth that we just now admitted. If we ignore this possibility to bring more love into the world by being together, if we give in to the temptation to lie because it's 'easier' or less messy or less scary...we'll suffer the consequences," he nods gravely saying this.

Anna nods. Yes, she knows this much is true. The years of living the lie with Erik have cost her dearly. She can't afford to lie to herself or God or anyone else like that again.

"If we love each other, and I do love you Anna in ways I never thought possible. Please tell me you know that." She nods. "Love always leads in the right direction. Love is the answer, not the problem." Anna nods, thinking of the ease and sanity that has come into her life along with Carlo.

It's true they balance each other in a way Anna stopped believing was possible. She also thought of the vast sea of emptiness her life would become without Carlo, without his laugh, his eyes…his touch. She reaches out to him, taking him in her arms, demonstrates what words can't quite wrap around.

"You're right. I love you Carlo. I love you. I don't want to do this without you. Any of it. You make me feel so special, so cared for and protected. I can't lie. This love is too big to ignore. It's what I want. To stay with you. To live with you. To always have you there by my side when I wake up. When I go to sleep."

The afternoon unfolds smooth and calm. Carlo and Anna are on the ground headed to the truck to go over the tile before they even know it. Plunging onward. Moving forward.

WITH SCHOOL OUT, the new 'neutral' pick up point for her visitations is Mother Reinhardt's house. Anna pulls in the driveway and waits for the kids to come out. Last time she waited over forty-five minutes, but she was too stubborn to walk to the door and knock. Today she only waits twenty minutes before Drew comes out lumbering his golf bag, with Betsy dragging her feet behind him.

This time Anna has a plan. After dropping Drew off at the country club—that's what she gets to be these days, a glorified chauffer for him. Anyway, after dropping him off Anna has a surprise for Betsy she hopes will earn her a whole evening's company.

"Bye Drew" Betsy says as her brother strolls away from the car with his clubs over his shoulder.

"I have a surprise for us…" Anna says with quiet excitement.

Betsy glares, arms locked across her chest.

"Well I see what you've done to your hair and it's very, well, interesting," Anna smiles, but it's thin and superficial. "So, I just thought a spa date, you know eyebrows, facial, get our hair done, maybe a manicure?" Anna says, fishing, glancing sidelong at Betsy to see if any of her suggestions take. Surprise, no blow-up. At least a partial success!

Betsy allows herself to be shepherded into the salon. She says nothing as Anna and the stylists and manager consult with about their schedule. Who wants to go first, what would they like do with their hair?

"Hair?" asks the manager, "Who's going to get their hair done first?"

Betsy speaks at last, "Well Mom I think you should get your hair done first."

Suspicious but excited, Anna agrees, "OK, what are you going to do while I'm getting my hair done?"

"Oh I'll just start with my eyebrow wax. You know, that stuff. Then when you're done we can have our mani-pedis together, you know sit and talk," Betsy says smiling, batting her eyes.

Feeling emboldened by Betsy's positivity, Anna asks, "And are you going to let Orlando work on your hair…let him spruce up that color you've got going?"

"Oh sure…yeah, of course," Betsy says nodding emphatically. "Sure…I can hardly wait." The excess ingratiating puts Anna back on her guard.

"Well OK then. I'll let him work on my hair while you get your waxing, then he can work on you," Anna says smiling as Orlando leads her to the changing room to slip on a smock for her shampoo. Betsy is led off toward the facial room.

Smiling to herself, Anna decides to have Orlando go ahead and touch up her color while she's there. Because Betsy seems so at ease, the extra few minutes shouldn't cause a monstrous scene, at least Anna hopes not.

As she sits timing her color, Anna watches all the mirrors to see Betsy emerge from the back. She hoped this would help the two of them get back to normal. Orlando comes and rinses her, combs through a light conditioner, and takes her back to his station for her trim. Anna grows more anxious. What's it been, fifteen, twenty minutes now and no Betsy? Where could she be? Orlando is starting to get snippy after Anna swivels her head for the hundredth time searching for Betsy.

"Anna darling, are you trying to ruin my work of art up here?" he says.

No I—could you just. Hang on a minute. Just let me go check on something and I'll be right back." Sopping wet and fully caped, Anna tiptoes into the back along the hallway of the massage and facial rooms listening for Betsy chatting with her attendant. Nothing.

She finally just breaks down and walks to the front looking for the girl who was doing Betsy's. Maybe they just keep missing each other. Maybe Betsy was taken in for her shampoo as Anna was in her chair getting her trim.

Anna finds the receptionist first. "Excuse me. I'm looking for my daughter. She was scheduled for a haircut after her facial and I just can't seem to find her anywhere. I mean, I'm assuming her facial is over?"

"What's her name?" the girl asks typing, checking the computer schedule.

"Betsy Reinhardt. She came in with me just about forty minutes ago. About yea high. Black hair?" Anna prompts.

"Oh yeah, her?" The receptionist asks confused. "She left about fifteen minutes ago.

"WHAT!" Anna shouts, louder than intended. "Are you sure? You're sure it was her?"

"Was she not supposed to? I mean, there was a car waiting for her and she didn't look lost or anything." the receptionist says by way of an apology. "Let me get Rina, we'll see if she knows anything. Rina's the one who did Betsy's eyebrow wax. Maybe she overheard your daughter on a call or maybe she said something to Rina?"

Rina says "I only worked on Betsy for a total of five minutes. Then she spent the rest of her time in the bathroom. When she finally came out she went straight out front."

"That must be when I saw her leave," adds the helpful receptionist.

Anna tries punching Betsy's cell number, only to realize the number she had was disconnected. Anna was tempted to call the police or Carlo. But what could she say. 'My daughter just snuck away from me. Get her back.' 'Oh wouldn't that look great in her court file.' When she finally stops attacking her phone, Anna realizes she has a message from a strange number.

"I just wanted to tell you. I'm not interested in your version of beauty anymore Mother. You don't have to worry. Karen's Mom picked me up. I'm fine. I just don't want to have to deal with you."

CHAPTER TWENTY

NEVER HOME AGAIN

In deference to the importance of her new home, Anna has Stanhope make arrangements for her to get the rest of her belongings from Erik's farmhouse. Funny, she can't even remember that last time she'd thought of it as 'their' house or 'her' house. Let alone 'home.' She moved into the Waterston house, such as it was, only the few things that came to her from the farm in garbage bags. There were things she missed, like her parent's wedding photo, for example, framed in beautiful antique silver and hanging in the bedroom hallway, and her grandmother's cornbread platter—her evening dresses, too. She only hoped that Erik hadn't destroyed or disposed of them.

"Dennis," she asked. "How hard will it be to get me in the front door to get the rest of my things from the farmhouse?"

"First things first." Stanhope says. "I've got an update on the housekeeper. I tracked her down. I spoke to her myself in person and she said she had no idea what I was talking about. Yes, she has been a housekeeper for Merry Maids, but she claimed to have no idea who Mr. Reinhardt was. On the weekend of the 23rd, of course, she wasn't at his house, couldn't possibly have called you. She left Merry Maids the beginning of that month. Because, wait till you hear this, she managed to get a rather cushy full-time job working for the city at the parking ticket window. That's where I spoke to her."

Anna is stunned, as much because she'd forgotten about the housekeeper as because the woman she is certain she spoke to is claiming the conversation never happened. And the fact that she now works for the city. Everyone knows how hard those jobs are to get. How did this former underpaid housekeeper get a plum position like that with the city, full-time with fringe benefits and healthcare? The whole shebang? "Erik?" she asks Stanhope.

"No proof of course, but that's party incest for you," answers Stanhope at the mention of Erik's name. "We know Erik's in with the governor, who's now in with the mayor. Ba da bing, ba da boom, LaShay is working full time for the city and suddenly has no idea who Mr. Reinhardt is."

"Lovely," is all Anna responds.

It took Stanhope almost ten weeks to organize Anna's incursion into enemy territory. A whole summer wasted. After six months of every other Friday afternoon torture sessions, Anna backed down to phoning the house to see if either child was available for their scheduled visit. Neither of them ever said yes. Neither of them ever even answered or returned her calls for that matter.

The growing string of twenty or so in-her-face rejections, and bouts of hysteria wore Anna down. After the incident at the salon when Betsy just disappeared, Anna got even more cautious. She began wondering if they weren't preparing to set her up to lose Betsy at the state fair or something. That way, Erik could complain to the judge that Anna was an incapable, inadequate guardian. She knew he'd do anything to cut her off, even if it meant using his daughter in some ploy.

Even Anna could only force her daughter to spend so many

hours of her life hiding in the bathroom before even she tired of
going through the motions, playing the role. It had been a month
since she even tried to force the kids to visit her. She wasn't sure
if the screaming and rejection were worse than the silent void just
yet. Maybe in a few more weeks she'd change her mind.

Not taking Betsy shopping for school clothes and supplies, not
being there to take pictures on the first day—knowing she was
missing all such things tore through Anna like bullets. But she was
still standing.

The school year had begun and finally, after weeks of hassle
and documented wrangling, of lists and counterlists, and amended
counterlists, Anna is allowed access to the house for exactly three
hours in the presence of a 'neutral observer,' Mother Reinhardt.

The old woman greets her with silence and looms in the
doorway of every room Anna enters. Without shame or guilt
Anna takes advantage of Mother Reinhardt's age, exploits her slow
reflexes and poor eyesight. Mother Reinhardt refuses to wear her
glasses out of vanity. Anna darts around faster than the old bag
can keep up, partly just to stay clear of Mother Reinhardt's person
and partly to gather unlisted items like her journals and files. Anna
stuffs Betsy's baby book into her pants and stashes Drew's infant
handprint in the bottom of the box of stored kitchenware she
packed.

Being in the house devastates Anna. Everything looks so the
same, so unchanged—yet so, so far away. Familiar things like a
sweatshirt fallen off the couch arm choke her up. The eerie
familiarity of everything is layered by a sense of fear and tension.
Fear she'll overlook something important. The anxiety that
something unlisted or unremembered will be discovered missing.

Anna takes pictures from the wall, but only those of her own
family. Her parents, her brother and sister and their families. One
of the extended battles of the lists excluded Anna from being

allowed to take any of the children's framed portraits. Anna stuck
to obvious things Mother Reinhardt dare not complain about
losing.

She tries to shake Mother Reinhardt so she won't be looming
when Anna walks by and tries to zip into Betsy's room. The first
step makes her dizzy. The familiar scent of Betsy's shampoo on
the damp towels (she's told that girl a thousand times not to leave
them on her bed) envelopes her. Anna delicately picks the towels
off the comforter and holds them up to her face. As she turns to
hang the towel from a closet hook, the sight of Mother Reinhardt
makes her jump.

Mother Reinhardt's lip curls into a snide frown. She looks down
her nose at Anna as if to say, "how dare you." Anna turns on her
heel, ignoring the old woman's derision. She raises the shade a foot
or two letting some light into the room. She can't help picking up
and shaking out crumpled put-it-on-but-didn't-wear-it clothes as
she assesses the room. Initially she told herself if she got caught
she'd pull out some jewelry, claiming it's hers. But as Anna stands
in her own daughter's bedroom that she'd furnished and cleaned,
she changes her mind and remains quiet. Anna was in some way
responsible for everything in this room. Why should she be shamed
for being in her own daughter's bedroom?

But enough. She didn't want to waste precious time, and she
had so little time left. No matter how many lists she'd made, she
couldn't possibly have thought of everything in advance. What
about that painting over the bed, the one Anna picked out on a
trip they took together?

'Better not…' she thinks, 'better not waste time on any bones
of contention, things Mother Reinhardt will argue about or dicker
over.' Thinking strategically, Anna avoids claiming ownership to any
items that could potentially draw conflict. 'Who gives a crap about
the wedding china, but the silver was from her Grandmother—not

a gift but her Mother's own silver, inherited from her mother. 'That was on the list so the old hag can't haggle over them,' Anna thinks with a sigh of relief.

In the basement Anna digs through boxes where they'd dumped everything left in her bureau and files, snatching up her few old memories, her own secret treasures, her yearbooks, her award for Best Essay. She was in search of her university diploma. She'd kept it in the bottom of her underwear drawer to remind herself everyday that she was worth something, that she'd earned this degree. In Carlo's house, scratch that, in her and Carlo's home she would frame this piece of vellum and hang it in the office where everyone could see it.

Anna walked out that afternoon knowing she'd left a veritable fortune of memories trapped inside Erik's legal paper fortress.

ANNA KEPT UP WITH HER LADIES, doing her part for the citywide garage sale, and helping Bernice update the school's certificates. As she worked with Clara and her faction, Anna fielded the inevitable questions of how she met Carlo and how she could get involved so quickly.

"Love," is all she answered. It was so unexpected it dumfounded the ladies who lunch. That, however, didn't put an end to gossip and speculation. Anna knew full well that she only heard about the top third of people's real opinions. Certainly there were those that grumbled among themselves, assumed she had Carlo waiting in the wings before.

At the citywide garage sale Anna felt the resentful glares of her so-called friends when Carlo donated rooms of his old furniture they could sell to help raise money for Big Brothers and Big Sisters. One bright spot of the event was the reappearance of the delightful Abby from Oregon. Janet had rescued Abby and her husband Carson from new-to-town anonymity at the Governor's Ball.

Now that they'd settled in a bit, Abby was pressed into service with the Jaycees as well. "Did you two find a house yet?" Anna wants to know.

"We're still looking Anna. Honestly my head's aswim with all the choices. I just don't want to make any mistakes. I'm starting to get how a small city like this operates, I think," Abby adds. "I'm starting to recognize how certain things like where we live and which clubs we join will have a significant impact on Carson's career. More than it should, if you know what I mean?" Abby says casting sidelong glances at Clara, the organization's president, and her cadre.

"How does he like the Inspector General's office?" Anna asks.

"Oh he likes it alright, there's just a lot of…well, let's just put it this way. Carson is beginning to understand why they had to go as far as Oregon to recruit a new chief investigator…" Abby says biting her lower lip.

"Getting messy already?" Anna asks.

"I don't even ask anymore," Abby says raising a hand to show how she prefers to shield herself from any more knowledge.

Even Abby started to notice how if Anna laughed or acted as though she was having a good time there were those who'd comment on the sly, "Yeah, I can see just how much she misses those kids of hers," with a sarcastic roll of the eyes. Or whisper with a sneer and a bitter laugh, "apparently Reinhardt wasn't rich enough for her. She needed to upgrade."

Bernice, though because, she'd seen the evidence for herself was forever trumpeting Anna's point of view for all the good citizens of Cambridge to hear. It was Bernice who brought Anna pictures of Betsy and some of Drew she took on the sly at the homecoming game. Drew was pictured hanging around with a much older crowd these days, an edgy looking crowd. Betsy looked haggard and exhausted in an oversized sweatshirt and baggy pants, alone in every shot.

It was Bernice who kept Anna posted of Betsy's growing string of absences from school, her drastic change in appearance—she dyed her lovely auburn hair to black—and her plummeting grades. Bernice only hoped she was doing Anna some good. She felt a bit like a Cassandra, knowing the awful truth and being incapable of doing anything about it…then sharing that truth with Anna, who couldn't do anything about it either. But Bernice was a mother, too. She knew if roles were reversed she'd want the truth. She'd want to keep abreast of what was happening, no matter what it was. No matter how bad it was.

CHAPTER TWENTY ONE

SURPRISE

Perhaps their romance sustains its dewy newness because Carlo is forever returning. The two of them celebrate a homecoming evening at least once a week.

This evening, Anna makes country lasagna. She's gathered her ingredients from far and wide and is ready well before Carlo's expected arrival. She's simmering and dicing when she hears his part ironic, part sincere, "Honey I'm home," as he makes his way in from the garage. Anna still runs to greet him.

"You'll never guess what I saw today," Carlo says with a smirk. Anna gives him a look as she stirs the stewing tomatoes. Distracted, Carlo asks, "Oh, and what are we making?" as he starts lifting lids and making himself a nuisance to the cook.

"Enough," she says steering him to a seat. "Now, tell me what is it you saw today?" distracting him again.

"Oh that's right," he says snatching a slice of prosciutto from the cutting board. "Oh this is…you're going to love this! OK, I'm deplaning this afternoon and there's a new jet on the tarmac. A Gulf I've never seen before. So I asked Bill--"

"Bill the security guard or Bill in the maintenance crew?" Anna interjects.

"Maintenance Bill. And he tells me that it's a recent purchase. It was just delivered for some local owner who's in the middle of negotiating a hangar and other things with the board."

"Someone else around here bought a jet?" Anna asks. "Who? Did you find out who?"

"Yes!" Carlo says doubling over in unstoppable guffaws. "Yeah," he cries, nodding, laughing so hard tears are practically rolling down his face.

Impatient Anna swats at his shoulder crying "Who? Who is it? Why it this so funny?" Carlo holds up a finger and takes an exaggerated breath to halt his laughing fit. "The new plane belongs to a local attorney Bill tells me. You know that guy from the TV commercials. The Enforcer?"

Now it's Anna's turn to laugh uncontrollably. "Erik?" she shrieks through her laughter. "Erik the miser bought a plane? A Gulfstream? Oh for heavens' sake, this is precious."

"Yep, talk about your inadequate masculinity?" Carlo says, breaking down into hysterics again. "Erik had to actually go out and buy a plane just to show the world…" he loses his thought in laughing again. "Just to prove that he can keep up with you…with me…with us I guess."

"Talk about your keeping up with the Jones's? Oh this is too good," Anna says handing him the spoon to stir the simmering sauce. "Here, keep stirring this, keep it moving, don't let it get too thick. I have to call Janet, she is going to have a field day with this." And Carlo nods, wiping tears from his eyes and taking over the sauce while Anna dials her cell.

THE GOOD NEWS IS STANHOPE is closing in on a date for the court appointed psychiatric evaluations of the kids. Even though the process drags on and on Anna at last acknowledges that the tide might be turning, that things are beginning to go in her favor at last.

Anna is truly grateful and excited for the first time in such an inexorably long time. She can hardly remember the last time she felt so good and upbeat about all aspects of her life. She's especially giddy today because she's having her first party at the Waterston house. Not just any old slapdash get-together, either. All of Anna's friends are gathering in honor of her birthday. Her first birthday since fleeing captivity, her first 'on the outside.'

Although Anna practically demanded to do the honors of cooking, Carlo managed to talk her into letting him have the kitchen at D'Ellarte's do the work and send it over.

"There's no doubt in anyone's mind that you can wow their pallets Anna." She opens her mouth to protest, but he continued. "Just let everyone cater to you for this one single day. If you want to cook for everyone, we can do it next weekend. Just let yourself be pampered, taken care of, for this special day? Please?"

He looks so anxious and so sincere that Anna caved without a peep. Besides, even she couldn't deny the food at the restaurant was always excellent. This way, she could be part of the conversation for a change, without cramming all her visitors in the kitchen.

They've been together at the Waterston house for going on five months now. The gardens are oceans of russet and yellow leaves from the ancient trees encompassing the old estate. School has long since been in session, and sweaters are being turned in for coats over night. Anna wonders if it will be too warm yet for a fire in the fireplace. She'll have to remember to ask Carlo his opinion.

Anna has planned exactly what kind of floral arrangements and extra touches will perfect the atmosphere of the whole house for a celebration.

She's had her birthday massage and mani-pedi, even a facial and her hair done as well, but the afternoon is creeping on and Anna grows anxious. 'Where is the florist?' she asks herself, looking out the front windows, scouring the streets for any sign delivery truck.

Even though she ordered the perfect floral arrangements a week ago and verified by phone days ago, she can't help pacing back and forth in front of the picture window awaiting the delivery.

It's not a truck that catches her eye, though. Across the street stands a dark-haired girl in a hooded sweatshirt. Anna swears she can feel the girl's eyes staring through the glass. It takes a few clicks for Anna to put two and two together. That's not just any misanthropic teenage girl staring at her house…that's Betsy. Without a thought Anna bolts out the door and down the steps, heading across the street.

She's not fast enough, though. Betsy takes off as soon as she sees Anna aiming at her. She disappears through the shrubs and bushes on the neighbor's lot. Anna plunges in after her, only to catch a glimpse of her hooded back as she pumps furiously away on a bike. The mystery rider is at the end of the block making the turn before Anna is free of the Queen Ann's Lace..

Extracting herself from the bushes Anna wonders at the sudden appearance of Betsy staring at her house. 'That sweatshirt is not near warm enough,' is the first thing she thinks, shaking her head. Betsy has plenty of school friends in the surrounding neighborhoods, definitely close enough to ride or even walk to and from the Waterston house. There's the Gleesons and the Hardwicks, both of whom have girls around Betsy's age. Betsy most likely did not bike ride from the farm, better not have in that thin-looking sweatshirt. 'Besides it's too dangerous,' thinks Anna. But that doesn't mean much. With Drew off doing his thing with his buddies all the time and Maggie, well, being Maggie, it's likely Betsy could very well disappear from the farm for that long before someone realized she was missing.

'Damn, damn, and damn again,' mutters Anna to herself as she crosses back home. She wonders if she should cruise by the houses of the likely suspects and search for Betsy. On the one hand, the girl ran from Anna, bolted, and Anna didn't want to make things worse. On the other hand, she showed up. Betsy knew it was Anna's birthday and she showed up! A small part of Anna is overjoyed at the profundity of the gesture. But the rest of Anna is spitting fury as she stands on the porch realizing, as usual, there is nothing, absolutely nothing she can do about Betsy's lack of someone to care about where she is and what she's doing.

Anna asks herself a thousand questions in the few minutes it takes for the floral truck to arrive as she stands shell-shocked on the porch, shivering in the chill. She watches without understanding as the truck pulls in the driveway. The poor delivery driver has to literally poke Anna in the shoulder to get her attention back into the here and now.

"Yes, yes that's right," Anna forces a smile. "I've been expecting you." She meant to be short with the delivery man for making her wait, but she is too stunned and confused. She has to remind herself, 'Today is my birthday, I'm having a party. People will be arriving in two hours to celebrate with me. This is my house. I live here with Carlo…' she brings her mind back up to speed as she points where each basket and spray of blossoms should be placed.

CARLO IS SURPRISED TO FIND ANNA standing in the kitchen in jeans and a T-shirt, staring into space when he arrives an hour later. But since he is also distracted and anxious, he simply suggests she might want to get ready.

Because the master suite is so well planned, both of them can get on with their toilette in comfort and convenience. Anna finally reenters the present moment enough to remember to ask, "How was your day? You're home even earlier than I'd hoped. Thank you." She smiles and caresses the back of his neck. She leans in to be held in his arms, where she sighs in a way that prompts Carlo to say, "Well we're not in that much of a hurry." Anna likes the way his mind works and pushes the dress and things she laid out off the bed while untangling her legs from her jeans.

The look of her there on the bed, all rosy and welcoming, overwhelms Carlo with feelings of love and comfort. Thoughts of how wonderful a woman, of how lucky he truly is to have her in his life—'that's it,' he thinks to himself. 'No time like the present.'

Carlo strides toward the bed, but instead of flopping down next to her he kneels at the bedside and pulls Anna up to sit facing him, "Oh," says Anna. "I like this game. After all, it is my birthday," she says moving to wriggle free of her panties, but Carlo stops her. She catches the look of gravity in his eye and gives him her full attention. "What's the matter honey? Is something wrong?" she asks with concern.

"Anna," he starts. Then stops. "Anna, I—Anna a few months ago I asked you to come live here with me. But I wasn't completely honest with you then." Anna tilts her head at an angle as if that will help her understand him.

"Well I don't mean—oh God. Anna, I love you and you're such a good woman, such a wonderful, wonderful woman," he sighs. "You're more to me than 'someone to live with' Anna. I wanted to ask you then. I wasn't honest then because I knew it would frighten you, but I can't wait anymore. Every day we're together I'm surrounded by your love and your goodness and I want to give you everything, Anna. I want to comfort you and protect you. I want to surround you with all the love and beauty that you deserve." Anna is tearing up, which in turn makes Carlo well up.

He is struggling to keep talking, "Anna you are not the kind of woman a man merely lives with. I wanted to ask you then…Anna, will you marry me? Will you be my wife?" Before Anna has the sanity to even form a reply Carlo is fishing in his trouser pocket, from which he extracts a small box.

Anna is kicking her feet like a little girl, she's embarrassed to realize she's clapping her hands in anticipation. She's holding her breath as Carlo opens the box to display the treasure to her.

Anna is confused. She gives him a quizzical look as she extracts the lovely Brighton key ring from the velvet-lined box. She holds the silver key ring, from which dangles a single key, in complete confusion.

Carlo, gleeful at catching her off-guard, takes it from her and positions the ring part of the key ring around her wedding band finger and slides it up. "Ta da," he says with great pride.

"Yes?" Anna responds, holding her hand as if it sports the world's hugest marquise-cut diamond. "Yes, absolutely Carlo. I'd love to marry you," she says laughing, drawing him into her arms, pulling him onto the mattress.

"You will?" he says, with a twinkle in his eye as he extracts himself from her embrace.

"Well yes," she says a bit petulantly.

"Don't you want to know what the key is for?" he asks as he rebuttons his shirt and hands Anna her jeans.

"Well, yes I---"

"Well, lets' get moving then." He interrupts as he cinches his belt and extends his hand to help her up. Anna scrambles into her clothes and is after him like a flash.

They make a silent parade through the house and out to his truck. He, of course, opens her door before getting in the driver's side and turning over the engine. Anna is in a daze, her mouth hanging open.

"Well what is it?" she finally squeals. "What?"

Carlo smirks silently. Anna knows him well enough to realize that no amount of begging or cajoling will break him down when he sets his mind. She simply crosses her arms over her chest and determines to remain as silent as he is. They could be going anywhere. Once they're on the main street off the park, that is. Carlo takes a familiar route past the dance studio, towards the beginning of the bike trail. 'No it can't be.' Anna thinks as their location gradually dawns on her.

Sure enough, he pulls into the lot among dozens of other cars. The hole in the fence around the al fresco patio is fixed and the lights are on. Carlo hands Anna out of her seat and guides her to the front door. The awnings are up. They stand there for a few seconds before Carlo lifts her hand removes the 'ring' from her finger and hands it to her.

Her hand shakes so much she can hardly...Carlo has to help her. The key slides in and Anna turns the lock, opening the door to her secret hopes and dreams, her lost future, her restaurant—Coco's Café. But inside is no longer dust and ladders and unfinished man hours. The lights reveal that most of the heavy work is complete; the counters and dividing walls, the tile and flooring. Anna looks toward the kitchen and Carlo nods. Anna runs from one end of the restaurant to the other, speechless one instant and screaming in shock the next. Her friends come out of the woodwork to take turns embracing her, squealing with joy, surprise, and delight.

Anna can't stop the tears. She turns and runs back to Carlo. "You've got to be kidding me? I mean how--"

"Shhh, a magician never reveals his secrets. I wanted to give you back your dreams Anna. If you're going to be my wife, then I want you to be happy," he says grinning broadly.

Anna recognizes her mother and father in the crowd and runs to embrace them, to cry and express her shock and excitement. After some more minutes of this gleeful chaos servers gradually appear, setting up a beautiful buffet near the big windows. Whoever wasn't scheduled to work D'Ellarte's tonight is serving drinks at Coco's Café.

CHAPTER TWENTY TWO

THE DREAM RESTORED

"Did you know?" demands Anna as she at last embraces Janet. Janet only smiles and shrugs, saying, "I'll never tell."

The guest list has been kept exclusive, Anna can't help but notice. Bernice and her husband are there, but she's the only one among her committee friends. The only 'true' friend among them. Her sister is here alone. Her parents, and Janet and her Steve as well. Janet made sure to include Abby and Carson. Then, friends of Carlo's that Anna has taken a liking to such as Dave the pilot and his lovely wife, Mick the project supervisor of the Waterston house reconstruction. Oh, and Sue, the dessert whiz at the restaurant, and a few others.

It takes Anna a while to acknowledge that she keeps searching the crowd for Betsy as well. 'If she appeared once, she could appear again, anytime,' Anna tells herself to feel less crazy. Before too long Anna is engulfed in the party mood, the excitement, the fun. Everyone is thrilled to have been part of such a big secret. Carlo really knows how to draw people together, that's for sure.

"When are you going to open?" Mick asks her. Anna spits out a piece of a puffed hors d'oeuvre as she howls in laughter.

"When am I going to open he wants to know! Uh, Mick, you do realize this is the first I found out about the whole thing, right?" Anna asks trying to gauge if Mick is teasing her or serious. She never can tell with his stoic attitude. But he cracks one of his rare smiles and Anna, relieved, gives him a whack on the shoulder for teasing her in her fragile, amazed condition.

After filling her plate Anna sidles up to check in with Dave the pilot's wife, Dana. Anna can hardly remember seeing a more beautiful pregnant woman. She sits next to Dana and silently grasps her hand in greeting so as not to interrupt the intense conversation going on.

Dave is talking "OK, so he tried to hire me away from Carlo, right? But of course I told him 'no way.' But he's so lost and at loose ends. Doesn't know the first thing about hiring a pilot." 'Ah ha, they must be talking about Erik,' registers Anna. "I take pity on him and give him the names and numbers of a few guys I know from flight school, good guys. After all, I'll be seeing them all the time. I want guys I like around the hangar," says Dave.

"He ends up hiring a decent guy I know, Grant. He moved his family from Denver for the job. Anyway, Grant is not at all happy to find out that he'll essentially be piloting the governor around. He ends up spending quite a few week nights and even some weekends in Chicago since the governor goes 'home' some nights and flies back down the next morning. Same on some weekends. So Grant's really frustrated, because he hardly gets to see his kids. When he's home during the day, they're at school. When he flies at night, the family is home without him," Dave explains. Janet nods, then tilts her head, indicating confusion.

"But wait wouldn't that be like…political patronage? Erik, or Erik's law firm, just footing the tab for the governor's work-related travel because some tax-payers are squawking? Isn't that illegal? Is that any different than buying him a vacation getaway to the Carribean or a set of golf clubs?" asks Janet.

"Wait a minute, wait a minute," interjects Steve. "I think I read something in the paper about this. Well, about the governor's travel expenses, anyway. There was something about some 527 organization that's chartering a plane and pilot to help the governor on his mission…"

"What the heck is a 527?" asks Dana.

"It's like a political action committee. Like the 'Swift Boat Veterans for Truth.' They're exempt from taxes and they can spend as much money as they want to 'discuss' candidates or issues. This one is called the 'Fathers for Families Alliance.' And because they feel it so crucially important for fathers to read to their kids at night, or something like that, they're making it possible for one father to see his kids every night."

Janet searches the faces of those around the table, "Fathers for Families Alliance? Has anyone ever heard of that?"

Some shaking heads. A few murmured no's.

"Still sounds illegal to me," Bernice's husband says.

"Is it?" Abby turns to ask her husband. "Carson here is with the Inspector General's office, so maybe he knows." Carson blushes and gives Abby a look through his eyebrows.

"Well there are pretty tight restrictions. Uh, fund-raising and political action committees aren't my specialty or anything. But I'm sure that these people have run their plan by the right kinds of lawyers to be sure it's all on the up and up," Carson says shrugging. "No one wants to go down on some technicality."

"Oh, you know how the politicians and the fund-raisers are. They all have their ways around obstacles such as 'regulations,'" Steve says. "Believe you me, if they thought there was a chance they were going to get caught they wouldn't be doing it. You can be sure they found some loophole to make it work in their favor."

"Well, I guess Fathers for Families feels it would be too much of an imposition to ask the governor's wife to do the obvious and move to Cambridge?" someone asks.

"I guess no one believes he's going to be around long enough to make it worthwhile, not even his wife," says Bernice's husband.

"Well, he manages to spend enough nights in Cambridge," says Janet with a nod. A few people laugh, but Dana, Bernice, and her husband obviously have no idea what Janet's hedging at. Ann kicks her under the table.

Janet kicks her back, saying, "Perhaps his wife has her own reasons for wanting him to commute and spend a lot of time away from home?"

Bernice blushes. Her husband looks uncomfortable, and Anna rolls her eyes at Janet. Dave and Dana devour their luscious dessert.

Because the guest of honor is obligated to circulate, Anna moves from her table to visit with others. She's effusive and incredibly grateful as she hops from table to table, group to group. She's afraid her mother and father must think she's drunk. She feels as giddy as a teenager. It's a bit as though she's in a dream, as if the people and the walls aren't real, that at any moment she will blink and it will all be gone.

She surprises her sister with an unusually warm and meaningful hug. "Now I think I get how you must have felt," Anna whispers by way of apology for her long-ago jealousy. Her sister looks confused, but holds her tighter.

After a few ticks, Katherine seems to get it, "Ah, you mean in love." Anna responds by jumping up and down. "Yes that's it! You've got it. That is what I was trying to say. You were happy when you married Mike, you loved him and couldn't wait to begin. I get it now. I get it!"

Words can't express how happy Katherine is for this new blossoming taking place in her sister. So she joins Anna in her tiny leaps of joy and excitement like a pair of long-separated sorority girls. "You get it now because you're really in love. This is what its supposed to feel like. Oh, my darling, I am so happy for you! So happy!"

Eventually Janet comes along to grab Anna's hand, and pulls her back until the two of them are alone. "Well?"

Anna nods, her smile bursting. The two hug and squeal and hug some more. "And I'm assuming you had the good sense to say yes?" Janet says, holding Anna by the shoulders.

"Yes! Yes, of course I said yes! Oh, so you were in on this? You knew and didn't tell me?" Anna accuses, bumping Janet's hip with hers, hard.

"Owwwwuh," Janet says rubbing her bone. "I knew he bought the restaurant."

"You did?" Anna says. "When did he do that?"

"A few weeks, or a month or so after you met him, shortly after you and I had a particularly interesting conversation about your relationship in the Thai restaurant," Janet says nodding.

Anna covers her mouth with her hands and lets the blush cover her face, knowing resistance is futile. "You're kidding me? He didn't?" Then she adds, "Hey, that was more like six weeks of knowing him."

"Way back then," Janet says. "Don't take this the wrong way, but he had to act fast before the lawyers froze all Erik's assets and he wouldn't be able to sell. Carlo had a very small window of opportunity. But then again, he's an unusually resourceful man."

"Did he buy it from Erik? I can't believe Erik sold it to him... to anyone?" Anna says.

"Oh no. Someone else bought it from Erik and Carlo bought it from them. Well, let's put it this way, someone else bought it for Carlo and he bought it from them." Janet explains. "Hey, maybe that's the seed money he used for the plane?"

Anna is relieved that Erik wasn't able to gouge Carlo on the price or anything. She finds she's also pretty excited that Erik doesn't yet know the place is back in her hot little hands again, that he couldn't keep her from her dream. She also worries a little if this isn't starting a war with him. But the drinks are flowing and music just started playing from somewhere, and Anna is the possessor of the key to happiness and she wants to enjoy it for as long as she can. Tonight. She turns to scan the crowd for Carlo—she can hardly wait to get her hands on him.

CHAPTER TWENTY THREE

AN ANSWER APPEARS

Carlo hired a reputable firm from Chicago to work in conjunction with Stanhope. They had an agenda that would deliver a divorce but leave the settlement terms open for debate ad infinitum, practically. Carlo and Anna meet with Stanhope to prepare him for their new approach. They have a wedding to plan, after all. They'd spent long hours debating, deciding, figuring out what's best to do.

They were going to let Stanhope's plan for the psych evaluation play through until its conclusion and reevaluate from there. The team working on Anna's case, who Carlo refers to as the 'League of Ivy Lawyers,' launched their first offensive to dissolve the marriage, meeting with surprisingly little resistance from Erik's legal entourage.

Anna is the one to solve that mystery. She discovers the answer while browsing the Sunday paper over morning coffee. In the announcements section of the paper she reads '…the engagement of Mr. Erik Reinhardt and Ms. Eleanor 'Ella' Hamilton-Lewis.' The stiff picture of the two of them speaks volumes. Erik looks as if he's aged ten years, his hair thinning and grayer than Anna remembers. There's a pitiable slouch in his posture that gives her pause. Even the pigeon-toed way he faces the camera speaks 'pity' to Anna.

Bernice calls to tell her the news while she was on the other line with Janet, who's hysterical. Anna sends the online version to Carlo's computer so he can have a good laugh when he gets back to the hotel that evening. That explains Erik's lack of resistance to pushing on with the divorce. It would be sad...if it weren't so hilarious. First the plane, now a fiancée? Anna was tempted to spread the word that she was pregnant just to see how long it would take Ella to get knocked up. 'The poor thing,' thinks Anna. 'She has no idea what she's gotten herself into. None.'

ANNA SPENDS HER TIME AT COCO'S getting details pinned down, planning for the opening. A lot of people come and go—line-cook and waitstaff applicants, the installers for the wine refrigeration, the tile guys—but Anna relishes being in the eye of the hurricane.

A few fellows in dusty overalls eat lunch, scattered at tables. Some college girls dot other tables, filling out waitstaff applications. Anna resists thinking that every girl with dark hair who enters is Betsy. Each one gets a double or sometimes triple take, though, so she can reassure herself.

This day is particularly busy for Anna. She has applicants coming and going like clockwork. Amid the sea of fluctuating faces, Anna sees her and knows without thinking that it is indeed her. Betsy is here at Coco's, standing alone with her hand on the entrance door, debating, deciding. Two people push out through the door, and Anna watches Betsy move aside without turning away.

When Betsy surveys the inside, Anna ducks down, hiding. She crouches and waddles along behind the counter, slipping behind the kitchen door where she can spy on Betsy through the window. Her heart is racing like she'd run two miles at top speed.

The girl enters, silently glancing around. She follows along with what she sees one or two others are doing. She retrieves an application and takes a seat far away from the others, right by the door where she can keep an eye out for Anna.

Anna watches Betsy watching everyone else, searching.

Betsy's gaze is sharp and thorough. Anna catches her breath as Betsy's eyes close in on the kitchen door, zooming in on Anna's face peering from the corner of the window, but she doesn't move. Anna didn't shift or hide. She stayed just where she was, not moving at all, just watching Betsy watch her. Betsy didn't move either, nor did she take her eyes off her mother.

They looked at each other unblinking. Passersby obscured them from one another for seconds at a time, yet neither one moved, or even seemed to blink. Betsy looks longer, leaner; she's lost that preteen roundness. She's grown taller in the five months since Anna had even attempted to force her to visit.

The line of Betsy's mouth has a new set to it, as if she's clenching her teeth behind her closed lips. Anna has never seen her daughter dressed quite the way she is today. She recognizes the scuffed Vans and even the outsized gray sweatshirt. If she's not mistaken, Drew's sweatshirt. Sure, Betsy wore sweatshirts camping or when chilled around the house in winter, but Anna never saw Betsy wear a sweatshirt like a shield, like body armor against the outside world.

In her head, Anna hears Erik's stream of complaints and criticisms at how Betsy looked, about what Betsy was wearing. Anna shakes her head. 'Why does she shove it in his face like that? If she'd just-- he wouldn't be so hard on her.' Then again maybe nice, child-bribing Erik manages to hold his tongue, refrain from badgering the girl in order to be the 'good loving' parent. Then again, more than likely, Erik has no idea what Betsy looks like or is doing. Unless things have changed drastically, he comes home well after she's supposed to be in bed and leaves it to Maggie or the housekeeper to be sure she gets into town for school. Someone else drives the kids and feeds them, or he simply leaves money for pizza delivery and his credit card for spending at the mall.

Anna had the presence of mind not to spook her. Instead, Anna watches Betsy. She pores over Betsy's face, trying to crack the code of the wrinkles in her brow and the angle of her slouch. If Betsy's father were to find out she was 'consorting with the enemy...' Anna didn't finish the thought.

A guy pushing a cartload of tile bears down on Anna. When she dips from Betsy's sight to make room for him, Betsy rises and slips out the door and past the windows like a flash. For a second Anna wonders where Betsy possibly gets her speed from. She briefly considers going after her, but quickly realizes it would only make matters worse. She's devastated, but knows the only thing she can do is hope Betsy comes back to her soon.

WORKING ON THE RESTAURANT, being with Carlo—any of it, all of it—is so far superior to receiving her updates about the divorce, about the psych evaluation battle. Anna is devastated when Stanhope tells her, "The judge doesn't have enough evidence of something wrong to even request, let alone demand, that the kids submit to such a screening."

Even though the Carlo's team Lawyers is having little trouble aiming for a dissolution of marriage now that Erik is on board for reasons of is own, Stanhope is getting all forms of flak and resistance regarding the kids. Erik's team seemed to show little resistance to the idea of psychiatric evaluations but once they got closer Erik's team went mad sending documents flying trying to block any hint that the kids' behavior 'altered' in any way that needs to be 'evaluated.'

The very idea of 'evaluation' is eaten away by writs and pleas and filings, until it becomes a 'declaration.' Erik claims he's not involved, not responsible for the fact that the kids refuse to participate in Anna's visits.

Stanhope informs her that "at this hearing, the kids are going be put on the stand and asked by the judge to state once and for all if they will or will not comply with your visits, Anna."

This is the price she's paying for her boldness. She dared to insinuate that Erik was up to something with the kids—that he was influencing, threatening, or bribing them to exile their mother. Without the necessary proof, she's in trouble for even bringing it up.

Anna is frankly sick of looking at the walls of Stanhope's office. She feels as though she's being chastised by the principal every time she enters. She's sick of his books and his ringing phone and his overflowing wastebasket. But most of all, Anna is sick of losing. Sick of watching so much precious time, so much lost time, slip through her fingers. She buries her face in her hands as Stanhope preps to brief her on what to expect, on what her choices are.

"For the most part, it's the judge who determines how much the child's opinions and wishes are taken into consideration. He decides if Betsy is put on the stand to answer once and for all whether she wants to come live with you, or see you as she's supposed to. If Betsy says in front of the courtroom that she wants to see you, her mother, that she's afraid of her father, afraid of making him angry. If she said that, the court would be hard-pressed to ignore her." Stanhope suggests.

Endless questions blossom in Anna's mind, "Will you be able to ask Betsy or Drew questions about the naked photos of Erik, and him chasing the kids with a belt?"

Stanhope looks at the ground and shakes his head. "No, since we don't have any corroborating evidence and we're not sure how Betsy's going to respond, it's in our best interest to leave it alone."

"But," Anna continues, thinking out loud, "under oath Betsy

would be safe to tell the truth, she'd be protected if she told the truth. Right?" While Anna wasn't so sure about Drew, whether he would break the silence, tell the truth, she was sure that if Betsy spilled the story, then Drew would back her up. Anna had noticed that over the course of her thwarted visits, he'd grown more protective and watchful of his sister. And that was only one thing she'd noticed over the course of their uncomfortable 'interfaces.'

Stanhope continues, "If, on the other hand, Betsy or Drew claim they never want to see you again, that they prefer staying with their father—if they say that once and for all in front of you and Erik and the lawyers and the judge..." Stanhope left the rest of the thought to Anna's imagination.

But Anna started thinking that if only Betsy could say how she really felt, in front of all those people—one way or the other—she would finally have her answer. After months of torture and waiting and not knowing, after months of confusion and self-blame, if Anna heard Betsy say those words out loud, then she would have to learn to let go, to move on, and to stop letting her heart be crushed. Or, if Betsy went the other way, Anna could look forward to rebuilding her relationship with her daughter. At the very least, Anna would finally know beyond any shadow of a doubt where she stood.

"Now, I want you to think long and hard about this Anna. We have, oh, two days, forty-eight hours, to respond. We could, if you want to, if you think this has even the slightest chance of blowing up in our face, we could cancel this hearing or eliminate the need for this hearing by withdrawing our earlier request," Stanhope says nodding.

Anna bites her lip and asks, "When do you need my answer?"

"By nine a.m. day after tomorrow," Stanhope clarifies.

Anna has forty-eight hours to decide on the biggest gamble of her life. It's too long. She can't stay on this merry-go-round of possibility for that long.

"What's your recommendation?" Anna asks him.

"You really want to know?" he asks.

"Yeah Dennis, what do you think I should do?" Anna asks.

"I think you should let it go forward," he says, rubbing his chin. "Withdrawing our request for the psych evals just because we're not getting exactly what we want makes us, makes you look... uncertain. As if you're afraid of what the kids will say or do. That they won't, you know, pick you."

"Well that's exactly what I am afraid of. That's precisely it. Because if she goes on the stand and says she never wants to see me again, wants me out of her life for whatever reason--"

Stanhope interrupts. "Now, let's not get ahead of ourselves. It's highly unlikely that the judge will permanently alter the joint custody ruling or entirely eliminate your visitation rights, no matter what they say. Even fathers in prison get to see their kids. Even if the kids are, let's say, reluctant."

Anna says, rising to pace. "Well no, but I have custody and visitation rights now according to the court and a fat lot of good they're doing me."

"More than likely, if that happened he'd schedule supervised visits like we talked about earlier. Visits in the presence of a neutral observer. Right, so in a way you have little to lose and only knowledge to gain." He then says more quietly, "that is, if you want that knowledge."

"OK..." Anna says, reaching for her purse. "I'll call you as soon as I figure it out."

Anna discusses her options with Carlo. She calls Janet. She spends two hours on the phone with her mother in Florida. They debate and discuss. They speculate and guess what Betsy, or Drew, or Erik will do, or might do.

The morning of the second 'day of decision,' Anna heads to the park along what's become her regular morning route. After seeing

Carlo off to the office, she walks, trying to purge the uncertainty that still lingers from her body. Should she, shouldn't she. If this, then that. The thinking is driving her crazy.

She wishes she'd had to decide on the spot, in the matter of the minutes after Stanhope told her. All the weighing and measuring is exhausting. But despite her inner chaos, Anna is relieved that something remains regular. Her daily routine is becoming 'normal.' The late fall chill hasn't deterred the usual suspects who walk the park each day. There's the blonde pushing twins in the jogger, and the old lady with the beagle.

She spends the rest of the second day going over and over the possibilities with Bernice. After all, Bernice is a mother, and she knows Betsy and Anna. Anna even calls her sister on the drive back home in the afternoon. But the simple fact is, no one can make the choice for her. They had their ideas and opinions. But Anna knows Betsy, knows Drew best. Only Anna knows what she stands to lose or gain, whatever the case may be.

As she pulls into the driveway, she's annoyed by the sudden cloudburst, the cold November rain. She tries to put on the wipers for one fast sweep, but accidentally turns up the volume on the radio, blasting. Discombobulated, hardly able to see through the windshield, at the last instant she reacts to a shadowy unfocused blob darting along the sidewalk between her bumper and the house. She slams on the brakes, music still blaring. Utterly giving up on the wipers, Anna rolls her driver's side window down to be sure the blob is intact and well clear.

Without the distortion of the rainy windshield, Anna makes out a kid on a bike, hood up and soaked through the skin but intact, apparently unharmed. 'Awful late in the year for that,' she can't help but think automatically. She addresses the radio volume problem and puts her hand on her heart, taking a deep breath.

The cyclist stops a few feet down along the sidewalk, turning to look at Anna. Worried that the driver may have had a heart attack, perhaps? As she exhales, Anna turns to see Betsy's face under the soggy hood. Neither one moves for a beat, and a longer second beat. Anna's hand flies to cover her mouth, to keep from crying out, to avoid spooking her. The rain is pelting. Betsy has to wipe her eyes to even see. She does so without moving any of the rest of her body. Then she shakes her head and laughs, holds her palms to the sky and turns to look skyward.

Anna does too. She cranes her head out the window and rotates her face to the sky. She sees what Betsy sees—the drops, like tiny missiles, tiny messages pelting the ground. They look to one another again. Anna tips her head and gestures to the warm, dry, and very empty passenger seat. Betsy shrugs, looks up into the rain again. As she pulls off away from Anna, she gives her head another shake and the hood falls back. Anna can see a wry laugh escaping as she disappears.

Anna wondered what would happen as the weather grew colder. She worried that foul weather might keep Betsy away. Even though all they did was stare at each other for a few moments from yards away, it was all Anna had.

She told no one. Not Janet; not even Carlo, or her mother, or Bernice. She barely allowed herself to even think of it.

The temptation to finally know where she stood, once and for all began to outweigh the declining opportunity. Anna worked to convince herself that no matter what the outcome is, she can live with it. The not knowing was gnawing at her insides, pulsing through her veins like poison.

In her heart, Anna believes that when push comes to shove Betsy could never betray her mother's love and deny to even see her. That would never, could never happen. And if, if by some strange stretch of the imagination, it did, Anna could just deal with it then. 'Seeing her here, her showing up today of all days,' she tells herself, is a sign. Of course, She feels instantly better, the decision made.

As soon as she pulls her tail end clear of the sidewalk and puts the car in park, she dials Stanhope's office. Well ahead of the next morning's deadline, Anna knows exactly what she wants to do. She tells Stanhope, "OK, let's get this done and over with. How soon can we schedule it?"

CHAPTER TWENTY FOUR

FINAL DECISIONS

The clock is ticking and the hearing is only days away now. Anna has scrubbed every floor in the house, all sixteen of them. She would have done the restaurant floors, too, if so many people weren't coming and going all the time.

Her mother is flying up to be with Anna at court, to see Betsy and Drew. The two of them stare at each other and wring their hands, together. There is nothing that can be said. 'Good luck,' 'I'm sorry,' 'Break a leg?'

"It's going to be OK," Anna tells herself. She hears her mother tell her the same thing. Anna finds herself reassuring her mother that, "everything will be OK, Mom, you don't have to worry." The thought passes around the room, from one person to the next, like a hat for contributions. The more repetitions that fill the hat, the more certain the outcome. Carlo and Janet and Bernice make their contributions. Even Abby and Dave and Dana add to the pile. Katherine adds a few by phone from Washington.

Initially, there is no reason to imagine anything strange in Abby's husband, Carson, calling to invite Anna to lunch—just that it's an oddly stressful time and he seems to be sensitive to that fact. But Carson is subtly insistent that she meet him at the gourmet sandwich shop near the new movie theatres. "No, it would be better if I didn't come to your restaurant, Anna," he says.

"Well no it's not entirely business," he says as a complete non sequitur before hanging up. Anna stares at her phone as if it has the capacity to decipher that bit of weirdness.

He's his normal charming self when she arrives half an hour later. He seats her near the fireplace and dashes off to fetch her coffee. After settling in his seat, Carson faces her with his elbows on his knees, head bowed, hesitant.

"Anna, now, I know this is a little odd. But your name came up tangentially related to something I'm doing for the job," he says clearing his throat. "You are aware of where I work?" Anna nods, unsure of what he's driving at. Yes, everyone knows he works with the Inspector General's office. 'What could this possibly be? They investigate state employees for misconduct, to get them fired, off the payroll. Anna never worked for the state? She is confused, and it must show on her face.

"Now, I can eliminate your name from even coming up in the paperwork on this if you can just verify for me when exactly you were divorced from your ex-husband, Mr. Erik Reinhardt." He nods and stops talking.

"Uh, it's no secret, Carson, that I'm still trying to get divorced from my ex-husband. What do you mean?" Anna says even more confused.

"No Anna, in the course of what we're looking into it came to our attention that Mr. Reinhold and yourself were divorced at an earlier date?" he says, hoping to lead her to the answer.

Anna's face forms an 'O.' Then another shock of recognition as it dawns on her, 'They must be investigating Erik'. As if he can read her thoughts, Carson nods. 'Oh no, am I going to be in trouble?' is her next thought. The doubt and fear flicker across her face, and Carson goes on, "No, this has nothing to do with you.

We're totally off the books here and, in fact, I'm kind of bending the rules. I just need the date of your earlier divorce and the date of your remarriage. We're trying to put some things, some financial arrangements, in context—on a timeline, if you will. The dates of that divorce are our only referent." He stops and sips his coffee. Anna does the same.

Anna gives him the dates willingly, and he commits them to memory.

"Sorry about all this. It just didn't seem necessary to have you come down to the office for an 'official' interview just to get this one piece of information verified. I figured it would be more convenient if we could just chat in private."

"Well, I hope that helps," Anna replies shrugging, not so subtly fishing for more information.

Carson rises to his feet and smiles. "Well, you won't be surprised to hear that that's more than I should have let you know. And I'm certain I can count on your discretion to keep this conversation confidential until everything comes out in the wash?" he says, giving her a conspiratorial wink.

Anna hurried home to her mother only to discover she needed to turn around and run out to the airport to pick up her sister Katherine, who decided to come in as well. The errands and hostess duties are an excellent distraction from the event that is the central meaning of all the activity.

Although they'd seen it at her birthday her mother and sister oh and ah politely at the beauty of the house, again. "Where did you find this ottoman?" "What do you call this color tile?" "It's rare you find a couch this pretty and this comfortable. It's almost always one or the other."

The melody of polite chitchat keeps them buoyed. It feels like a vigil over failing hope. Will hope die or will hope be revitalized, restored, and brought back to life? Everyone works to make hope more comfortable, to convince hope to remain with them for good.

The closer the day draws, the more quiet the women become. Carlo asked Anna over and again if she wanted him there, if she needed him there at home, or in court. He instinctively knew that her mother and sister would have a far better chance of being helpful, and he gave them room. All the other court dates, Anna thought it best for Carlo not to come along. His presence would only antagonize Erik further. She maintained the policy for this hearing as well. As much as she could draw comfort from his presence, the benefits do not outweigh the potential ramifications.

Carlo goes to his office each morning and tiptoes around the women in the evening. He cancelled all out-of-town trips for the time being, not only to be near for the big day at court but because the pilot's wife, Dana, was almost due with her first child. Nothing was important enough to drag Dave away from his wife at such an important time.

THE NEWS THAT THE GOVERNOR IS the focus of an 'on-going probe' is a welcome current events distraction from their own problems. Local NPR correspondents were on national broadcasts, explaining how yet another Illinois governor is under investigation.

"What's it for this time?" Katherine wants to know as she collects the breakfast dishes.

"Either they're not saying or I'm not understanding it," their mother says.

Anna doesn't even register the news or the conversation, because she's on the phone with Stanhope going over and over what's supposed to happen tomorrow. Anna's grateful that he's being very patient, very supportive and considerate to her now. They may have started off rocky, but she was discovering that he did have some strengths—perhaps more those of a friend than a ruthless attorney. But Anna needed the patience and compassion of a great friend at the moment. The fact is, Stanhope's years of experience couldn't help him influence or control what could happen in the morning.

Sometime in the late afternoon a strange sense of calm descends over Anna. She's stopped feeling jittery, the acid in her stomach has stopped churning. Her mind quiets, and there was very little talk at the dinner table. Everyone goes through the motions of going to bed, although who could sleep?

An hour later Anna heard someone rustling around in the hall. She found her mother peeking through the crack in her bedroom door, as if Anna were five years old and her mother was come to turn out the light.

Anna took her mother by the hand, and they went and sat in the living room together.

"Mom there's something I want to tell you that made me feel better. I saw something that made me absolutely certain that tomorrow will turn out for the best. That everything will be OK." Anna tries to moderate the sixty-watt inner grin that has been growing since the afternoon.

"You know the day I decided to go through with this hearing?" Anna asks her mother.

"Sure I remember. We talked for hours the day before and went round and round. When you called me back the next night, you were absolutely certain." Her mother says. "I wondered what happened, what made you commit to one over the other?"

"I haven't told anyone about this yet, Mom." Anna takes both her mother's hands in her and speaks as calmly as possible. She's afraid her voice will betray her since she's not once talked about it. "I've seen her Mom, Betsy."

Her mother raises her eyebrows in hope, then lets them drop again as confusion sets in. "What do you mean you've seen

Betsy? You've talked to her? You know what she's going to say or do tomorrow?" Anna's mother says with growing excitement, squeezing Anna's hand, her eyes glinting.

"Well. I've seen her. She's come by the house and the restaurant. I've seen her three, no four times now. The first time was on my birthday. Before the party, I was looking out the window and saw this ragamuffin in a sweatshirt staring at me from across the street. I ran out to her, but she ran away."

"You didn't talk to her?" her mother asks.

"No, no talking. But don't you see Mom, she's coming to look at me, to watch me, to see me. She misses me Mom. She misses me and she wants to come to me. She wants me in her life but something is trapping her," Anna says.

"So this is how you decided?" her mother asks.

"Yes. Betsy was my sign. That's what happened to me this afternoon, why I was so calm, why I'm so calm now. I just know that the right thing has to happen. It wasn't a coincidence she passed by my house that particular rainy afternoon precisely when I was about to pull into the driveway. It couldn't be. It was a sign that everything is going to be OK. Oh, you should have seen her Mom. Don't get me wrong, she looks like a wreck—remember that when you see her tomorrow. She's dyed her hair black. She's lost weight. She looks like she never sleeps."

"That doesn't sound good" Her mother exclaims.

"She looks like a wreck, but that afternoon despite the rain, despite the cold, she was glad to look me in the eye, happy to be seen. She just looked like a flash of her old self. It's been so long since I caught a glimpse of that girl, but it was there that day." Anna says as she breaks into tears for the first time in a very long time considering.

Anna lets her mother hold her as she cries. Although their lives were not deeply steeped in religion, it is not uncomfortable for

Anna or her mother to suggest they pray together. They do so now, silently and with dignity.

In the dark of the night, a mother and daughter facing the unknown bow their heads in hopes of receiving a little of God's grace. And so they wait.

CHAPTER TWENTY FIVE

THE FINAL STRAW

The morning flies by in a blur. Anna can hardly tell if she is awake or in a nightmare. Anna sits behind her lawyers, the whole swarm of them agitated because Betsy isn't in the courtroom—or Drew, for that matter. Everyone knows they are being called today. So where are they? That is the whole point of this legal exercise, after all. As Anna sits there absorbing the tension in the courtroom, she shakes her head wondering if this is what she wanted after all.

Both the kids are to be put on the stand this morning. Neither side was willing to allow the conversation to take place in chambers—the kids one at a time, alone with the judge. No one wanted that.

Anna was sure that being alone with the judge, another scary authority figure (very much like their father), would not be particularly conducive to getting them to open up. But as she can recognize only now, neither will the wood-paneled courtroom. Anna wonders what she'd been imagining, because this wasn't it. She hadn't anticipated a bevy of anxious adults waiting to pounce on a couple of damaged kids. Her fear was that without friendly faces and moral support, the kids would be more likely to grunt and hardly answer, which would maintain the status quo—not work in her favor.

Anna felt certain Erik had his own reasons to fear the kids speaking to the judge privately in chambers, behind closed doors.

When Betsy is called to the stand, she's ushered in from the back of the courtroom by a bailiff. Her father was already seated behind his team, alongside his shiny new fiancé dressed in mourning chic.

It looks as though the bailiff is half dragging half carrying Betsy by her left elbow. Betsy sort of hangs at an odd tilt from his big hand, helpless, scuffling pigeon-toed. Betsy sort of swung ever so slightly every few steps. Although her clothes should have looked normal—trousers, a blouse and sweater—they instead looked like some kind of costume. Her hair is back to a supersaturated exaggeration of her true auburn, yanked into an awkward ponytail. This gives her already pale complexion an even more translucent quality that doesn't respond well under the fluorescent lights.

As the bailiff strides past Anna, Betsy swings from three o'clock to six o'clock, looking over her dropped shoulder to lock her mother's eyes. She traps Anna in her gaze and holds her there for the duration of the walk to the front. Anna registers the silent scream hiding behind the steeliness of Betsy's eyes, in the slackness of her face.

Betsy looks like a refugee. Certainly the judge can see that, the lawyers. Even Erik would have to admit that Betsy looks like hell, bony and in a state of shock. She's practically catatonic for Pete's sake. Anna wants to fall to her knees screaming, 'what have you done? What have you done to my little red-haired baby girl, Erik?'

A stifled moan escapes involuntarily from her in the courtroom.

But the judge smiles at Betsy in a doting kind of friendly way, as if her battle scars and gaunt, slouchy appearance are quite normal. He explains in a calm voice what the bailiff is there to do and that she'll be taking an oath that required that she be completely honest, because everyone there is interested in her well being. Everyone wants what's best for her.

As Betsy places her hand on the bible, she glances around the entire courtroom. She looks at her father, bites her lip, and then swivels to fix her stare on Anna, where her focus remains. Anna can feel Erik and the lawyers stealing glances at her, at where Betsy is staring. Betsy lets her arm drop like a lifeless doll when the bible propping her hand up is removed. The bailiff reaches out to steady her as the momentum of the flopping arm unbalances her.

'Does she look drugged? Is that what's wrong with her?' Anna stops herself from whispering to Stanhope. Anna scrutinizes every muscle flex in Betsy's face and body to decipher what might be going on behind those eyes. 'Are they filling up with tears? Is she refusing to blink to keep the tears from overstepping their bounds?'

Anna pulls her attention back to see how other people are reacting to Betsy. Do they look worried, sympathetic, concerned? No. Nothing. Everyone seems to behave as though there is nothing odd or unusual in Betsy's behavior, as though she's not just limply hanging there, absolutely trying to pretend she's not there—that she is anyplace else in the entire world, in the entire universe, but there in that courtroom.

In that instant Anna finally gets it, that Betsy has retreated within to hide herself from this unbearable situation. Betsy has completely checked out of her body and is floating somewhere slightly above and beyond herself as she sits in the hot seat nodding to the judge, staring unblinking at her mother. Anna sees for the first time that the pain, anger, and fear she thought Betsy was aiming at Anna is simply aimed out…at anyone, at everyone, at the whole ugly situation.

Betsy is all porcupine quills and petulance not because she hates Anna, but because Betsy is trapped in her own particular brand of inescapable pain. Betsy is at the mercy of those who say they love her yet are torturing her, tearing her heart out. Betsy has been retreating from the torture that her everyday life has become, the constant tearing at her emotions. Rather than stay present and be torn in half, Betsy has withdrawn within her own armor, revealing nothing in hopes of putting a stop to the ongoing madness.

Anna hears it from somewhere deep in her body…'save me.' It's not loud or urgent. It's flat and lifeless and a little bit underwater. 'Help me,' more clearly this time. Anna looks around, holding her hand over her heart and trying to slow the racing of her pulse. She breathes slowly in and slowly out. She pushes all other thoughts and worries from her mind and concentrates all her focus, all her energy and powers of observation, and empathy, and understanding. Anna gathers all these within herself and zeroes in on Betsy. "Please, help me, save me…Mom?"

The feeling is so powerful, the message is so clear to Anna, that she's startled at the sheer volume of it, shocked that she'd been deaf to it until this instant. She looks around to see if others sense it. No, the judge is asking Betsy questions to get her comfortable. "What grade are you in school?" "What's your favorite subject." Things like that. To Anna, it is all happening in slow motion. His words drag out in stupefying denseness and sluggish gravity, then drop like cannon balls all around Betsy who pleads at her mother with her eyes.

Once the message behind Betsy's pleading eyes breaks through Anna's consciousness, she can't stop it or turn it down. 'Please. Stop this. Don't make me…I can't do it. Someone help me.' Betsy looks to Anna like trapped prey on the Discovery Channel. When the predators pick off a runt and then run it down, toy with it, break its resistance. When the camera catches the eye of the prey that knows its fate. This is what Anna recognizes in her daughter's eyes.

To the whole of the courtroom, Anna blurts, "Stop. Stop!" It comes out, out loud, perhaps to wake her from her stupor. Everyone in the courtroom freezes. There is a reactionary hush. Betsy actually straightens her head and shoulders and takes her mother in once again, head to toe, as if only just recognizing her. Stanhope turns to shush Anna, with the whites of his eyes showing all around. She shakes her head at him, making the cutting at the neck gesture, 'cut,' 'stop,' 'hold it.' Stanhope just stands there with his jaw on the floor while silence envelopes the court.

Anna makes the universal sign for 'time out.' Stanhope responds correctly, apologizing to the court, requesting a moment to please confer with his client. He turns on Anna with teeth gritted, blazing through her with his eyes. His ire doesn't cow her. "Stop this now. Immediately," Anna says.

"Anna" he forces through his teeth. "Do you know what's going to happen if we screw this up? What's wrong with you? This is what you wanted? She's about to break, isn't that what you wanted?" His forehead has a vein pulsing with such ferocity Anna can hardly keep her mind on what he's saying.

"Look at her for God's sake Dennis...LOOK AT HER!" Anna takes his face in her hands and swivels his head around to look at Betsy. He shrugs loose, turning on Anna again. "So? What?"

"This is killing her. This is...she's begging me to help her. She doesn't want to—No she can't do this and it was wrong of me, wrong of us, wrong of Erik, wrong of all of us to demand that it go this far. Dennis, I was wrong and I want this to stop right now." Anna spits out with as much control as she can muster. "Can't you see? She's damned if she does, damned if she doesn't. No matter what she answers, she's going to pay the price. And the price is too high."

Stanhope requests an emergency break to talk Anna down. Everyone in court rolls their eyes at the delay, except Betsy. Anna is pretty sure she saw Betsy take her first full breath in what looked to have been months, according to the difficulty of it. Betsy struggles to heave the air all the way in. And as she is 'escorted' from the room, Anna is certain without a doubt she saw something else in her daughter's eyes as well; gratitude, recognition, relief.

Luckily Stanhope is teetering very close to his wits end, as he runs out of steam for arguing with Anna fairly quickly. The lawyers' are on the blower with Carlo. Since he's their meal ticket, they need his approval. Carlo asks to speak to Anna.

"Hi honey…are you doing OK over there?" he asks her.

"I'm doing better now," she replies cryptically.

"Oh yeah," Carlo says, "How come?"

"I just realized something," Anna replies. "Something important."

"Oh yeah…" says Carlo. "What's that?"

"This is killing her Carlo. I took one look at her today and I don't know why I didn't see it before, recognize it a long time ago."

"Recognize what honey?" Carlo prods.

"How much pain she's in. That I'm part of the cause. That she's trapped in this terrible, horrible situation that I know all about. I lived it. She's just a little girl Carlo. I can't keep doing this. If this means I have to let her go, to lose her to save her anymore pain, any more grief than she already faces on a day-to-day, minute-to-minute basis living in Erik's sick world. Then that's what I'll do."

"Are you sure?" Carlo asks her.

"I've never been more sure of anything in my life. That's what she's been trying to show me—she's fading away, dying, letting go a little bit more each time. I have to make it stop. I can't do this to her." Anna succeeds in clearing away the looming sobs, because she at long last knows what she has to do.

Carlo tells the lawyers to do what Anna wants, and they do.

They bring the proceedings to the most gracious and least jarring halt possible. They claim illness, and when questioned about rescheduling they are vague and say, "We'll shoot you some potential dates," to the opposition.

The whole thing is shut down and they are clearing out in a matter of minutes. Anna cranes her head around to catch a glimpse of Betsy, out in the hall somewhere. But instead she sees Drew leaning languidly against the wall down the hall. When Anna catches his eye he doesn't flinch or shy away. Instead, he puts his hand to his heart, closes his eyes, and bows his head in the tiniest acknowledgement of Anna's sacrifice.

By three o'clock in the afternoon there is nothing anyone can do except keep watch over her, for which she is grateful, but all she really wants is to be left alone for a while.

Another day comes and goes and all Anna wants is for them to leave her alone in the dark in her bedroom. Let her stare at the wall or ceiling for an hour, or for ten if she feels like it. She just wishes they'd all quit interrupting her, just give her like a whole day without chirpy heads poking around the door. "You know, you'd feel better if you ate something Anna." "C'mon, it's a gorgeous crisp afternoon, the leaves are just starting to fall. Come for a walk Anna. It'll help you feel better."

'No it won't,' is all she thinks as she turns silently toward the wall. 'No it most certainly will not.' Anna is beyond certain. The canker that eats at her, the sore the suppurates is the fact that she was so wrong, so selfish, refusing to recognize the full depth of Betsy's pain. How could she have not known sooner? Why did she assume that Betsy's rage was at her, about her, rather than seeing it for what it really was? Just pure misery directed out toward the safest, most understanding and reliable person Betsy had…her mother. It was her mother's obligation to ease her daughter's pain, to hold her and comfort her.

Not being able to do so was driving Anna quietly mad, because now she understood. Now she got it that Betsy acted out against her because doing so was 'safe' compared to aiming her anger at Erik, or her friends. What choice did the poor child have?

Lying in the darkened bedroom, cursing the sun for even pummeling her shades, a worn dry sob escapes her as she curls into a fetal position around a pillow. She's lost her kids, but did something heroic.

She's replayed the scene over in her mind a thousand times. Each time Anna crumples once again, dry sobs echoing into the dense foam of the pillow. Silent screams drive into the mattress.

But even as she wallows around in her bedroom cave Anna knows if she had to do it over again she'd make the same choice, but she'd do it sooner. She'd always vote for her daughter's peace, sanity, and well-being over her own needs. She'd do it again. So, there was no solace but time and there was no 'right' and there was no 'solution.' Anna had to cut out her own heart to save her daughter's. She could see Betsy evaporating from within, becoming one of the walking wounded. Anna recognized that she had the power to remove one layer of chaos and misery from her daughter's daily burden and that was about all she could do for her. So, she'd done it.

In the comfort of her dark room Anna thrashes around to her other side, facing away from the relentless glowing drapes. She covers her ears when she can't stop the words from replaying in her memory. How could she have been so ignorant, how could she have let it come to this? These questions strike Anna so hard they seem to draw blood. How could she have been so blind to Betsy's pain for so long?

Anna prayed only one thing over the course of the following weeks. 'Please let her understand that I did it because I love her. Not because I gave up on her. Please God, that's all I ask. Please let her know. Whisper to her that I haven't given up on her. I'll never give up on loving her. Let her understand. I love her. That I did this for her.'

CHAPTER TWENTY SIX

JUST DESSERTS

After a day or two of prodding and watching, Anna's mother manages to get her out of her room for a walk one day, to make dinner the next. Katherine, of course, had to get back home right away. Anna remembers Katherine slipping into her dark room to give her a kiss on the forehead before she left.

Even her mother has to get back to Florida. Anna's father would be getting anxious alone. So, Anna goes through the motions of her day to show her mother that she's alright, that she'll be OK.

Once she's finally alone again Anna is tempted to relapse into hibernation, but instead decides to go to the restaurant. She'd forgotten for a time that she has responsibilities, plans for her future. But every minute she aches as she constantly adjusts to a future that excludes her daughter, excludes her son. It all hurts.

In the evenings she curls up on Carlo's lap, and he lets her be. On a good night she'll watch whatever movie he's put in, and even laugh where she's supposed to. Although there is dinner on the table every night and she goes to the restaurant every day, Carlo can see she's only going through the motions. But he admires her for even that. It takes strength and determination to go on when it is so much easier not to.

This particular Friday is a 'good' night for Anna. Even though it's been a week and a half since the hearing, she's showing some signs of coming back to life. She even picked the movie for a change. But just as they are about to curl up on the couch, there is a knock at the door.

It's Dave.

Dave and Carlo confer in the entrance way for a minute before coming into the living room. At Dave's prompting, Carlo turns the channel to CNN. It's a weather update, but the ticker at the bottom of the screen reads, "Illinois Governor Kasovitz arrested on federal charges of racketeering...three die in riots in South Florida's hurricane disaster zone...'

Carlo wipes his face with his hand as if he can change the image of what he's seeing. Then the weather update is over and the images come into focus. There it is, the governor's perp walk from the plane. In the dark.

The announcer says, "Sheriff's officers are escorting Illinois Governor Kasovitz to the station. The governor is under arrest as a result of what is reported to be a sting operation targeting political abuse of the now notorious 527 organizations."

The news anchor goes on, "The governor's plane was greeted upon landing by not only a large gathering of Chicago's finest, but by representatives of the FBI, the FEC, and from the State's Office of Internal Investigations."

The television showed Erik's plane taxiing toward a roadblock of police cars and tactical vehicles. Carlo could swear he saw the shadows of a SWAT team in the background. "Sure, as if the governor is going to come out guns a'blazing?" he wonders aloud. She only looks at him, eyebrows raised, hands over her mouth.

"We're joined by Sun-Times reporter Ken Jenny who in his recent profile of the governor dubbed this plane you see the governor emerging from as 'The Governor's Partisan Plane.'"

This is a field day for reporters and the media. They are feasting on the rich meat of political scandal.

Dave finally speaks. "What I came by for Carlo is...you see this guy?" he says pointing to the TV screen, to the pilot also being escorted from the plane and taken into custody. "That's Grant. He's an old friend of mine Carlo. We went to flight school together. He moved his wife and kids here for this job, pretty much on my recommendation. I want to go up to Chicago and bail him out. I know there's no way he is in anyway involved, but I'm afraid he'll be railroaded."

Carlo stands and claps Dave on the shoulder. "Let's figure out if there's anything we can do that will help. If it's worth going up there, that's what we'll do."

"I'm really sorry Carlo I hate to ask you for such a big favor, but...I--"

"Let me get the 'League of Ivies' on the phone to see what they can start doing from up there." Carlo says as he leads Dave into his office.

Anna finally comprehends the full impact of what's happening. The news drones on. "The aircraft was supplied by 'Fathers for Families Alliance' to transport the governor home to his children every weekend. In addition to the governor of Illinois, three other individuals are also under arrest tonight in connection with this alleged conspiracy. "

When images of Carlo's hotel downtown start appearing, Anna calls the men back into the room. "Hey...you two, you're going to want to see this."

As they emerge from the office, a helicopter shot of the hotel fills the screen. "At least it looks good," Anna says. Carlo rolls his eyes. The camera picks up on the line of sheriff's vehicles lining the entrance drive. "Officers have also arrested well-known political fundraiser and director of the governor's reelection campaign,

Tony Roscoe." An irate half-dressed Roscoe is escorted out the front doors of the hotel for the camera.

The phones instantly go mad. The office phone, Carlo's cell, even the house phone brringg brrriing, beep beep, blip blip. Carlo heads for the office phone, checking the caller ID on his cell to see which was more urgent. Anna answers the house phone, but the person on the other end hung up.

Dave slides onto the couch, mouth hanging open.

The television drones on. The talking heads take over. "Tony Roscoe played a pivotal role in Illinois Senator Martin Black's successful campaign four years ago."

The other anchor interrupts. "That's right Jen, but Roscoe was quietly put out to pasture when Senator Black was drafted to run for president." Then there is a clip of Senator Black being interviewed by one of the two anchorpersons. The interviewer is asking. "Is it true Senator that Tony Roscoe was run off your presidential campaign because of his reputation?"

The senator responds "Mr. Roscoe played a valuable role in helping me gain the honor of the senatorial seat that I now have. Was he run off? No, absolutely not. Mr. Roscoe is an adept manager who is in demand all around the country."

But Anna no longer pays attention. The ringing of her cell phone startles her. "Hello?" she says.

"Anna?" sniff sniff. "Anna, its Maggie?" "Anna please…its Dad…the police were just here at the farm. They took him with them. I think they arrested him…I- I…please Anna…please." Then she breaks down crying.

"Maggie?" Anna says in shock and alarm. "Maggie? Are you and your sister OK? Is Drew there with you? Are you guys OK?"

Sure enough, the next image that flashes up on the screen is Anna's farmhouse, Erik's farmhouse. "Also under arrest in the conspiracy is local Cambridge attorney Erik Reinhardt, who is the chairman of Governor Kasovitz's reelection campaign."

Dave turns to call Carlo back in as they watch two sheriff's deputies wrestle Erik from the doorway and he stumbles a bit on the top step. Erik is blinded by the flashes and cameras. He tries to shield his eyes with his hands, but as he raises them he becomes aware of the handcuffs. So, he lowers them and puts his chin on his chest.

Most important is what Anna sees in the instant between Erik's exit and the door slamming shut. In that instant Anna sees Maggie shielding Betsy who crouches a few feet behind the door screaming before Drew slams the door shut. Anna's mind struggles to wrap around the timing. This must have happened an instant ago. Yet here was Maggie on the phone.

"Maggie?" There is sobbing on the other line.

"Maggie, first of all turn off the TV and the radio. OK? You've seen enough."

"OK," Maggie sniffs. Anna hears the clicks of electronics going off in the house.

"Now, I want you to turn off all the lights in the front of the house, the porch, the sitting room, everything. I want you to have Drew go upstairs and look out Greg's bedroom window to find out if all the reporters are gone or if they're still there..."

"OK," answers Maggie. The she gives Drew his instructions.

"Anna, will you come out to get us. I'm scared. I don't want to stay out here. I was going to leave, but they were crowding the driveway and I was afraid I wouldn't be able to pull the Escalade out without hitting someone." Once uncapped, Maggie's anxiety overflows again.

"Of course. Sure I will. You don't need to stay out there all alone. I'll be out as soon as I can." Anna is already slipping into her shoes, groping around for her purse while still talking Maggie down.

Carlo points to the phone in Anna's hand and raises his eyebrows. She nods. "Do you want me to go? Or Dave?" he whispers to her while she manages Maggie. Anna holds up a finger.

"What did you say Maggie? Drew saw how many cars and vans?" Silence as she waits. "Oh, OK, but they were leaving he says, right? How many are there left, would he say?" Anna asks. "OK, just a second Maggie. I'm getting in the car. Hold on."

"All the news vans and crews seem to be leaving to follow Erik to the courthouse, or jail, or whatever. I'm going to go out and bring the kids here, if that's alright with you?" Anna says quietly, holding her phone to her chest.

"Is it going to be safe? I don't want you having to run down any reporters or anything?" He says kissing her on the cheek and wrapping an arm around her shoulder. "I have to run over to the hotel and calm everyone down before I go take care of anything else."

Anna nods saying, "OK, keep me posted."

They each head off on their own missions, Dave accompanying Carlo until they can get back to helping his friend Grant.

CHAPTER TWENTY SEVEN

RETURN TO THE FOLD

There is nothing but dust and debris scattered around the front of the farmhouse when Anna pulls up. She dials the house as she arrives to let the kids know it's her headlights they see pulling in the driveway this time. "Oh, wait till you guys see what a mess they left," she says. She sees where chunks of the lawn and landscaping have been churned under by thoughtless drivers. The house is dark from the front, just like Anna told them—good.

"I'm coming around to the back, so I want you guys to come unlock the kitchen door for me, OK?" Anna says as she wheels all the way around to the back door. She pulls the car up as close to the back steps as she can. Just in case. Just in case *what* she doesn't quite know, but it does feel rather spooky and odd out there.

As soon as she puts the car in park, the kids are tumbling out the back door and down the steps to the car. Anna quickly clicks unlock so they can climb in. Betsy pops in the passenger seat, eyes like saucers, but she leans all the way over the armrest to put her head on Anna's shoulder for just that instant before yanking on her seat belt.

"That's it?" Anna asks. "You don't want me to come in? You

guys don't want to pack anything, bring anything with you? Clothes, books, computers?"

They point out the lumpy backpacks and duffel bags in the back seat with Maggie and Drew. "OK," Anna answers. "What about keys? Did you lock the house up?"

Maggie answers, "Yes, we locked it," holding up her keys and jingling them a bit.

"OK, great. Well, Maggie what about your car? Or the car Daddy lets you drive? Do you want to take a car into town with you?"

"No...uh. We can come get it tomorrow or the next day or something, though, right? I just don't want to drive it by myself," Maggie says.

"Well OK then. I guess we're off." Anna says as she puts the car in gear and heads home to the Waterston house.

It's dark and the kids are silent as they pull away from their home. Anna avoids the radio in case a news break comes on. Betsy doesn't even commandeer the CD player, she's too stunned. Anna wants to ask questions. She wants to scream and cry and shout, but she remains silent as they drive through the dark night, until her phone rings.

"Hello?" She mostly listens, asks few questions, and ends saying "Be careful. I love you." She says it without thinking, but then is worried that hearing her say 'I love you' might upset the kids. She glances around in the dark. Nothing.

She clears her throat. "Um, that was Carlo. He's going to Chicago to take care of something, so you guys won't meet him until tomorrow I guess," Anna says awkwardly. No one responds. They continue driving in silence.

As they emerge into the house through the garage, the first thing Anna wants to know is, "anyone hungry?" She gets grunts and nods of approval. She leads her troupe into the kitchen, turning on all the lights as she goes. They stand around the kitchen island eating the cheese and crackers Anna pulls out while she browses the refrigerator and pantry for something to make.

Seeing the speed with which they attack the cheese Anna brings out more, slicing it thin. She grabs grapes and trail mix, anything ready to eat, and puts it on trays. By the looks of them, they'll be asleep before she manages to make anything more complicated.

"Hey I know. Why don't, here, come with me," she says picking up the tray and leading them out of the kitchen and into the living room. "Why don't you guys just spread out here?" Betsy leans in to help Anna make space on the coffee table for the trays of snacks. They share a smile.

"Mom, I'm dying of thirst. Where do you keep the drinks around here?" Drew asks. She comes back with some bottles of Jones and Snapple for them to pick from. Betsy still goes for the lemonade, Anna notices.

Maggie says, "Hey, pass me that peach tea will you?" and Drew does. They start talking to each other at last. Anna breathes a sigh of relief. "Who wants that last piece of provolone?" Drew asks as he lunges for it, racing Maggie. "Hey, don't eat all the M & Ms out of the trail mix Betsy," Drew teases.

"Hey Mom. Can we turn on the TV or something?"

Despite the bizarre circumstances and the months since they've been together, the night begins to feel normal. Or what normal felt like for the past decades.

There is no schmaltzy crying and group hugs, but there are smiles and gentle teasing. As Anna takes to the couch to operate the remote Betsy leans up against her, curling her feet up under her. Anna reaches for the throw on the reading chair and tucks it around Betsy, who snuggles gratefully into it then looks up into her mother's eyes.

There. Anna sees in Betsy's face relief, gratitude, and love. Drew catches the instant of contact between his mother and sister and he blushes and looks into his soda bottle, smiling. Then he complains about the impossible selection of TV shows. "Don't you have any decent movies around here or anything?"

Maggie has tears in her eyes as she brings a pillow down on her complaining brother. She glances at Anna to see if she's going to be in trouble for abusing the furniture but Anna only laughs, extracting a throw pillow from behind her and lobbing it at Maggie.

Anna is taken off guard when the phone rings. "Hello?"

A woman's voice on the other end sounds as if she's been running. "Hello Anna? It's Dana."

"Oh my—Dana, are you OK?" Anna asks, remembering the girl was due to give birth any day now.

"Well, that's what I'm calling about; you know Dave's gone with Carlo. And Grant's wife can't leave the little ones at home alone…Anna, I was wondering if , whooo whooo," she takes a little break. "If you could drive me to the hospital?"

The kids are shocked to see Anna leap up screaming. "C'mon c'mon! Dana's about to have her baby. We've got to go." It takes her a minute. "Oh, wait. I guess we can't all go. Dana doesn't need an audience. Ummm. OK, I have to go take a friend of mine who's in labor to the hospital. Does anyone want to come with…" Betsy raises her hand, nodding vehemently, biting her lip. Betsy made it clear that wherever Anna was going, she was her shadow. "You two will be fine here by yourselves?" she asks Maggie and Drew.

Drew answers laughing, "Uh, yeah Mom, we'll be fine. That is, unless you're expecting any camera crews or anything." Maggie hits him with the pillow Anna threw at her.

AT THE HOSPITAL BETSY HELPED ANNA, taking her turn holding Dana's hand and getting ice chips. It was only very early labor yet.

Anna tried to shoo Betsy off to get soda or coffee for her if Dana's contractions got too intense. Betsy wasn't falling for it. She held Dana's hand and screwed up her face and bit her lip for as long as Dana squeezed…hard.

They were soon rescued from the job by the return of Dave. Anna had called the tower and asked them to get ahold of Dave. When the tower radioed Dave and Carlo the news, they simply turned around heading for home.

Betsy was asleep in the visitors lounge, wrapped in Anna's jacket, a few hours later when the news came. Anna and Carlo sat holding hands just next to her. "It's a boy!" Dave shouts. "A boy!" as Carlo rose to clap him on the shoulder and Anna leapt to give him a hug.

"What are you going to name him?" Betsy asks, sitting up awake and smiling.

Anna takes Betsy to get a peek at baby Ben through the nursery glass.

Tears spring to her eyes at the sight. "He's so tiny Mom," she exclaims. "He's so little, I'd be scared to hold him I think."

Anna puts her arm around Betsy's shoulder. "No you wouldn't, not if he was crying and he needed to be picked up and fed. You'd do just fine."

"Were you scared when I was born Mom? I mean, was I really that little?" Betsy asks, no longer even trying hide her tears.

"Yes. I was scared. I was afraid of how tiny you seemed. But you were mine and I loved you, so the fear went away. I picked you up and held you and it felt like heaven, and I knew at that moment I'd love you for the rest of your life no matter how big you got," Anna answers, crying now too.

"I love you Mommy. I missed you so much." The tears grow into sobs, "I'm sorry Mommy. I didn't mean to--" The sobs turn to hiccups and Anna holds her daughter in her arms, saying "I know you didn't baby. I know. No I'm sorry. It's OK. It's going to be alright. Everything's OK now."

A DAY PASSED, AND THEN ANOTHER. No one spoke of going out to the farm for any reason. Anna tried taking all three kids shopping for clothes for the coming school days. It didn't take her long to remember what a nightmare such an exercise was, but she was grateful even for the arguing and eye-rolling.

Four days passed before Erik's lawyers phoned Stanhope to phone Anna, to inform her that she has Erik's *permission* to "shelter and care for" her own children while Erik remains behind bars. This message came about an hour before it hit the news that Erik was turning himself in after being out on bail. He deduced that it was in his best interest to start serving his time while awaiting trial. Apparently he had nothing worth staying out for once it became clear that conviction was inevitable, that the evidence was irrefutable. When his criminal lawyers determined that either way, no matter what, best-case scenario, Erik would serve time, he went right back into custody to get the clock ticking, getting it over with as fast as possible.

He didn't even bother to try and see the kids or call.

When Anna sat the kids down to update them, Maggie tentatively asked, "Does this mean we can go get my car?"

"Yeah," Betsy said "can I finally go get my clothes?"

Anna looked confused. "We could have gone any time…you know that. Why didn't you ask?" They all left the question hanging, because it didn't matter. Now that they knew precisely where Erik was and that he wouldn't be dropping in, or showing up while they were out there, they were ready. No one even asked if they would be staying out there, living out there. As day after tentative day went by, things got less distant, less edgy, less weird.

Anna recognized that a Rubicon had been crossed the first

time she shouted over them in an attempt to quell their arguing. Things were gradually growing more routine, more normal.

AS ANNA WIPES THE REMNANTS of her experimental fruit and juice shakes from the counter, Betsy plops down on a stool opposite her mother. In her best John Wayne, Betsy asks, "OK bartender, what do you have on tap today?" Anna pushes three chilled silver malt cups toward her.

Wherever Anna is, Betsy is sure to be tagging right behind. In the kitchen, in the freezer, in the office…it's as though once lost and now found, Betsy can't let her mother stray too far from sight. While another mother might complain that Betsy's 'too tied to the apron string,' Anna will not.

Betsy sips one, then another, then goes back to the first as if she is a connoisseur tasting the finest of wines.

"Don't you dare," yelps Anna when Betsy bulges out her cheeks looking for a place to spit. She snatches the mixing sleeves from her daughter's hands laughing. "No way, nu-uh, don't you even think about it."

The final menu is coming into shape. The opening of Coco's Café is only weeks away. Anna recruits Betsy's help in cleaning up her mess so they can scoot home. "After all," Anna reminds her daughter, "Dana is coming in for dinner and bringing baby Ben. You don't want to make them wait do you?" Anna teases, flipping her towel in Betsy's general direction.

THE WEATHER IS TURNING SUMMERY early. Even though school still has weeks left to go, the day's highs already crawl into the eighties. Carlo balks when he enters the kitchen to Maggie's screaming.

"I did it! I got in! I got in! Oh my…I'm so happy! Can you believe it?" She runs to Carlo, showing off the acceptance packet from Northwestern, where she will go in the fall. She decided to go into law to protect other families from what happened to them.

Obviously, everyone else is all 'celebrated' out. Anna returns to her dinner preparations. Betsy asks the voice on the other end of the phone, "You hear that?" She says, handing her sister the handset. "Here Maggie, talk to Drew."

Drew opted to go away to a high school in Florida for golfers. The humiliation of his father's conviction hit him the hardest. The school was his reason to get away from the constant reminders and smart-mouth hazing of his so-called friends.

Anna can hear him holler in Maggie's ear from across the entire kitchen. Carlo takes it all in, astounded. He never quite imagined what it would look like when his dream came true, but he was beginning to get the picture. Sure, sometimes he still felt a bit on the outside in the company of Anna and her children. But he was pleased with how things were slowly but surely getting better.

Anna continues concocting something wonderful in her kitchen, and Betsy stands in the doorway waving Carlo to come with her. While Maggie overflows, filling her brother in on all the details of her achievement, Carlo follows Betsy into the dining room.

Before the mail so rudely interrupted them, Anna, Maggie, and, Betsy were poring over maps and atlases spread out over the table. There was a big one of Europe with colored sticky dots all over it. Carlo leans over attentively as Betsy begins pointing out all the new orange dots she's added to the map.

"These are all the stupid golf courses Drew says he wants to see while we're there. Only one of them *isn't* in Scotland. See?" she says pointing.

"Which ones are your colors again?" he asks, although he knows full well. "Yours is the one on Florence here, right? The purple one?"

The whole family has been throwing their two cents in to the process of mapping out a European tour for their collective honeymoon. They're scheduled to depart the week after school lets out, only days after Drew flies in from Florida. Anna thinks it's going to be a bit of a rush dashing out of town so quick, but worth it.

"Why can't we just stay another week?" Betsy pouts at Carlo. "If we could, then I wouldn't mind wasting five days in Scotland waiting for Drew to chase little white balls around."

Anna strolls in from the doorway, where she's been watching. "You know perfectly well why not," she says tousling Betsy's ponytail. What they *told* her was that Anna couldn't be away from the restaurant longer, that Carlo had a construction project scheduled, and that Maggie needed to get ready for college. But the truth was, it involved the visits the judge ordered, saying, "…even a convicted felon has a right to a relationship with his kids." Trying to reschedule them takes so much paperwork it's nearly impossible. The trip to Europe can't be any longer because the kids visit their father at his minimum-security detention center once every six weeks.